The Last Man to Hit .400

A Love Story

Stanley W. Beesley

PEGASUS BOOKS

Pegasus Books
3338 San Marino Ave
San Jose, CA 95127
www.pegasusbooks.net

First Edition: September 2016

Published in North America by Pegasus Books. For information, please contact Pegasus Books c/o Christopher Moebs, 3338 San Marino Ave, San Jose, CA 95127.

This book is a work of fiction. Any resemblance to actual persons, living or dead, events, or locales is entirely coincidental.

Library of Congress Cataloguing-In-Publication Data
Stanley W. Beesley
The Last Man to Hit .400: A Love Story/Stanley W. Beesley– 1st ed
p. cm.
Library of Congress Control Number: 2016950294
ISBN – 978-1-941859-50-6
1. FICTION / Sports. 2. FICTION / Romance / Sports. 3. SPORTS & RECREATION / Baseball / General. 4. FICTION / Thrillers / Suspense. 5. SPORTS & RECREATION / Baseball / History. 6. FAMILY & RELATIONSHIPS / General.

10 9 8 7 6 5 4 3 2 1

Comments about *The Last Man to Hit .400: A Love Story* and requests for additional copies, book club rates and author speaking appearances may be addressed to Stanley W. Beesley or Pegasus Books c/o Christopher Moebs, 3338 San Marino Ave, San Jose, CA, 95127, or you can send your comments and requests via e-mail to cmoebs@pegasusbooks.net.

Also available as an eBook from Internet retailers and from Pegasus Books

Printed in the United States of America

For Carly

"Life's so uncertain when
matters of the heart
Arrive to divide us and
keep us apart."

Michael Ray Little
Singer/Songwriter, Tulsa

"If you don't think too good,
don't think too much."

Ted Williams
Left Fielder, Boston Red Sox

Batting .400 for a Major League Baseball season? Absurd. Never again. Hitting .400 is the most sacred and secure mark in all sports, and will never be done again. Never by a superstar, and never, ever by a .259 lifetime guy like Paul Demeter. It's the last month of the season, the world is watching; and promising 17-year-old journalist, Sylvia Kerrigan, knows if Demeter finishes at .400, some writer will nab the Great Story. Sylvia aims to be that writer. She is young but not a kid. She was tear-gassed at Occupy Tulsa, she had her stomach pumped at the OU/Texas Game, and she was assaulted hanging out with a friend. Any other qualification? Easy. This ballplayer, this unlikely hero who abandoned his family years ago, this Paul Demeter? He's her old man.

The Last Man to Hit .400

A Love Story

PART I

The Last Man

The last man to do it was the incomparable Ted Williams, the greatest hitter who ever lived, and it was so long ago that Reagan was a Democrat, America was pretty sure Japan wouldn't dare attack, and civilized people herded other civilized people into pens before slaughtering them like animals.

Even if you know squat about baseball, you know that no hitter will ever bat .400 again. The idea is absurd. Today's game makes it impossible, with its healthier, better-trained athlete wearing gloves the size of catfish nets, and the advance scouting, which can pick at a hitter's every imperfection. The season is longer, while you have the glare of *ESPN*, *Fox Sports* and the pressure of talk radio putting every facet of a ballplayer's personal life out there for millions to see and hear. Then there's the trans-continental travel and hotel existence.

Never again will a player hit safely four times out of every ten at-bats for an entire Major League season. It is so hard to hit *.300* that if a man manages to do that for ten or twelve seasons, they put him in the Hall of Fame. Wade Boggs and Rod Carew came close to .400, and George Brett came even closer. They were great left-handed batters, with decent speed who made good contact. They flirted all summer with .400, but they failed late in the season.

The pundits agree that no superstar of today will ever do it. But they say records are meant to be broken, so it makes sense that someday a whiz kid out there—maybe not even born yet, is going to come along and do it again, right? *Wrong.* Experts say .400 is the one mark in sports that's untouchable. Can't be done again! Not by the great players today, not by a future great, and never, ever, by a 38-year-old, good-field, lifetime .259 guy like Paul Demeter.

Credentials

In one of the college brochures that came to the house, I read an article that said most people wait a long time to learn their purpose in living. I figured that made me mighty damned lucky. At 13, and quite by chance, I hit upon why I was born. I needed an elective class, and being the exact opposite of an athlete, I opted for Journalism.

I figured I could score at least a *B*, selling the Henry Clay School newspaper, *The Compromise,* on Fridays at lunch. The job was taken. How about I run copies and staple stuff? *Taken*, they said, so I would have to write.

"What do I write?" I asked the teacher, Mr. Atherton.

"Write what you know, Sylvia. So… what do you know?"

I told him I knew a little something about a lot of stuff, but the only thing I knew a lot about was sports, especially baseball.

"We *have* a sports reporter," Mr. A said. "You don't want to do fashion or gossip? You like politics? You could report on the Student Council meetings."

I did the gag gesture, so he would know exactly how I felt about that.

"You might give the weekly GPA report?"

"Nah, it's the same six nerds every week."

"You could be a copy editor."

"I don't think so, since I am currently rocking a cool *C-minus* in language arts."

Again I mentioned sports, and he relented, saying I could help cover the big high school football game against Booker T. Washington.

"But only stats," he warned. "Yardage, scores, turnovers, stuff like that. Nothing else. And stay out of the way!"

"Sure thing."

Cool. I could do this: keep stats at sporting events until the kiosk job freed up again. Plus, I would get in games free. Then something exciting happened at the football game that changed everything for me. When a BTW quarterback sack turned into a shoving match, which turned into a brawl, which turned into a riot, which landed on *CNN,* well I just happened to get *way* in the way.

When benches cleared, stands emptied, and the boy reporter who was supposed to get the story ran away in terror, I grabbed a notebook and hit the field running. For the price of a black eye from an errant linebacker fist, I found my life's calling. I cornered a few players and two coaches for quick interviews. I scribbled notes as I zigzagged through the melee, and then I stayed up all night, turning them into a story that would be published under my by-line as the lead the following week.

Mr. Atherton said that what I had written was powerful stuff that transcended sports, a piece that was a commentary on pent-up community resentment and economic racism. I didn't know about all of that. I only wrote what I saw, heard, felt and knew, but I was hooked.

My bags are packed. I am almost ready to hit the road on a trip to write a great sports story, maybe the greatest ever. I see Jodie in the atrium, working herself up for one last-ditch effort to talk me out of going. First though, before I hug my mom farewell, I am meeting Wahoo (not a nickname) at the Dairy Queen for a goodbye milkshake. I told him I'd prefer a beer, but he said he'd prefer I didn't drink and drive.

I re-check my bag: smart phone, notebooks, iPad, laptop, markers, scorebook and binoculars. All good. I'm set. "Back in thirty, Jodie," I call out.

"Okay, honey," she answers, forcing a smile.

I had snagged a massive moment during junior year, and though it didn't pad my journalistic credentials in a professional sense, it gave a boost to my self-esteem as a writer and stimulated my muckraking juices. I was pretty certain the school board was firing the girls' assistant basketball coach, not because she was incompetent, but because she was lesbian.

"What are you going to do about it?" Jodie had asked.

"I don't know. Something."

After public testimony from both sides at the special meeting—the LGBT topic was never mentioned—the board recessed in order to go into executive session. I snuck down the hall behind them.

Just before the door fully closed, the over-zealous clerk spat out, "We'll nail that dyke bitch now!" as I captured it on tape.

When Mr. Atherton read the first draft of my column the next day in his office, he took off his glasses, stood, looked between the venetian blinds out the window and sighed. "Kerrigan, this is the finest thing you have ever done—perhaps the best work *ever* done on *The Compromise*."

"Thanks, boss." I beamed. "That's nice."

"Too bad it will never see the light of day," he said. "You'll have to tear it up, and I'll have to ask you to surrender your flash drive too."

"No sir, Mr. A," I pleaded. "You can't *do* that! You've never killed anything I've done before. You can't!"

Mr. Atherton wouldn't look me in the eye as he explained that there was no freedom of the press in public schools, and though he respected and applauded my fine effort on behalf of a woman who was clearly getting a shitty deal, he was the father of three young children, and his wife was undergoing chemotherapy for breast cancer. He couldn't risk losing *his* job, which is what would have undoubtedly happened if he published my column in the school newspaper.

Then his eyes came back around to mine, and he told me that he wouldn't ask me to give up the tape, but that if I trusted him, I could voluntarily hand it over for his safe keeping. Then he could begin a conversation with his superiors to see if that information would have any effect on the coach's case.

I did, he did, and it did.

We never spoke again about my dead piece, but a month later, the coach was quietly offered her job back. She declined, having already been offered a similar post at the community college at a higher salary.

If a person is more upset than Jodie is about this upcoming journey of mine, that would be Wahoo. It is sweet of him to buy me a milkshake, since we are no longer *seeing* each other. He took our break-up like a man, meaning he yelled, and when he saw he wasn't getting anywhere with that, he teared up and wheedled.

I smile when I see him in the booth. Since we've become *just friends*, I've had the distance and time to realize he is a good guy. Deep down, I think he is as relieved as I am. We hug. He aims a kiss at my cheek, but his lips hit my eye. Thankfully, it is closed. We laugh.

"It's dangerous," he says. "You thought about that? Your car is a piece of junk."

"I've considered the risk. Greatness often requires pluck," I say. "Anyway, Moby Dick will make it just fine. I have no doubt," I lie.

"I wish I had your guts," he says, slurping his straw.

Liberal Pansy Crap

Jodie couldn't see why anybody would ever call in, unless they were masochists, and she certainly couldn't explain why *she* listened when she wasn't forced. The loudmouth radio host berated callers and interrupted them if he didn't like what they said.

She would have never known about the station if Mrs. Ford hadn't designated her to drive the coaches to Tahlequah for Great Expectations sessions on Thursdays.

"They won't make it past the titty bars if you don't take them," her principal had said, handing over the keys to the school van. "Besides, they *like* you."

Right. They like me, Jodie thought. They like me so much they slap my hand when I try to dial up *NPR*. They yell at me to turn off the 'liberal pansy crap' and put it on *The Game*. At 10:00 every morning, the rant began. Oh, lord.

The host liked to pick on certain sports figures, and his target this summer—all summer—had been Paul Demeter. He called the man a fraud. Today, the radio in the atrium squawked. The host yelled that it would be bad—in his humble opinion—if a sacred mark like .400 was achieved by a so-so player like him.

Sylvia returned from the Dairy Queen. When she heard the radio, she entered the atrium to turn it off, but Jodie backed up to it.

"I want to hear," she said.

"Right. I forgot, Mom," Sylvia said. "You're the lady who forces herself to watch an hour of *Fox News* every night."

"So. You are leaving soon?"

"Right, and you will attempt once more to block me."

"No, dear, I will not. I have come about-face. As I consider it more and more, I now have all the confidence in the world in you," she said unconvincingly.

What she actually thought: *My child will be loose in the world, away from my protection, on a crazy mission in an unreliable automobile. She is going to get hurt. No matter how it turns out, she is going to be damaged, and I am scared to death, because smart, tough, curious, dogged Sylvia is also, undoubtedly, going to learn too much. I should stop her.*

"That would sully everything," the radio blowhard shouted. "Listen to me—it would be like a darn three-hundred yard career, third-down back suddenly breaking the NFL rushing record. It would be like a Nick Collison-type NBAer (now I do love Collison, don't get me wrong) in one season erupts averaging 34 points a game—or some Dot.Com Tour guy, known only for pissing down his leg under pressure, in one year goes crazy and wins the Masters, the US Open and the PGA. Nope.

"Should be a star that hits .400, though I personally think it will never happen ever again. As it is with a fraud like Demeter, the big thing hanging over all of it is the doubt. People don't know whether to praise him or censor him. The Doubt, ladies and gentlemen. Cheer him or boo him? Root for him or hope he goes away?

"This Demeter phony, he's only had two good years his whole career. And back then I was like, okay, he might turn out to be a Boyer, Hart or a Kubek kinda guy, y'know, a really, really solid player, but never a star. Turns out he's a flop. Never done a lousy thing after that! Lifetime he's like .250, and now this one season, he's in Ted Williams territory? Please! C'mon, really?

"Now he's up there hitting the ball with Ty Cobb, Honus Wagner, Shoeless Joe Jackson, the greatest names in the book? Jeez! Just look at the great hitters who never got close to .400: Musial, Rose, Mays, Gehrig, DiMaggio, guys like that. And now we're supposed to believe Paul Demeter?

"Last year he hit what—look it up for us, would you, Aaron?—Two twelve? Thank you—he hit .212. Last season this fraud hit .212—at 39 years old! What's that, Aaron? Thirty-eight? Oh *excuse me*, he's 38."

After eight minutes of commercials for erectile dysfunction, hair restoration and testosterone replacement therapy, the host continued.

"Let's go to the phone lines. Light 'em up, folks," he bellowed. "Let us know what you think about Paul Demeter hitting .400. He got a chance or no?"

Jodie snapped off the radio. She brewed a cup of chamomile, and took a tablet from the shelf. The yellow of the paper brought the heat of the day back into play for her. Moving to a window, she remembered every window in the house was open. She'd vowed not to turn on the air conditioning until mid-afternoon. The electric bill was outrageous. Scarcely a breeze rustled the curtains, their vague movement in the sills like old people dancing. She sat, sipped and simmered, filling two pages with her slightly masculine slant.

When Sylvia had asked Jodie if she had noticed Paul Demeter this summer, she'd been coy with her answer. Actually, she'd done more than notice. She had watched anytime Sylvia and Jack were out of the house. Not a bandwagon voyeur, she'd looked for the odd television schedule over the years and taken a peek when she felt like it. When Paul was a Cardinal and sported a goatee, when he was with the Tigers and filled out the home white pants nicely, and when he was back with the ChiSox. She watched with curiosity when he played first base for Houston. She was furious about being furtive when she needn't be. The dues were paid.

When they were not much more than kids, Paul was so shy he barely talked on the radio. How is he handling the smothering fame? She didn't know how he could stand it: mics always in his face, reporters asking *can you do it?* but never listening to that answer or others because the one question they all got around to in the end was *How?*

During spring training, he was the rage of the Cactus League, ending any discussion of him not making the team. In May, his batting average hovered around the .390 mark, and the media noticed. At first, he got softballs: *How you feeling this year, Slugger? Anything different at age 38?* And, *You're batting almost a hundred-fifty points higher than your career mark— how is that?* He laughed, and the reporters chuckled with him.

His answers were articulate, self-deprecating and were not answers at all. He gave credit to his teammates, which was bullshit. He wasn't getting any help from them. He was alone. *This was him, damn it!* She understood the painfully solitary experience a batsman went through at the plate. All the clubhouse solidarity in the world—the opposite of what Paul was receiving from his teammates—wouldn't swing the bat for a man. In the box a hitter takes his own licks.

At the All-Star break, when Paul was hitting .408, the media had become less amused. Interviews and press conferences grew hostile. Writers and broadcasters turned bolder. The lob questions stopped. The "hah-hah" phase was over. More quantifiable explanations were needed for an increasingly skeptical media and public. "Boos" now mixed with the applause he received in stadiums across both leagues.

Jodie stood in the closet without remembering the walk over. She reached above her head to a cubby where she kept hats. She took down a cigar box that her father gave her—the kind you didn't see anymore, since men didn't smoke as much. In elementary school, it housed crayons. She remembered the bittersweet smell of wax and tobacco. It had remained sturdy all that time. In middle school, photos lived there. The box was heavy, though it now only held paper—envelopes, most unopened. Back at the sofa, she rested it on her lap.

She had ordered the envelopes by date and kept them together with rubber bands. One of the bands had rotted and broken apart, leaving the envelopes lying loose in the box. She opened the end table drawer and found a new rubber band. Using her father's ornamental unit knife as letter opener, she ripped a decade-old envelope along the fold and let the crinkly paper fall to her thigh.

On The Road

I hate to, but I'm going to have to turn left. Whenever I plot an itinerary, I make sure to x-out as many left turns as I possibly can, because when I turn the steering wheel to the left beyond ninety degrees, Moby Dick's cacophonous horn blares like the cornet section of the fifth grade band. Then I have to pull over and get under the hood with gloves and a wrench to turn it off. Yet if I don't turn left, I will have to drive four miles out of my way and execute a cloverleaf of right-hand turns to get back to the turnpike, and I'm late enough getting started anyway. Can't be helped. I turn. Five miles later, and after at least six vehicles have pulled over to let me by, I am able to pull into a rest stop and pop the bonnet.

I check my phone. Two texts: one from Jodie, who wants to know if I am drinking water and not texting while driving (Duh!), and another from Wahoo, who just wants to check in to see how I'm doing.

I would have gotten away a lot earlier if Jack had kept out of the war that Jodie and I were waging this morning when she found the cigarettes in the console. Why he stuck his face in the middle of it, I can't begin to know, since Jodie needs no help, and the only attention he ever pays me is when I forget and come downstairs in a Kowalski and panties.

Jodie's mama lion instinct was strong this morning, and she had me almost whipped into compromise when Jack got off his lank ass and said his piece.

"Up yours!" I told him, and it was on.

He knew better than to touch me, but that didn't keep him from dog-cussing me out in front of god and everybody. I was right back at him. Jodie whirled on him too, and said, "Jack. Don't swear at my child!"

Way to go, girl! It chilled him some, but still he planted himself and tried to high-hat me.

When our imaginations ran out, Jack and I stood on the sizzling concrete, glaring at each other and sweating like a couple of tapped out MMA sluggers who weren't sure the match was over or who had actually won.

So Jack threw down his hands. "The hell with this!" he said and stalked off to the garage.

While Jodie resumed explaining to me the evils of tobacco, she kept looking at the garage, like she ought to go in there. I told her that what she ought to do is run the sorry sonofabitch off.

I seriously do not know how Jodie can be so overwhelmingly predicted to find them. She can do so much better. She is still attractive—check that—ravishing, not a bitch, and sharp as a tack. There *have* to be some decent men out there somewhere. I tell her this all the time, but she doesn't really listen and goes all Edna St. Vincent Millay on me.

"I cannot say what loves have come and gone,
I only know that summer sang in me a little while,
That in me sings no more."

She allows that she loved, honestly and truly loved—but once in her lifetime, and she messed that up. She is convinced that one time is it. *Blah! Blah! Blah!*

After Jack split, I spent another half hour arguing with Jodie. In the end, she took my pack of cigs and field stripped each one, letting the tiny bits drift to the blacktop. I put up a fight only on principle, since I had a whole carton in the trunk. Thinking she was victorious, she tired of talking, and I finally got on the road.

Up ahead, where the Will Rogers makes a long, easterly loop, I see that both lanes are backed up at least a mile. Bad accident most likely. Sure enough, twenty minutes later, I get close. I count six emergency vehicles, with their red, blue, and gold lights on fire. Not a wreck, though.

A Toyota van sits on the shoulder with a flat tire, and I see a large number of brown-skinned people in various stances behind and beside the vehicle, some lying down in the grass of the right of way. The men and the older boys are handcuffed. Women and children, looking tired and scared (more tired than scared), sit on the road shoulder and in the tall Johnson grass right of way. No shade anywhere in this swelter.

Doesn't require a Mensa membership to figure out what's going on here. Coyotes cram two dozen poor, desperate people in a vehicle meant to carry nine—probably picked them up in Tulsa. If they make it to Springfield, or even Joplin, everything is okay. The group can break off and go in different directions in safer, more secure vehicles—except they don't make it to Joplin. They blow a tire in Oklahoma.

I ignore the trooper, whose power-curl biceps twirl a harsh, impatient circle, ordering me through the bottleneck of traffic between parked cars, semis, fire trucks, ambulances and patrol cars. I don't care. I pull off on the shoulder.

"You'll have to vacate this area, young lady," an avocado-shaped sheriff's deputy says through my window and in front of my face.

"I'm just going to give those kids and ladies some water..."

"No, you're not. They are fine."

"No, sir. They are *not* fine. They look like they are suffering."

"Professionals will help them. We have this situation under control."

"Sir, they need help now."

I get out of Moby with my water jug in my hand.

"This is none of your business."

I stand in front of him. "Yeah, I think it is."

"Miss, I am ordering you to get back in that vehicle and leave this vicinity in an orderly fashion."

"I'm only going to give them a little drink."

"No! You are not!" the deputy yells. "If you do not leave this area immediately, I will place you under arrest."

I walk toward a woman who cradles a boy of about three in her arms. I feel a yank on my forearm, which makes me drop the water jug. It hits the pavement on its top, knocking the lid loose. Fresh ice-cold water runs off the shoulder and into cracks on the dirt's surface. What doesn't run off evaporates almost instantly. The woman looks in my eyes. She is too exhausted for expression.

"See all the good you done, smart aleck?" the deputy says. "Shoulda minded you own business."

He cuffs my hands behind my back, route-steps me to a patrol car and deposits me in the back seat.

I guess I'm pretty far down on their list, because two hours later I'm still sitting in a police station office, and I haven't been booked or finger printed or had a mug shot. I haven't even had my one lousy phone call, but that's okay. I'm not exactly looking forward to talking with Jodie about the auspicious beginning to my monumental journey. I imagine my end of the conversation:

So, Jodie, can you drive up here to this little border town and get me outta jail?

Yes, that's right. I said jail.

What's that? You told me so? Yeah. Yeah, you did.

Yes, I will pay you back, Mom.

Here comes a town cop. At last I'm going to get some movement! A farmer in dusty overalls and a priest are with the cop (no, this is not the start of a joke). The farmer speaks first. "Hello, Miss Kerrigan, I'm Tom Bourland. I'm a public defender in Ottawa County, but I'm more of a dairyman than a lawyer. This here is Father Montoya. He and I are working with the people who got brought in with you. Ordinarily, I'm dressed more conventionally for my law job, but this was kind of an emergency, so they had to get me down off the tractor to come in."

Then Father Montoya tells me the woman I tried to help told him about me, and he and Mr. Bourland convinced the town authorities that they had more than enough on their hands with the alleged illegals without worrying about throwing the book at a young Good Samaritan—even if she was snotty and did disobey a direct order from an officer of the law.

"Meaning?" I ask.

"You can go," Mr. Bourland says.

Outside, the farmer/lawyer unhooks Moby from the back of a huge, honking John Deere. I hug his neck. I thank Father Montoya and shake his hand, and then I get out of town as fast as a cat let out of a dog pound. Somebody might change his mind.

Since I had only the one smoke when I crossed the Verdigris, I allow myself another, feeling the calming effect immediately.

I cross the Neosho. Once in Kansas, I take to the two-laners. I'm no longer in a hurry, and I enjoy easing through small river towns with main streets that haven't totally tossed the towel to Target, Kohl's and Home Depot.

It is hot, absurdly hot for September—for any month, and so dry a handshake could knock you both down. The whole country is burning up, and the Southwest is especially sunbaked and arid. You can't turn on *The Weather Channel* any night without hearing Roy Dale and Myrtle swapping Dust Bowl yarns about the drouth.

All Moby's windows are down, because his a/c locks up after fifteen minutes. The hot wind swooshing my face feels like the suffocating air from the floor fans that were supposed to cool us in Hard Rock's casino kitchen. Thank god I was relieved of my dishwashing position there for skipping work to cover the flash mob at Occupy Tulsa!

"So what?" I told Jodie, who is perpetually worried over money, "When I get old enough, I'll go back there, deal blackjack and write an exposé on the corruption in Indian gaming."

Since Jodie was already upset that I was going to be living outdoors on Riverside with "a bunch of hippies," I went ahead and told her I was not accepting any of the scholarships that my S.A.T. scores had secured me. I told her that college was on hold—a little white one, that was. The whole truth was that I have decided college is a total waste of my time, and I am not going at all. But I felt like that would have been piling on.

Since I'm close, I veer off in this prairie village to pay homage to Mr. William Allen White. Evidently, the day could scorch kiddos and grandmas, because the park is as empty as Adele's happy song collection. Nothing moves above the burnt earth but the wings of locust and cicada, and they sound muffled.

At the statue's base, I settle in the ginger ale-colored grass, open my mini-cooler, and remove the sandwich of meat loaf, onion, jalapeno and mustard Jodie that prepared for me last night. I pop an icy, sweating PBR tallboy—good thing Jodie didn't check the cooler—and toast the big man before taking a drink. His stuff was a bit maudlin, but he was a pioneer. What he wrote about his deceased daughter struck me hard and stayed with me long.

My late start and border diversion meant I couldn't be at the ballpark in Kansas City. I will miss tonight's game, but tomorrow's a matinee. That's another reason I am not in a hurry. No need to rush into the city now. I will find a place to stay up the road and close in, so I can coast over in the morning. I'll miss a lot of traffic with my some times troublesome auto that way too.

I guess I slept, because the next thing I know, a man with thick patches of corn silk growing out his ears sits in the grass beside me, going through my cooler. He jumps.

"Don't scream, girl. You'll have the laws down on us."

"I'm not a screamer," I tell him. "If you're hungry, go ahead and have those deviled eggs. I've eaten."

I spy a woman, whose face is polished wax and as yellow as an Easter chick. Her animated eyes lock on the other can of beer in the ice. I nod, and she fishes it out. She squints hard at me, pointing. "Your hair."

"I know," I answer, holding out my hands, palms up. "I get that all the time."

The woman puts the can against one cheek and then the other. I hear the sizzle.

"Child like you on the road alone," she says. "Don't let the bucolic setting fool you."

She and the man take the beer and eggs to a concrete table, set among a copse of pecan trees. "I appreciate it!" the man calls out.

It feels good to be back on the road. Moby doesn't have cruise, but he is kickin it on down the line pretty good, and I set my mental right foot to a steady sixty-eight per, leaning back.

"C'mon, buddy—you're doing fine," I whisper to him.

My car and I are trek buddies, and I talk to him like I'm sure highwaymen, cowboys, knights and other road warriors of bygone eras conversed with their horses and mules—coaxing, cajoling and otherwise encouraging their performance.

Freedom

The day did not begin significantly for Paul. He woke with no lingering dream to parse, no omen—either pleasant or dark—to energize him. He didn't feel dread or a sense of being exceptionally well. Nothing in the morning suggested it was going to be anything more than it was: an icy, hazy November day.

He reached behind him and under the sheet for Elizabeth's fine, long bare leg. A sharp pain reminded him that she'd ridden her bicycle back to her own apartment. He also remembered they were over—her and him. She would not be in this bed with him again. She left his apartment grim-faced, taking everything with her but her scent.

He felt sad, but not overwhelmingly so. He was very fond of her, but he was not in love with her—just as he admitted, finally last night, that he will never be in love again.

"You will do much better," he told her—as if that sappy expression was going to make her feel fine.

It was true, though. She was pretty and practical, and she had, as she liked to phrase it, a natal hourglass that was losing sand rapidly. He felt helpless to explain to Elizabeth, as how to anyone, that he was finished with love.

He hadn't loved since Chicago, a long time ago. He could admit it now. He was done pretending. Being in love, he slowly realized, was like being truly religious—you couldn't fake it. Either you were or you weren't. Either you believed or you didn't. He was not going to be in love again. He was finished with it.

He realized it sounded silly and outrageous to think it, let alone say it. It was also silly to think this was a new start, but that's what it felt like. The notion was huge, but not impulsive. The idea had taken its time, living with him, settling on him like loneliness, slowly, and painfully at first, yet when accepted, what a release! A guy could climb mountains with such spirit.

After Chicago and Jodie, his relationship with Elizabeth was the closest thing to genuine he'd permitted himself to have with a woman. He was a ballplayer, and plenty of desirable females were attracted to a professional athlete, who though not a star was at least somewhat famous, single, and led a glamorous (to them) lifestyle. A little black book had not been required. Numbers he had in his head, if not always the right names. He was not proud of the history. In a previous generation, he would have been a cad; in this one, an asshole.

At that moment in the darkness of the bedroom, his head felt ready to explode, and he was sick to his stomach. How odd? Headaches seldom plagued him, and he'd had only the one glass of wine with dinner. Fully awake now and sitting up, he felt pain in his groin area, and when he reached a hand between his legs, he brought it away sticky with blood. He patted his forehead and felt a lemon-sized bulge above his right eyebrow. What the hell? What have I done? he wondered. He wasn't in a wreck; they didn't leave the apartment. He wasn't in a fight; the only person he saw all day yesterday was Elizabeth. *Think*. After she left, he went for the walk in the blackness and spitting sleet to sort his thoughts. He remembered thinking he should cross to the other side of the road where there was more light. He would when he turned around.

His underwear was bloody stiff. He stood, and the pain and wooziness overwhelmed him. He remembered the bicycle. Yeah. A bicycle. He'd heard it first, a rider pumping furiously in the mist. Then he saw it briefly, hurtling out of the dark. What was this idiot thinking, riding a bike in the dark on such a forbidding night? The front tire hit him first, smack in the balls, and the force sent him up past the handlebars and over the rider. He landed on his head. He didn't remember returning to the apartment.

The First Crummy Motel

I find a place on the interstate in a town associated, if I remember my middle school history, with the John Brown troubles. The motel is a dump, and I tell the young Asian male at the desk that I will have to check out a couple of things before plopping down cash. I am resigned to staying in crummy places. Most homeowners use lawn services manned by rangy college boys now, so I didn't get to mow that many yards after the axe fell at the Hard Rock. The only other cash I have is the advance Jodie gave me on the last four child support payments I would be getting.

With a serious look, the kid says, "Certainly, Miss," and pitches me a key.

I scope out the pool. It is tiny, more like a hot tub than a pool, but clean. You always check the pool before sealing the deal at a cheap motel, even if you aren't planning to swim. If they neglect the pool, a highly visible amenity, you think they're going to give a hoot about the rooms?

I feel the guy at the desk stretching his neck and ogling me. He is thinking any girl— young woman—who travels alone has got to be easy. I let myself in the room and crank up the a/c full throttle. It huffs and puffs, but it puts out a frigid blast. It will do.

I pay at the desk as the Asian eyeballs me gravely. I guess he hasn't read the report that says tending the night desk at a zero-star motel is not the same as casting a vote in the United Nations. I give him a look, just in case he is getting any ideas. He gulps and looks contrite, so I ask about dining prospects. He points to a couple of vending machines. So many choices! I settle on Funyuns, white powdered doughnuts and strawberry pop. My hands full, I walk to the room.

I suffer a momentary lapse, get careless and leave the door ajar as I carry stuff in from the car. I am bent over, checking the lumpy mattress with my tush in the air when the creepy desk guy puts one foot inside the room.

"Get the hell out of here!" I yell, slamming the door.

He doesn't get all of his foot out of the way and yelps in pain. I don't care if I broke it.

"I am bringing you ice, Miss," he says, trying not to groan.

Oooh! "Oh! Thank you. Just put it down by the door, okay? Sorry about your foot. You can go away now."

"Yes. I am going away now, Miss."

Jeez! I snatch the ice bucket and my laptop from the car and then I slot the dead-bolt and latch the chain-guard. I tilt a chair and wedge its top under the doorknob. Door secure, I turn on the ball game. I miss Paul Demeter's double to raise his average to .401, but the Royals suck, so he will get four more at-bats.

This season Paul Demeter is different. Well, that's obvious, but I see it early. I see it in his face, in his eyes, the way his shoulders relax, how his hands set the bat an instant before he pulls the trigger. Pitches that used to tie him in knots—anything low inside and sliders medium outside—now he is killing. I see it in April, then in May.

He finishes tonight two for five. The second hit is a push bunt, placed perfectly up the first base line. It has to be perfect because he bats from the right side, and he isn't that fast. I study his face as he calls time and jogs back down the line to retrieve his cap. I follow the close-up of his face as he plops his cap back on where it settles atop his shank of blondish hair. Think a taller Timberlake—minus the dimples. He lifts his smiling mug and waves toward the fans, who answer him with equal portions of cheers and jeers.

How can I be so sure about Paul Demeter? Easy! I have dissected practically every televised at-bat of his career. I probably know Paul Demeter's stance better than he does. I know what pitches are his weakness and which ones he turns on. I know what pitch count he has struck out on most in his career. That would be two balls, two strikes!

His career until this season has been disappointing. A *can't miss* prospect in college, he graduated in three years and was drafted by the White Sox. Chapter and verse, I know his quick rise through the minors and how he landed in Chicago. After a disappointing rookie year with the Sox, he settled down and had a very good sophomore season, hitting .301, and making the All-Star team. The next season was good too, as he hit .292, won a Gold Glove and was an All-Star again. He looked a lock to be a fixture at third base for the White Sox and the A.L. All-Star team for the next decade or so. But then bad luck settled on Paul Demeter, like fog over Lake Michigan.

I don't like to dwell on it. I'll only say his misfortune was tangled up in family and leave it. Anyway, following a long absence from a woman and a child, he returned to Chicago, but not to them. Not long after, they went to Tulsa to stay without him.

Whether related, nobody knows, but Paul Demeter became injury-prone. Majorly. He tore an ACL, sliding into second, and was sidelined for most of his fourth year. He came back too soon from rehab and re-injured the knee, and he tore his Achilles from favoring the knee. One spring, pneumonia sidelined him until after the mid-season break. From there, it was downhill. Not speedy-of-foot to begin with, the injuries slowed him further, and infield hits turned into outs. The White Sox traded him to St. Louis, and there the slide gathered speed. He became a journeyman, known for defense, playing for eight different teams—whoever needed a first, second or third baseman—in both major leagues, plus humiliating AAA stints in Louisville and Charlotte. He never hit over .255 again, and during the last two years, he sunk to .219 and .212, clinging to the bigs by a glove.

When the press coverage had reached ridiculous proportions this summer, he announced he was through talking to the media. I imagine he was exhausted from all the thinly veiled, accusatory questions.

When the season ends, all the great sports writers will swarm him. No matter—I know *I* will be the one who gets the real story. Yes, it is brazen of me. But true. Fortune has given me a great break on the angle, but at the end of the day, or season, that lucky inside track only gets you so far. Luck gets me in the door, but talent rules in the end. Talent gets published… usually.

My best work had come this spring, when three months short of graduation, my class was going on without me because I was a few credits light. I told Jodie I was quitting school to cover the Occupiers on Riverside Drive, where I spent twenty-nine fun-filled days with the protestors (Jodie later told me the experience taught her that she could not actually die from worry.)

I slept where they slept, ate what they ate, went to the bathroom where they went and got routed by bayonetted, gas-masked cops like they got routed. I knew the story I chronicled was both powerful and revealing. I also knew it screamed for a wider voice than a school paper's reach.

"This is pretty good stuff," the *Sentinel* editor said as he stared far too long at my chest.

"But?" I rasped, securing the top button of my blouse. My lungs and throat still burned from the CS gas.

"I'm sorry. What?"

"'But!' You were about to say, 'This is pretty good stuff, but …"

"Oh, right. Yeah, I guess I was. This is pretty good stuff, but you are very young and lack experience, and so… this is a mature subject. But if you want to leave it with us, we'll study it some more. If we think we might use some of it, we will give you a call."

He didn't call. The next Sunday, in the feature magazine, a *Sentinel* reporter who had not put in the time or the sweat equity with the Occupiers that I had—this reporter gave his own account of the experience. It was written well and factual, but it was not as well written, factual or poignant as mine, and it was rife with bald-faced plagiarism of the most crooked stripe. It was plain to see he had taken full paragraphs of my stuff, and with a middle finger poised over the thesaurus key, he had re-shaped the sentences as his own. I was flat assed robbed!

I was pissed, and so was Jodie. She wanted to take my back-up copy down there, shove it under their eyes and raise high hell. I told her to calm down. If we actually got in the door, my flimsy copy would prove nothing. Who the hell was I anyway but some high school dropout who was role-playing as a reporter?

If you know me, you will say I have the talent, and you will be right. Then you might also say, yeah, but I'm young—just a kid, and you will be wrong. I am not a kid.

I have been tear-gassed by cops on the east bank of the Arkansas, I had my stomach pumped from an accidental overdose at the OU/Texas game, and I was sexually assaulted, just hanging out with a friend.

Not that I'm recommending any of the above as desirable rites of passage, but you can see my level of maturity. The first two life-altering events are well documented, though I never told anyone about the other. Some secrets are so heavy that you don't see how objects as frail as the human psyche and soul possibly can hold them in, but I forced myself to do just that.

The boy, Kevin—he would have claimed he was only fooling around and that the situation got only a little out of hand. He said he was sorry, but he didn't think he hurt me. He's the brother of my former best friend. He used to be my friend. I try to avoid him, but that's problematic. It's a small town. We know the same people, and we went to the same school, until I quit.

The main reason I don't tell anyone—Jodie. I am afraid of what she would do if I toss this nugget her way. I don't want Kevin's life ruined over a mistake, no matter how it hurt me. Could I have used a little motherly devotion right about then? Sure, I'm not going to lie about that. I could have. But I weighed the options and sucked it up.

I could have touched *The Sentinel* for a little travel money and per diem and maybe even a "press pass" for this project, but I have pride—a lot of pride. The primary reason I don't approach them is because I would have to stoop to allowing them in on the reason that my story will be like nobody else's, and that includes the biggest names in the business. And that is for sure—straight up because this unlikely hero—this Paul Demeter, who is trying to run down .400—he is my old man.

After the game, I lie on the uneven bed and stare at the pockmarked and water-stained ceiling. This week, I have been excited, practically giddy. All summer, I had plans to work on, and now the opportunity is here. I take stock. I am still geeked about what I am doing, and I am sure of my plan, yet a tinge of disquiet creeps in, maybe even a little trepidation? *How could it not? This is natural, right*—at the threshold of one of the big ones, after all?

Verging on one of life's *moments*, yeah—I'm flying straight into grown-up territory, without the advantage of college's four-year safety net. I am not a schoolgirl anymore. I am practically a woman. *I got this.* I fluff the pillow that I brought from home, stick my face in it and try to fall asleep.

I sleep like a baby: I wake every hour and cry.

Daybreak

I start coffee with my little road fixins. Today is a dash of Columbian bold and two spoons of Verona x-bold. Some people are horrified that I mix. "That's drinking you don't mix," I tell them. "You do whatever you like with coffee." I love coffee. So glad Jodie wasn't a prude about it and let me start young.

"You're old enough for a period, you're old enough for coffee," she told me.

"Same-same for booze and sex?"

"Don't test me, young lady," she answered.

I strain with the jammed motel window crank and finally get enough of a crack so that I can re-direct the smoke from my morning cigarette. Takes a lot of nerve to post a *No Smoking* sign in a dump like this!

It's about time to run. I know running and smoking seems "counter-intuitive," which sounds fancy, but it is really just *PC* for stupid. I think of it as a balance thing. I wait until the sun's first light. I might seem intrepid, as Jodie claims, but I'm not about to run in a new place in the dark.

Running usually clears my cobwebs after a restless night. Wearing the snug green Dry Fit shorts and matching top I borrowed from Jodie's closet, I stretch. The same office guy from last night limps by on his hurt foot, pushing a service cart between buildings. He looks at me with the serious eyes again, but he doesn't speak as he walks on. I whip my head around in a snap so I can catch him staring at my ass. I blush to see that he isn't.

Whenever I run, walk or drive in a new place, I usually find myself beside a stream. I have a river magnet in me. Today, it is working. Beside the green water is a path of pea gravel—perfect for running. I run for twenty minutes up and eighteen coming back down. It is already ninety degrees, so I have a good sweat going.

I wish the pool were bigger. I'll have to hydrate before entering the stadium, and though it is sacrilege, I will limit myself to one beer at the game.

The motel guy holds a giant butterfly net.

"I will clean out the pool for you," he says with the serious face.

It is hard not to laugh. You could clean this little thing with two swipes of a toothbrush.

"I appreciate that, but I am not swimming this morning. I am sorry about hurting your foot, but you shouldn't have snuck up on me like that."

"Yes. I am sorry for that, Miss. Have a nice day."

The One

She was the one. Aqib was sure. She had the good face, and by that he meant an honest, practical face that belonged to a serious person. His plan called for a very serious one. Her face was also pretty, though that was not a necessary factor in his plan.

He had not expected it to be someone young—especially one so close to his age. He checked his list. He re-packed his bag to be certain he had everything he needed: water jug, two changes of clothes, his jimmy—that could also serve as a weapon if matters came to that—and a foiled two-pack of condoms that some guests had left in a room.

He smashed his cell phone and left seventy dollars in the cash box. He didn't enjoy robbing the motel, but weren't the owners trying to rob him? Trying to rob him of his future without him even having a say? He helped himself to another twenty.

He was ready… more than ready. He turned out the lights. He locked the office door. She was still at the pool, sweating out from her run. Soon, she would go in the room and take a shower. Then he would make his move.

Keeping it Professional

I aim Moby toward Kansas City. The radio is unpredictable, so for news and entertainment, I turn to the slick little unit I found in Jodie's underwear drawer.

"This looks handy," I remember saying to her. "What is it?"

"It's called a Walkman. *Every*one had one back in the day. And stay out of my panties."

"But yours are so cute!"

I plug in the headphones and scroll. I stop on *CBS Sports*, and big surprise—the first name I hear is Paul Demeter. Imagine that! I'm way past being shocked by my father's sudden and seemingly ubiquitous fame. Before he clammed up, he was on the morning and late-night TV news and talk shows, as well as the covers of the major magazines. He gave interviews in every major league city paper, and he used to appear at press conferences after each game since May.

"Baseball is back, and Demeter is a big part of it!" the Columbia professor of sports economics says on the Walkman. "Attendance is up in both leagues, and the thirds have it! One-third of America thinks Paul Demeter is the savior of baseball and is hoping he hits .400. The second-third couldn't care less about baseball, but they are tuning in to see what the fuss is about, while the back third is positive he's cheating and is hoping he fails. Either way, his quest of hitting .400 has re-energized the country's interest in baseball.

"The steroid-era soured America on baseball. People were disgusted by the use of PEDs. The fans were duped. Now they are back—at least this summer, and they are watching and waiting. That is why," the professor says, "Heaven help Paul Demeter if he *is* cheating, because they will hang him from the flag pole in Fenway!"

I get a text. It's early for lunch, but I can get a sandwich to take to the game. I pull over to a place to check my phone. It's Jodie. She wants me to call. I buy a pork chop hero before I punch her number.

"Jack moved out," are the first words from her mouth.

"Whoo-hoo!" I yell, slugging the air. "Ole Jackie Boy gets booted to the curb! Hubba-dah hubba-dah! Well done, young lady. I hope you kicked him one time for me."

"Uh-not exactly. He left *me*."

"Either way!"

Bad form. I hear a tiny sniffle. *No more Jack slams, Idiot.* I wish I could put my arm around her. I hurt for her, but I am glad Jack is gone. Jodie is so much better off—think addition by subtraction— but that doesn't make her feel better. I know I sound like a callous little ingrate most of the time, but I do love Jodie very much, and I wish her life were happier and less complicated.

"So today is your first game?" she asks. "Are you excited?"

"A little bit. He's cheating."

"Who? Jack? It doesn't matter now," she sniffles.

"No. Paul Demeter. He's cheating."

"No one knows that, Syl."

"C'mon, Jodie. Hitting .400 is impossible. You know it!"

"Not one person has found a single shred of evidence that proves he is cheating."

"You *are* paying attention!"

"How could one not? It's just silly. Paul Demeter is everywhere. You can't go any place that his face or his voice or someone else's voice talking about him doesn't pop up. You'd think people would have better things to do than to indulge in such trivial pursuits! Even the guys at OZ were watching *ESPN* yesterday when I went in for a new pipe."

I hold my tongue. My mother and I have agreed to disagree on the use of marijuana in *la chez* Kerrigan. I used to tell her she was a hypocrite not letting *me* indulge, while she smoked up a storm. Jodie's comeback, of course, is that her use is purely medicinal. We don't talk about it, because it results in the same old dead end. I exaggerate, of course.

Jodie is not a pothead. In fact, she is the reverse. She is such a prude. She makes sure the dog and cat are outside before she lights up. I laugh at her because she is so Prissy Mae about dropping even a speck on the floor or furniture. She takes the sissiest little puffs and inhales like a mosquito. It really is about her headaches, which are a real *mother*! Still, I worry about her getting caught. Oklahoma is the reddest of red states. She would lose her job, and they'd probably send her to prison for life.

"Do you expect your father to be happy to see you?"

"I expect nothing. He may not be glad to see me, but he won't toss me, will he?"

"No, he won't throw you out," Jodie whispers. "But you expect him to tell *you* things he won't tell others? Things like, 'why no personal contact with you for twelve years? Not a card at Christmas or a phone call?' *Those* kinds of things?"

If she meant to stun me, she hit the nail smack on the head. I stagger and sit on a concrete bench. I do recover, but only after a long moment's silence.

"I will be keeping it strictly professional," I murmur.

Jodie is quiet for a few seconds.

"And, you'd feel fine tricking him?" she asks.

"*Damned* fine! He's cheating. Why shouldn't I? I hate him!"

"Syl—of all people, I know how much you've been hurt."

"That's why I knew you would understand what I have to do."

"I'm sorry," Jodie says. "You needed a father."

I shake my head so hard that I think I hear my brains slushing around.

"No. I didn't need a *father*; I needed him! I needed the man who told me he would be with me always."

"He *loved* you…" Jodie consoles, blowing her nose

"He *left* me!"

"He left me, too, Syl." Jodie says, hesitating, sounding like she is on the verge of making a special point, but she changes her mind. "He left us both."

I know that. *Damnit, I know that!* I also know Jodie's life is about to change—at least for a while—when my story comes out. She and Paul Demeter have somehow managed not to leave much of a paper trail in all these years. It's why she and I have been able to fly under the radar all summer. That will all change with my story.

"Are you eating right?" she asks.

"I've been gone two days, Jodie."

Always Swinging

Paul needed to check something that had been bugging him since the bike wreck. More than halfway to his destination, he almost turned back when he realized he hadn't put in his contacts, but he was up the road and hadn't crashed yet. So what the heck? Drive on. It was not the first time he'd forgotten his eyewear recently. He'd been forgetting other things too.

He thought the exceptional vision and the bad memory might be tied to the knot on his head. He should have gone to the ER the morning of the accident for the concussion protocol at the minimum. Funny, but like the other times, he was able to drive on to his destination without crashing into anybody or anything. It was "funny," because since he was ten, he couldn't walk down the sidewalk without glasses.

Vision wasn't the only thing changed in Paul since the accident with the bicycle and his acceptance that he was no longer playing the love game. He felt a sense of release and resilience. He didn't feel it immediately, so when it eventually kicked in, he didn't make the connection at first.

He felt such a load had been lifted off. When he realized the feeling wasn't leaving him, he got used to it. It felt good! He rolled his shoulders. He thought he'd lost fifteen pounds, though when he weighed himself this morning, and he was at his playing weight since college: one-hundred ninety-five pounds.

A cold wind gust shook the truck, but he was creeping along, so he lost little control on the slick road. He wore gloves, ear muffs, a thick windbreaker and baggie sweat pants. A bat standing on the floorboard leaned against his knee.

"Always Swinging," the junkyard of a driving range and batting cage, was open… barely. The snow on the ground didn't keep four old duffers from slashing at balls down range. The one cage was predictably open. He woke an undernourished, harshly pretty teenager, slumped at the window, paying up and giving her a ten-dollar tip.

"An hour okay?"

"An hour?" she said with a slight frown. "I was gonna close when the old guys got done. In fact, I was gonna try to run them off before they caught pneumonia. A couple of them already have colds."

He started to say something to her. Somehow she reminded him of Sylvia. She looked bright, and she was probably a little sassy. She would be Syl's age. About. All he said was, "I won't be long. Thank you."

He had not touched a bat since the last day of the season, so he missed the first fifty-mile an hour pitch from the machine. He laughed at himself. Had the golfers seen him whiff? They had. They waved and hooted. They probably thought he was a softball hardcore, getting an early start. He cranked the dial to "Red Hot Heat," the highest setting, which was touted as eighty-five, but was more like seventy-eight, seventy-nine.

He took his stance, which had not changed a skosch in over fifteen years. Most players experimented with changes, but not Paul. He used the same lazy, hands tucked close to the belt, knees slightly bent, shoulders a tick off level stance as always. Of course, plenty of hitting coaches had hinted that his below-average career screamed for him to consider some changes. None said it better than his friend, Fungo Kerrigan.

"Bud (he was always "Bud" to Fungo), it's not like you're Musial or Mays. Those two never changed their stances either, but then you could blindfold and handcuff them, and they would still hit .300 off God."

He strode into the second pitch and hit a ball so hard that he thought it might rip a gash in the cage's hurricane fence. *That felt good.* He saw the incoming cheap ball so clearly he could almost read the label on it, and he was surprised at how hard he hit it. He'd hit balls hard before, but this was different. Something unusual happened when he hit this ball, because *he saw the ball come off the bat!*

No big deal, right? Players all the time talked about seeing the bat meet the ball when they made solid contact. Paul hadn't joined that conversation since his two All-Star seasons. Babe Ruth said he could count the *threads* on the ball when he hit it. Mantle claimed he saw every ball he ever hit, drunk or sober, as it left the bat. But that was Mickey *Damn* Mantle!

For the last decade, when Paul swung on a pitch thrown by a major leaguer, it was all he could do to try to make contact with the dang thing—never mind seeing it come off the bat. After the two good years, the game had never again slowed down that much for him.

He swung on the next pitch and distinctly saw the ball explode off his bat, and he heard it slam, like a rifle shot. He made solid contact with ball after ball, and each time, he saw the ball leave his bat. He didn't know how long he swung, but he knew he was onto something. *Swing, swing, the same swing, the same feel, the same sweet faint kiss of the bat, the same violent jingle at the fence.* He didn't know what was happening, but it felt good. He felt good. The machine stopped.

"Closing up, Sir," the girl said, astride a bicycle.

The golfers were gone. *Was that an hour?* It seemed like five minutes. He didn't hesitate. "Here, a hundred bucks. Take it. Let me hit. What's left, put in your pocket. I'll lock up."

The girl said, "I watched you. I've never seen anything like that here. Mind if I watch more?"

"Naw," Paul said, frowning. She wasn't dressed for this weather. She had on cutoffs and flimsy sweater. Maybe that's all she had. "You're fine," he added.

He lost track of time. He took off the gloves and ear muffs. Hours passed like minutes as he swung at balls. Ball after ball, seeing each one detonate off his bat—he hit and hit, never tiring. Each swing of the bat was a sweet jolt to his gut and a tickle feeling in the tips of his fingers. Something big was happening, and he went with it, hitting baseballs in contentment.

When the day grew grayer as heavy clouds rolled up, he didn't see them. He saw only the machine balls in the advancing darkness. When pellets of ice bit the exposed flesh of his hands, neck and ears, he didn't feel them. He stripped the windbreaker, swinging to an inner rhythm. He'd never been a dancer, but he imagined it was how Baryshnikov felt when he was in a zone.

He didn't feel the cold or exertion, swinging as if he were set free because… he was! He was never going to love again, and that gave him freedom. He'd made a terrible mistake—walking away from a woman and child in Chicago, never even giving them a chance.

Maybe he'd loved them too hard, too fast. He'd made an awful blunder, and he was finally, finally past it. What he possessed once, he would never have again, so he was going to quit looking. He was free of that. Could that realization, in some way, transfer over to hitting a baseball? Probably not. Certainly not. But what was this feeling, then?

Elizabeth was crazy to ride a bicycle along a dark street—just to tell a man one more thing! She would have probably claimed she couldn't see for the tears in her eyes. She would have said she didn't mean to hurt him—if anyone had seen it and come after her. She might not have hit him and run—if it had been anyone else.

Elizabeth would be fine. God, how could she *not* be? A man would find her and count himself the luckiest guy in the world. They would have a child. Paul knew well how a child could bring joy to a relationship… or tear it apart.

"That was stupid good," the girl said.

Paul jumped. He'd forgotten the kid was there.

She had to be freezing. Her nose was red and runny, and her cheeks were grayish blue. "Don't forget to lock up, and thanks for the money," she said before peddling off into the flinty, dark night.

Paul knew an old hippie who was a mechanical genius, so he asked Lyman to take a look at the pitching machine.

"How fast can you get it up to?"

"How fast you want it?" Lyman asked.

"They say Randy Johnson threw a hundred-four. Make it that fast."

When he was finished, Lyman smiled at Paul.

"Now it's not exact. One pitch will go one-o-five, another one-o-three, but you got that basic range. Here—take this tool. You can't get to that gear without this. And for god's sake, be sure and turn it off every time you leave. We don't want a kid wandering in here by accident and getting himself killed! For fifty bucks, I'll come back and disable that gear when you're ready to leave town."

As a Major League ballplayer and hometown lad, Paul had a standing invitation to hit indoors at the university, but he'd never availed himself of the opportunity. This winter, he did not miss a day, not even Christmas, hitting the ridiculously fast pitches at the frozen range. He worked a deal with the kid in which he gave her three hundred dollars a week, and she gave him his own key. It was too much money, but she looked like she needed it.

Most days were frigid, so he always had the cage to himself. The old timers who swatted golf balls every day never left without huddling at the cage for a while and cheering him on. They shared their hot coffee thermoses with him, sometimes spiking them with whiskey.

Most days the girl, who he now knew was almost exactly Sylvia's age, watched, too, standing with her fingers hanging in the wire of the cage.

"You better not do that," Paul told her. "You might get hit by a foul ball."

She shook her head. "You don't hit foul balls."

He hit for four hours daily, sometimes in the morning, but more often in the afternoon. On several occasions, he hit until dark, like he did the first day when time went away and he experienced dramatic freedom. He kept no track of his swings, freeing his mind of all but the process. He later calculated that if he hit, say one hundred-fifty balls an hour, he would have taken close to fifteen thousand swings by New Year's Day—far more than he had in all his former off-seasons put together. He had never trained so intensely all his career. He had always stayed in shape, but intensively working on a particular part of his game like this? No way. And the funny thing? It didn't feel like training. It felt like freedom.

The day before he left for spring training he went a last time to the batting cage. The sun was just coming up, and the old men hadn't arrived. He warmed up swinging his leaded bat when a beat up Civic pulled into the parking lot. The girl got out carrying two tall cups of coffee.

"Here," she said, handing him one of the cups. "I thought you would come today."

"Some ride you got there," he said. "Thanks for the coffee."

"You're welcome. It's sixteen years old and has over two-hundred thousand miles on it, but it runs good. I got it from my cousin. The one time in a month my dad didn't come home high, he drove it and said it was probably a fair deal. I used the money you gave me. I feel like I have a little freedom now. Thank you."

"Glad to help."

"I have a feeling you are going to have a good season," the girl said.

Deaf Heaven

Though the Royals suck, and it's the last month of the season, leaving them with no chance for the playoffs, the stadium is already packed. I feel the exhilaration in the air as I walk in. Fans are here to see a very mortal ballplayer stalk an immortal number. The great Royal favorite, George Brett, who threatened .400 in 1980, will even throw out the ceremonial first pitch.

I take my seat in the right-field bleachers, slathering my face, neck and arms with SPF 80. I wear my favorite frayed and faded Levi cut-offs and a smart, sleeveless blouse that I found in a second hand shop on Brookside. My Boss sandals protect my feet. I try to flatten my crazy hair, but I give up. I pull my visor low until it touches my sunglasses, and taking my binoculars from my bag, I open my scorebook and jot in the starting lineups. The first name I write in the cleanup spot is that of my long-lost Daddy-O.

Play ball!

I watch William 'Fungo' Kerrigan jog in from the bullpen until he passes under my seat. I forget his age, but he's kept in good shape. My grandfather and I are not exactly destined to be BFFs. I know he has me down for a little bitch that's too sassy for her own good. Fah! And this from the *Good Housekeeping* model family member!

We thought after jail and two years exile in Japan, William was done with pro baseball for sure. No team would touch him. He tried to catch on with a juco in Texas or Oklahoma, calling around, but nobody needed anybody. Jodie told him he could be a bus driver or a custodian at her school in Tulsa and he could stay with us (she got a half-hearted okay from Jack; she didn't consult me, because she already knew the answer).

William thanked her by saying he was "no damn janitor." He was ready to give up and go back to Japan, where they said he would always have a job, when Texas called. The new manager was Lavernicus Thibodaux, a buddy of William's. He was looking for a bench coach. The only caveat to William's returning to baseball came straight from the Commissioner himself—he was not allowed to so much as even hold a fungo bat again.

At the tail end of last season, the Rangers lost a shortstop and third baseman to injury. Backups filled in the last twenty games, but they needed an infielder as their sub.

William told his boss that Demeter was over in Milwaukee, and they weren't using him much. "He's only hitting about two bucks, but it's his glove we need," William said.

Thibodaux asked William if Demeter had been with him in Chicago?

"And St. Louis," William answered.

"Wasn't he your son-in-law or something like that?"

"Something like that," William admitted. "He ain't hitting much, Vern, but he scoops up grounders like a power vac sucking up dirt balls."

"Call him, then," Thibodaux said.

And that's how my father and grandfather ended up on the same team.

William stops in the outfield, turns and looks up in the bleachers like he's looking for someone in particular. He scans with piercing eyes, partly shadowed by the bill of his cap. That's crazy; he can't have spotted me in so large a crowd. I scrunch down in the seat and stare at my lap.

Same as last night, Paul Demeter gets mixed reactions from the enormous crowd when he steps in the batter's box: roaring applause and thunderous boos. He touches the bill of his cap to both sets of reactions. He smashes the ball tonight, but on three savage line drives, he is robbed of hits by spectacular defensive plays.

Using the binoculars, I watch Paul Demeter's face for his reactions to the outs. Will he curse and spit? Go to his knees and trouble deaf heaven with bootless cries? Literally, an inch or two in either direction and each ball is a base hit.

He grins slightly, shakes his head and even jokes with the first baseman who made one of the catches. The man grabs the mitt, still on his hand, looking at the pocket and laughing. He is certainly a lot more good-natured about it than I would have been. I'd have pitched a fit that Billy Martin would have been proud of, but that's me.

Today, his average dips to .399.

Before the Trouble

Before the trouble with the attorneys that sent him to prison, William Kerrigan had been a legendary infield coach—maybe the best ever. Wielding the extra-long, ridiculously thin eponymous stick like a wizard's wand or third arm, he peppered crisp grounders, dribblers, worm burners in the hole and handcuffers at infielders.

Opponents gawked, and fans came early. He scalded balls within inches of where the shortstop or third sacker needed to be. Feisty, he'd have three balls on the way to three basemen at the same time. He challenged with Texas Leaguers, just past the reach, and towering pop-ups that got lost in the clouds.

It was like watching a baseball ballet, with players leaping, jumping and stretching for batted balls. He even provided the accompaniment, berating, praising, cajoling, cussing, whistling and all around coaching them up the entire time.

William thought he was still in good enough shape to put an infield through their paces, but they didn't let him. He missed the smell of the dirt and grass. He missed the hands-on feel to the magnificent game.

A Different Angle

I sneak a smoke as I finish my notes in the bleachers, and then I walk down a ramp. On my way down, my grandfather steps from behind a pillar. I bump him hard, bouncing backward.

"You look ten years younger in jeans and a Polo—no ball cap," I tell him. "You'd think it would be the other way around. Y'know, dressing for a young man's game, you oughta look younger. How'd you find me?"

"You're obvious." He scowls. "Girl alone in the bleachers, writes on a laptop, keeps score, dresses goofy, and hair that no hat is going to hide. You after money?"

"Bastard!"

"So?"

"Actually? I'll be saving him money. When I turn eighteen, his child support's over. You're not going to tell me I ought to go home?"

"No, because you wouldn't listen to me. I hear you're not going to college."

"Yes, I am not. I am a writer."

"Like your mother is a writer?"

"Jerk!"

"Are you leaving?" he yells.

I turn. "Why? Am I getting smaller?"

"Hold on. Come back here. I meant, 'do you write short fiction and poetry?'"

"I am a journalist."

He nods, mulling this over. "Right… for the school paper, wasn't it? So, if not for the money, what're you doing here? Just curious, like everbody else?"

"I wanted to pick my time, plus I had to earn enough to do it my way."

"Do *what* your way?"

"Cover the story here, at its end."

"Whew, Sister! There's a long line…"

"You think I don't know that? The competition is stiff, but my take will be a one-off, original. It originates from a completely different angle than anyone else's. I'm the only writer who won't be disappointed when he fails."

We let that hang in the air between us.

After a long, still moment, I look straight in his lion-colored eyes.

"How's he doing it?"

He scowls. Then chuckles. "You actually think I'm going to have that conversation with you, standing out here under a stadium?"

"I can't think of a better place."

"Well, I'm not having it. You seriously mean to follow us across the country?"

"That's the plan."

He snorts and hands me a card. "Tuesday, then. Chicago. Lunch at this place. We can discuss Paul, and then we can generally catch up on things. If you don't make it, I'll know that old rig of yours finally blew up and left you stranded on the side of the road."

I almost say, *Don't worry. I'll make it, but what have we between us to catch up on?* when a sudden movement snags my eye. I blink twice. I am stunned.

"Excuse me a sec, William."

I cannot believe my eyes. I point to a concession stand that is closing. "See that kid over there? I need to talk to him."

"That Hispanic kid?"

"Asian. I'll be right back."

I cannot believe what I am seeing. I squint hard to make sure my eyes are not leading me astray. They aren't. The damn motel guy is here at the ballpark. It is the ice bucket Pakistani kid. He is obviously following me. Stalking me! He trailed me to the border, to the city, to the stadium! The nerve, the gall, the perversion!

"What the hell are you doing here?" I say to his back. I am surprised my voice is under control, because I am so angry.

"I like baseball, Miss?" he says, turning with the same serious face he used at the motel.

The vendor tosses his change and slams the aluminum overhang shut.

"Right. A kid from Islamabad likes *our* national pastime. And he happens to appear near me at a game attended by forty thousand people. What a coincidence!"

Such a serious look. He isn't actually menacing-looking, with his frizzy little starter mustache and grave auburn eyes. His hands are delicate, with almost feminine-looking fingers. He is about six feet, a string bean. I could knock him down myself, and I'm not big. He is harmless. But he *is* following me. *Eck!*

"So, I am running into you again, Miss," he says after taking a sip from a soda.

"No. You are not *running* into me. You are following me. That is called stalking, which is a crime in this country. That cannot happen. It's way beyond creepy. You can go to jail. You can't expect me to believe you are here for the baseball?"

"Oh yes," he says, as if he were telling me he loved his mother. "It is not as exciting as cricket, but I am loving when the hurler strikes down the batsman."

"Out."

"Miss?"

"It's out—strikes *out* the batsman… er batter."

"Right."

He takes a long, noisy slurp of the drink, like he is dying of thirst.

"I am also loving when the field men make interceptions of the batted balls."

"Interceptions? You really know your baseball. Don't follow me. You should leave. You know, this is weird. If I see you again, I'll call the cops on you."

"Okay. Nice to run into you. Goodbye and be safe."

"Friend of yours, up here in KC?" William asks after I stomp my way back to him.

"He's a creep, and he is following me—stalking me. I can't believe it!" I watch to make sure the guy exits the gate. He still walks with a limp. *Good!*

"*That* kid? I'd say he looks pretty harmless to me."

"He's the office boy, janitor and maid at the Kansas motel I stayed in last night—a cheap loser of a motel. Now he's here. What would you call that?"

"I'd call it a lot of cojones… if he really has a crush on you."

"A crush? OMG! Please!" I look again, and he's gone.

"It can be a small world, Syl. Maybe you're giving yourself too much credit. Maybe on his day off, he thinks he will check out all the fuss about Paul Demeter over in the big city? A lot of people are coming to the ballparks for the first time this season."

"Never mind," I groan.

"Or, he could really be sweet on you. He's not a bad-looking kid, and obviously he's a hard-worker. You could treat it as a compliment. Shoot, I've never had anyone cross a state line just to be with me."

"Ooh! I cannot believe you just said that. You telling him?"

"Paul? You want me to tell Paul about you?"

"No!"

"Okay then. I won't."

"Look. I mean… I'm not ready. I know that at some point I will have to confront him—face him, but not yet. I'll wait. If I get close to him too soon in the process, I don't know what I might do."

"What are you afraid of?"

"I'm afraid I might plunge my pen deep into his lying eyes."

William takes a step back.

"Isn't that being a little dramatic?" he asks, his piercing eyes looking at me in a new way.

A Father's Lie

This is beyond ridiculous. I am being stalked. Me! Sylvia Kerrigan! Personally!—not some poor chick with a mug shot in the Metro section who has her wrestler-boyfriend beat up the guy who's helicoptering her. I don't feel particularly frightened— mainly because of the incompetent nature of the guy doing it, but it feels creepy. Weird! Oh well, I signed on for this. I know the risks. A writer sacrifices for her craft.

Maybe I imagined it, but it seemed to me my grandfather looked at me with a different perspective when I said that about Paul Demeter. It was like he took me seriously after that. I'm a little surprised he didn't object. Paul Demeter is more than a friend to William. I won't say like a son, but pretty damn close.

Still, he didn't defend him. He knows better. He knows what Paul Demeter meant to us and did to us. It is still alive in me, as vivid as yesterday.

We lived in Chicago. Paul Demeter came for me in my limo, the Thunder Chicken—the fat-tired, three-wheel stroller we put hundreds of miles on when I was a baby. He ran me all over the place. We ate up miles like popcorn. We wore out three sets of tires. When I was very small, I napped in the buggy, and when I stirred, he told me how many people stopped and commented on the cute child with the crazy curls.

When we school kids waited with teachers for moms and nannies in nice cars, my dad, the White Sox player, the third baseman—who taught me to read by going over scouting reports on his lap—rounded the corner, like a wild man, behind my golden chariot on one wheel.

I was the rage. We careened off curbs and vaulted across the river as we raced the route home at speeds not recommended by the manufacturers. It was glorious—me standing, face to the wind, as Paul Demeter ran and sang to me. Almost home, we stopped at The Hand, and he got an onion bagel for Jodie, a sesame seed for him, and a kid's pizza slice, cut in two, for me.

Jodie hated that he got pizza, because by the time we got home, I wore most of it on my face and in my hair. I asked him if we could be like this a long time, and he said we could do better than "a long time."

"I will be with you *always*, he said. "Always is way better than a long time!"

At first, I wouldn't believe my dad left us. Not *could* not, but *would* not—not for good, anyway. He would never do a thing like that! He loved me too much.

Even as a child, I should have seen it coming. I should have known, the way a child knows, to expect something bad to happen—if not bad, at least something very different. Nothing had been quite right in the small apartment, or in my world, since the day I found Jodie on the floor in a small lake of blood.

I knew something big was up the morning Jodie went all yoga on me after he was out the front door, asking me to sit. She told me that with this trip, Paul wasn't coming back, but I was not convinced. In my mind, he was gone on the road with the team (despite being aware that the season was over), and he would return as usual.

After weeks went by with no Paul Demeter walking through the door to grab me up, I considered the facts, commanded myself to grow up and ripped up all pictures I had of him, (even his rookie card, which would be worth a freaking fortune right now). Jodie had laminated the card for me, so I had to get a butcher knife to cut that hard plastic.

Jodie and I moved back to the house in Tulsa, where we've been ever since. I wrote, *I hate you, Paul Demeter* forty-six his (jersey number) times on the inside cover of my two favorite books. (I was five, remember?) I wanted to curse him, but I couldn't remember enough of the words I'd heard from my grandfather, who didn't use them around me much after Jodie scolded him.

I kept up with my dad on TV just to see him fall on his face, and mostly he did. His fine bat from the two All-Star years went AWOL. He could still field his position like a maniac, but the pop from his bat was missing in action. I watched as many games as I could, except for the west coast games on school nights.

In second grade, he showed up at the house, just like that. Jodie knew in advance, but for some reason, she didn't warn me.

"Don't you dare do a stupid thing like getting your hopes up," she warned/threatened me a minute before he walked in the door. "He's here on business. Period."

When he saw me, he did a weird thing. Instead of hugging me, he shook my hand and glanced over at Jodie. The only time I'd ever shaken hands with anyone else until then was at kindergarten graduation when, Mr. Roberts showed us the proper way. That is how I shook Paul Demeter's hand—firmly, like I imagined business people shake hands, though lacking energy.

"It's not a car jack," our principal had admonished, "So, don't pump it up and down like you're about to change a flat."

When we finished shaking hands, Paul gave me a smile. Again, he looked at Jodie with eyes that were different.

He spent the night with us, but instead of sleeping in the room with Jodie, he ended up on the futon in the atrium. Jodie gave strict orders I was not to come down and bother him in the night. I wanted to, but I obeyed. To my wonderment, I was sort of afraid to see him.

The next morning was no more hopeful. As I was forced to go to school, my father shook my hand again, with the same odd look in his eyes. I had perked up some during the previous night when Jodie told me she and Paul would be going to the courthouse. People went to courthouses all the time to get married, right? I made a deal with my pillow I would no longer fight Jodie over all the green mess she consistently put on my plate—if indeed that was their errand.

I didn't take the stupid bus home, because it made too many time-consuming stops. Instead, I ran, cutting through Colonel Phillips' backyard. I had to kick at her big Doberman—the dog that she told everybody was sweet as sugar plums, though it had already bit two FedEx drivers.

I ran in the house calling for Jodie and Paul, only to find the two of them drinking coffee and talking at a table in the atrium like they were a husband and wife who were discussing everyday issues. I experienced a jarring return to reality when it appeared to me that both had just finished a good cry.

Cautious though undaunted, I sidled up, checking fingers for gold rings. It turned out they needed to see a lawyer at the courthouse because Paul was buying our house for us, and they required legal assistance. Dang! Pretty dull stuff. I didn't know our house even needed buying.

Only thing, Jodie refused at the last minute. She wouldn't accept his offer. And was that what the crying was about? Later she told me it was huge of him to offer, because he didn't have to, just like, she reminded me for the jillionth time—he didn't have to pay monthly child support either, since he and Jodie never officially married and he wasn't my real father. This last is such *boosh-wah-zee* from Jodie.

I know the difference between a real father and a fake father. A fake father wouldn't take a comb and a brush every day and do battle with a head of hair like mine, or wipe my bottom when I couldn't do it myself, or buy me wedding cake snow cones, or sit up with me when I am sick, or let me scrootch onto his side of the bed at night when there's a Bigfoot under my bed.

But all this probably belongs in a different story. I remember sitting there, and the only thing I could think was:

We can accept the piddly child support, but we're too proud to let him pay for the house?

I should've been happy that Paul Demeter felt a little something for us. Instead, I felt real sorry for myself and descended into a fatherless funk, lasting through cursive, Accelerated Reader, multiplication tables, half a mouthful of teeth and tee-ball. I was not a happy camper, but on my eighth birthday, I decided to take the high road and forgive him.

My school sponsored a week in which we wasted valuable class time participating in pukish role-playing games, such as "Trust," "Loyalty" and "Forgiveness." In spite of my fierce reluctance, some of it rubbed off on me.

So one Saturday, I woke up early and filled my jeans with seventy-nine dollars from my birthday. I stuffed my bag with clothes, a toothbrush, PJs, my Woobie and notebook. I told Jodie I was pedaling over to Zoe's. You can actually do that in our neighborhood—ride your bike or walk over to a friend's without the fear of being stolen and sold into sex slavery.

It's as if every household designates a member to stand at the front door or the picture window and stare out at persons going by on the sidewalk. If a lost driver finds himself on our streets, he will not make very many laps before he'll be surrounded by residents offering directions. If a person drops a phone or handbook or wallet stuffed with cash and comes looking for it, she will find it still there, safe, untouched, and guarded by five neighbors. Our area is pretty safe.

In no time, I rode my bike down the opposite direction on a one-way boulevard and into the crowded downtown Union Bus station. The first person I encountered was an old homeless man, who did not turn out to be old at all, but he looked that way before I got close.

"You really shouldn't be here," he scolded.

I remained undeterred, because I'd worked out a plan. I would stand out in the covered area where the buses arrived and departed, and when I saw one with a "Wichita" sign above the windshield, I would simply get on it and hide under a seat or in the bathroom.

Yet when I went out there, I saw such a confusion of people in panic, carrying overstuffed bags, scurrying and knocking others aside to find the right buses. There was also the clamor of hissing brakes and yelling and a loud speaker trying to talk over all the commotion. I became frightened.

So I went inside, where it wasn't so crazy, and I sat on an empty bench. I would go to Plan B. Once settled, I would work my nerve up to walk over to the ticket window and lay my money down. Then I would shove across the letter from Jodie, telling the bus people that her 12-year-old daughter (*Sylvia is small for her age*) has her permission to go see her father, who lives in Kansas and can't wait to see her.

If they asked why my mother didn't come down herself and buy the ticket, or why the sloppy penmanship on the note looked more like a third-grader's, I was prepared to tell them my mother suffered from early onset Alzheimer's and couldn't safely drive a car. I would further explain that their own handwriting might not look so hot if they couldn't remember when to use a 'g' instead of a 'q.' I was pretty sure that would shut them up.

The groundwork for putting this option into play took longer and was more wearisome than I thought, and the next thing I knew, I was waking from a two and a half hour nap, during which I had drooled slobber down the front of my sweatshirt. When I looked up, I found myself staring into the eyes of three of TPD's finest.

Of course, when I hadn't come home for lunch, Jodie called Zoe and found out I had never even been to her house. While I slept on that hard wooden bench in a dank and dirty city bus station, surrounded by drug addicts, homeless people, pick pockets and honest families going back home; an

Amber Alert had been airing on radio and TV stations over all of Northeastern Oklahoma.

A Foolish Thing

Aqib knew he did a foolish thing, going back into the stadium, but when she didn't come back to the car one-half hour after most of the people left, he got worried and thought he should go see if something happened her. He had to be careful, but he saw one lone drink stand still open, and he was very thirsty. Of course, that's where she saw him. His heart beat wildly when he thought of how he almost ruined everything.

He thought he came out of their confrontation okay. She didn't buy his baseball alibi, but he thought she was not suspicious. She thought he was a stalker. That was funny. That was good too, because she would not suspect what he was really about. She seemed very smart, but she couldn't possibly have a clue why he needed her.

He was smart, too. He tried to appear frightened when she threatened that she would call the police, so she would think he was long gone and would never trouble her again. He *was* very frightened of the police, but he knew she wasn't going to call them. Not her. This female seemed to be the kind who handled her own problems. That's why he chose her in the first place.

He was hot, very hot, but he had trained for this. He took a long drink and then went through techniques to slow his breathing. Soon, he would be asleep, and his heart would beat more slowly. He concentrated on thoughts of the breezes blowing through cold mountain passes in the foothills of the Hindu Kush, and soon he slept.

In the Spring

On the third day of spring training, Lavernicus Thibodaux had called William Kerrigan to his office.

"Fungo, I guess we're going to have to let your buddy, Demeter, go,"

"Yeah? You call around?"

"You know we did. I hate it, but ain't nobody needin a 39 year old, .200 hittin infielder. I don't care how good a glove he is."

"He's 38, Vern."

"He got anything he can fall back on? Selling cars or insurance? Anything like that?"

"I don't think so."

"I thought you might want to be the one tells him, and all."

"Thanks a lot."

Leaving the skipper's office, William heard a commotion at the batting cage on C Field. He stopped and listened. Someone was pounding balls, the crack of the bat ringing solid and crisp in the desert air. It even had an echo to it.

He headed that direction. Regulars on the wire watched a hitter, clobbering balls off a machine and making a racket doing it. William had heard that exact sound only one other time—with Albert Pujols in the cage.

The hitter in the cage was Paul Demeter. One of his Ranger teammates hanging on to the outside of the cage yelled, "Can't get away with that shit no more, Dem."

"Yeah, they got tests for everything now," another called out.

"I want some of what this cat's been smokin!" somebody added.

"Paul, you found the Fountain of Youth or what?"

"Dude is killing the ball! He wearin that machine out!"

"Yesterday, he about knocked a hole in the fence."

William stepped into the batting cage and called loud enough for all to hear.

"Bud, I need to talk with you." Under his breath, he added, "Let's get you outta here."

"What's up, Boss?" Paul asked, smiling as they walked away from the cage.

"'What's up' is I'm watching you tear the hide off dadgum balls, while I'm trying to think of a nice way to tell you that your baseball career is probably over."

"Oh yeah?" said Paul, the grin still firm.

"So, I just came from the skipper's office. Thibodaux confided in me they're going to give you your outright release. Before you ask—they called around. Vern asked if you had other things you could 'fall back on.' A real *caring* fella, that guy!"

"I think he is going to change his mind, William," Paul chuckled.

"That so? You are looking pretty damn sure of yourself for a guy about to get cut. Hell, you look *younger*! What *are* you up too, Bud?"

The next day was Sunday, meaning they had the morning off, so William drove Paul across town to a high school football practice field where a young man waited for them.

"What's going on?" Paul asked once he studied the male figure leaning against a goal post. "We're gonna catch hell if anybody finds out this guy is out here."

William folded a bag, roughly in the shape of home plate.

"Grab a bat. Let's see what yesterday was about. This kid ain't a machine."

Brad Bradley, a rookie hotshot right-hander who would make the starting rotation once the season started, didn't look any happier to be there on a Sunday than Paul did.

William donned a catcher's mask. "Not to worry. The kid's probably headed to Cooperstown at the end of his career, but he can't play poker. He owes me cash, but I said

I'd forget it if he came out for this little party we're throwing... *and* kept his yap shut."

Not one more word came from any of the three. William dug a line with his heel—a half-foot on the other side of the twenty-yard-line for the kid to toe. Then he squatted behind the bat bag and held up his catcher's mitt. Paul took his stance. The kid wound up and threw.

The sound of the ball hitting the catcher's mitt rang out, like a rifle shot. William knew that if he hadn't caught the ball in front of his face, he would have been a dead man.

"You waitin on Christmas?" William growled while wringing his mitt hand.

Paul stepped out, casual like, but he kept an eye forward. "Where was it?"

"Belt-high, perfect strike," William cackled. "If I catch a glimpse of it headed toward your melon, I'll try to holler out."

"Thank you kindly."

Paul swung on the next pitch, but his bat caught nothing but air. He whiffed at the third pitch as well. He blinked hard as if something was in his eye.

"Something get under a contact?" William asked.

"Naw, I'm not wearing contacts."

"Whoa now!" William yelled at the pitcher while ripping off the mask and throwing the mitt on the goal line. "We're done here. He doesn't have his specs. This man's blind as a mole. Why didn't you say something, Bud? You could've got yourself killed."

"I'm good, William," Paul laughed.

"Like hell you're good! You can't see crap without glasses."

"I see fine now."

"All of a sudden?"

"Just like that."

"Bullshit! I was born skeptic and don't believe in miracles."

"Try me."

"Fine. What's that billboard say down the street a ways?"

"You mean the green one that a woman parked her car under where four kids—no five—are getting out?"

"Hell if I know, showoff! I can't see that far."

"Well, it reads, *Fifty Dollars Free Play at Arrowhead Casino.*"

"You had that laser surgery?" William grunted.

"Nope."

"And all of a sudden you can see perfectly?"

"I don't know if it is perfect," Paul answered, "but I can see better than I've ever seen before. I can see stuff now that, before, I didn't even know was stuff."

William opened his mouth, but nothing came out. He shook his head.

"What exactly were you wanting me out here for anyway?" the kid pitcher asked, speaking for the first time. "The man cannot hit me."

William picked up the mask and mitt.

"Damned if I know! Nothing, I guess. Let's get the hell out of here. My knees are killing me."

"Not yet," Paul interrupted. "Throw me another," he called to the pitcher.

"I already struck you out, Ace," the rookie groaned.

William glanced at Paul, who smiled with the bat nestled in his arms.

"Why are you smiling? You look like a kid waiting on homemade ice cream at a picnic. You sure look casual for a man whiffing at hundred-mile-an-hour fastballs."

William nodded toward the pitcher. "Give him one more!"

The right-hander glared, angry. He wound-up, kicked and threw pure gas. Paul swung and connected. The crack of the bat was solid and loud—the way it sounded the day before in the cage. The line-drive would have been a one-hopper to any fence in baseball, and for the first three-hundred feet it never got higher than a basketball goal. William spat in the grass.

"Even a dumb hog finds an acorn ever once in a while. Try this one!" William challenged, showing a change-up sign that Paul couldn't see.

The rookie rocked and fired, and the ball whistled in, belt-high, making a rushing sound like a cartoon locomotive. Just before it reached the plate, it vanished. When Paul swung at it, it disappeared again and didn't reappear until it slammed off the right-hand goal post—crossbar high, a hundred yards away.

"Shit!" William said to himself.

"How long we gotta do this?" the kid pitcher said thirty-five minutes later.

His shirt was soaked through and sagging. Paul had missed only two of his pitches over that time. The kid had shown him everything—heat, four seam, change, curve and slider. Paul hit all pitches well. Most of the hits were line drives, reaching the school buildings on one hop.

William patted the rookie's wet back.

"Kid, we need to get you out of here. We'll give you a complex before the season gets started. Go on! Get, and be quiet."

"Don't worry," the rookie scowled.

At the truck, William tossed the equipment and turned to Paul.

"How long we known each other, Bud? Seventeen, eighteen years? Like that?"

Paul's forearms glistened with sweat. "Yeah, like that. I'm sorry, William, but you would've probably laughed." He slid his bat onto the truck bed and smiled.

William shook his head, his eyes darkening. "Laughed? There's nothing funny about this at all, Bud. That shit-eatin grin on your face will be gone if you try to mess with that stuff."

Paul stopped smiling, but not by much as William continued.

"Fella as smart as you knows you can't get away with those things anymore!"

"You wanna stand by me tomorrow when I take my pee test, William?"

"No thanks."

"I'm not cheating."

"Never said you were, Bud," William sighed, shaking his head. "Still and all?"

"A couple or three things changed on that night I had the accident."

William spat on the ground. "You mean the night you got run over by the mystery bike rider and should've gone to the hospital?"

Paul nodded. "After that night, I started seeing things better. I'm talking about my vision. I don't know if it was from the knock on the head. I never saw a doctor, but it was better—much better—and for the first and only time in my career, I spent the entire winter working out and hitting baseballs. I mean *really* hitting balls and getting in shape!"

William frowned and shook his head.

"Bud," he said in a low voice, "that would have to help *some*, sure—but good god, man! You're 38-years-old and hitting like A-Rod when he was 23! Eyesight, training, and dedication in the batting cage is gonna help, all right, but not *that* much. And even if it did, you'd have muscle-bound, twenty-twenty gym rats all over baseball, and that's not happening. Ever! Baseball's not that kind of game. You said a couple three things changed. What's the other?"

Paul looked down. For the first time in the morning, the half-smile was gone from his face. He began to speak, stuttering the syllables that stumbled off his tongue, unintelligible. He looked at William. "Well, that's the rub, Fungo," he said as he massaged the back of his neck. "That third thing—that's the most important one. It's the crucial one, and it's a little hard to explain."

"Uh, huh. I'll bet it is."

"You'll throw a fit."

"Try me."

"I'm through with love," Paul said.

William leaned his head sideways.

"How's that again?"

Paul repeated the words, "*I'm through with love.*"

William snorted and clapped his hands. "You're done with love? Yeah, me too…or will be pretty soon, they say."

"I told you, William," Paul said, shaking his head. "I knew it. That's the *thing.*"

"What thing?"

"That third thing."

"You mean the reason you're tearing-the-cover-off-the-ball *third thing?*"

"That thing—the reason I am freed up to hit like I haven't hit since college, even better. The ability has always been in me, but for so long, I was unable to call it back up, to tap back into it. Now, I am free. I am done with love. That's it."

William took off his ball cap and flung it through the goal posts like the game winning field goal. "Damn it all to hell, Bud! You are going to be in a lot of trouble, and I would've rather you told me you'd been beamed up by an alien spacecraft, and they zapped you with magic dust. But love? That's what this is all about, huh?"

Paul didn't answer. His look said enough.

"Well, buy me a horse and call me a cowboy," William said sadly. "Why don't you tell me you're taking something, and that there's no way in hell they can check it? I'd rather you tell me that. I wish you'd told me you saw a mad scientist in Switzerland. Why don't you just go ahead and lie to me, Bud? It would do so much better? I'd feel a helluva lot more at ease if you came up with a giant whopper than reach out into fantasy land and pull down a silly movie twist like that."

"See!" Paul laughed.

"I'm trying to be your friend here, Bud."

"I know. You are more like family. Speaking of family—how are Jodie and Sylvia?"

"Don't go try to change the subject on me."

"I'm not.

"They're fine, but what have they got to do with this?"

"Maybe everything," Paul said.

Huntsville

The confrontation with my grandfather irritates me, but I need to get over it. William Kerrigan will have to be involved at some point. I am counting on that. If Paul Demeter is at or close to .400 near the end, the security around him will be ridiculous. It may be impossible for me to get close without credentials, and even those might be worthless when it gets crazy. It will be madness.

William can get me near to Paul Demeter. He was a sneaky-Pete, getting himself in and out of tricky places like Cambodia and Laos, so he should have little trouble getting me in to see a ballplayer… if he wants to. That's a big "if." Our relationship has never been fluffy.

When they let him out of Huntsville, Jodie was presiding over a reading conference in St. Louis, so it fell to me to go pick him up. It took forever, because I was fourteen and had to take the back roads. He drove back.

We weren't out of the shadow of the walls when he started. "Before you ask, Anna was with me practically the whole time in there."

"I wasn't about to ask."

"Your Nanna talks to me. I hear that tangy, twangy Texas song that flies out her mouth when she opens it. Can you hear it?"

I snuck a peek at him, quick-like, to see if he was about to run us off the road. He didn't look wild-eyed, so I gave him the benefit of the doubt. He'd been locked up, after all.

"You okay?" He laughed.

"I'm fine. I'm not the one hearing dead people."

A few minutes passed as he stared hard up the interstate. "Your grandmother's sudden death disoriented and demolished me."

"Well done, William," I said, sitting up straight. "That's a good start. I'm ready—ready for you to really cut loose so we can have that serious, soul-baring talk that grandparents and kids are supposed to have. The one we haven't gotten around to it yet! Don't worry—it won't be like we're bonding or anything… so much as it will be you, having been locked up so long, needing to get a bunch of crap out. Even so, it should be a major breakthrough in our relationship. Kinda like Reagan, Gorbachev and The Wall."

"Losing her hit me harder than prison by a long shot," he offered.

"You know we're going over ninety, right?" I looked at the needle, astonished that Moby still had that kind of speed in him.

William's chin was almost touching the top of the wheel and his hands were dry. His eyes were steady and as bright as sapphires. "Some mornings," he continued, as if I hadn't asked a question, "I couldn't walk in a straight line more than ten feet. I might be hearing Comanche or Yiddish, for all I understood what people said to me. Levis fell off my ass. Time—that lying slut—didn't make a damned bit of difference either."

After listening to that declaration, I did not consider it odd at all that neither of us spoke a single word the next one hundred miles. *Let it be, Sister.* So I just sat reasonably still, looked out the window at hot fields where cattle lazed in the shadows of billboards, and let my mind wander.

Well, William wasn't the only one missing Anna. When I came down with mono in fifth grade, Anna announced I would come live with her and William until I got well. She would be my teacher as well as caregiver. Mornings, when I was strong enough, Nanna accompanied me through the obligatory texts the school sent: math, grammar, spelling, science and American history. But after lunch and a nap, I attended *L'Academie Nanna*, which convened in the huge bed of the guest room, lit by brilliant rays of sunshine and dedicated to the *The Three "Ls": Latin, Lincoln and Layers.*

"Versed in Virgil's tongue, no recognized language should ever intimidate you," Nanna explained. "All you ever need to know about the history of your country and how to conduct yourself among other persons—you will find in Sandburg's volumes on Abraham Lincoln. And, by understanding the structures of the atmosphere above you and the soils beneath your feet, you will always know where you fit in."

Made sense to me!

During free time, I read on my own. That year, I read all of Twain and Alcott, most of Dickens and as much Hemingway and Faulkner as I could stomach. What books weren't already on Kerrigan shelves, William toted from the public library by the bagful.

On days when I was weak, I watched *ESPN* news and games or Nanna read to me. Sometimes it was Shakespeare, while at others it was the *Oz* books by Ruth Thompson. William sometimes pinch-hit, and in a pirate's voice, read from Clair Bee, Kahn, Plimpton and Feinstein. He humphed and grumped and acted like it was a pain in the butt, but once I overheard him talking to Anna.

"Naw, it's my turn, and I think the kid'll like this new stuff of Deford's."

A Horrible Place

Aqib was sad… at first. He was sad at first that he was not dead—sad because that meant he was not in the afterlife, but still in that horrible place. He had only slept rather than died.

Why did he ever think this was a smart thing to do? The heat and space were suffocating. He was desperate for something to drink. He tried to urinate in his empty water jug, but he was so weak he could hold neither the jug nor his penis, and he urinated on himself.

He willed himself to think other thoughts. He filled his mind with contemplations to steel his resolve. He deliberated horrible deeds. Mentally, he drew up an enemies list. On it went those who drove them out, who burned them out, who stoned them, who humiliated their sites of worship and gathering—those who hurt him personally.

He saw those people in his mind's eye, but they had no faces. They were blank, so it was difficult for him to focus on them. The lack of focus helped as a distraction, and for a precious few moments, he thought of something besides knowing he was probably going to die in such a horrible place.

W-W-J-D?

I take a chance and run in the dark because I want to get on the road early for Chicago. I stick to the inter-state frontage road, where there's plenty of light. I jog three easy miles. I feel pretty good for having tossed and turned most of the night on a lumpy mattress.

Moby waits until we are perfectly midstream the Mississippi River bridge to start making noises. "Not now, Moby, not now…" I say as I pat the dash. "C'mon, Man, you can make it!"

The engine sounds fine, and the ride is smooth. Still, I have to address the noise, so as we clear the bridge, which takes almost forever, I ease off the highway to park under a gigantic elm, killing the engine. I wait. Stillness… Extreme quiet, but for the low rattle of a mocking bird in a honeysuckle bush. I hear the noise again, faint and muffled.

After I lift the hood, I can feel that the engine is hot, but not stressed. I still hear the noise. It is only a scratch now, not a tap. I try to pin down the source. As I walk around, I stop at the trunk. *Something is in the trunk!* An animal? How the heck?

I realize it is probably one of the cats I saw hanging around the Jefferson City motel I stayed in during the previous night. It must have crawled around in the undercarriage and managed to find its way into the trunk. The same thing happened to me before—when Jodie's cat got caught under the hood and would have been cut to small pieces had I not heard her yowls and stopped and rescued her. I exhale.

"Silly cat…"

Wait a minute! I thought just as I was about to open the trunk. *It might be a possum, and possums can be fierce when cornered or scared, and they have razor sharp talons.* I reach in the back seat for the six-iron I carry on the road. I had removed it from Jack's bag, thinking it the one club he probably wouldn't notice gone—except at the dinner table when he said, "Can you believe this mess? Some low-life nicked my six-iron from the cart when I went in for a beer and sandwich at the turn. Man, I hit that club sweet!"

Oops! Oh, well, sin loi, Jack-san.

I raise the club high in one hand as I turn the key with the other. When the lid flies open, I will take a quick hop back, ready to strike if the creature comes out clawing and gnashing. I take a deep breath, immediately wishing I hadn't as an overwhelming urine stench fills my nostrils. *Whew!* The animal must have become terrified and peed all over itself and my trunk!

I gulp a mouthful of fresh air, throw open the lid and jump back, with the golf club poised high and in both hands. Well, it isn't a cat or a possum or a raccoon. No animal springs out. It isn't even animal… it is human! What the heck? A man?

It is a man! And he isn't in the best shape, as you can probably imagine. He is dirty, and piss soaks his clothes. He barely moves as he bleats there, like a hurt animal.

"Water!" he says.

OMG! I dash for the Topo Chico that I keep in the console. *The poor soul!* I can't help but flash on those unfortunate people in the van on the turnpike. This guy is probably an illegal, confused about which vehicle he was getting in. How the heck did he get in there? No telling how long he has been in the trunk!

I try to think. Did I go in there at all at the motel? No, no, I didn't. I haven't opened the trunk since the park in Kansas! I hold my nose, thrusting the bottle in the opening. "Drink. Drink!"

I hear a sucking sound, and then a long belch. I shove another bottle in. "Drink!"

Then I hear a suck, belch and gag. I make the mistake of sticking my face in the trunk just as the person vomits Mexican fizzy water and bile on the front of my shirt.

Eck! I stand there with puke in my hands and dripping down my chest. This guy is in a bad way. *I've got to get help. Yuck, just yuck!* Then I hear a chilling, terrifying sound coming from the human in my trunk. It is a sound that strikes at my core. It makes *me* want to throw up!

It sounds like, "Sorry I am vomiting on you, Miss."

I slam the trunk closed, still holding the club high in the air. *Huh? I am imagining things. No, no—Hell no! This is not happening!* I look frantically around to see if anyone is witnessing the event. No—no, of course not. This is not happening. This goes way beyond bizarre!

This is *not* Paki-Boy from the Kansas motel in my car who stalked me to a ballgame in Kansas City! No it is not! I *so* do not have time for this! I am on a mission. What is happening only happens in bad movies that try to be funny, but fall short. I know what to do. I will pretend this didn't happen. I will drive down the road as if an Asian person who stalked me is not now, nor ever has been, a stowaway in my trunk. But what if he dies? He looks bad—that would be murder… or at least manslaughter. What if I pour him out of the trunk and drag him under the big tree, where he will have shade? I will leave him water. Some good person will come along and help him. Sure someone will! And if it goes all wrong, and they try to pin it on me, I can plead self-defense because the creep *is* stalking me.

This is a totally different deal than those poor, innocent illegals. This guy is a criminal… and a pervert! Then, of course, I think: *W-W-J-D? What-Would-Jodie-Do?* Oh, no—Dear God help me! I know *exactly* what Jodie would do.

Jodie would take him in her arms—pee, puke, filth and all—and personally nurse him. The least she would do, and I mean the *very* least, would be to take him to the hospital and sit with him until she was sure he was out of danger. *Aw, I hate this!*

Jodie did not raise me to run off and leave someone in this bad way. She would be horrified to think I even contemplated it. I wipe my hands on my jeans and open the trunk again.

"Are you going to throw up some more?"

"I don't think so, Miss."

I look back inside. He is dehydrated, weak and lucky that last night, the oppressive heat had let up a bit… or he might be dead now. Check that. *Would be dead!*

"This is so stupid! Here is more water. Don't throw up on me. Drink it slow."

"I am thanking you, Miss, for saving my life," he says from the trunk.

"No, I'm not," I snap back. "Heck no—don't say that! I am not saving you—you don't owe me anything—anything except to get the hell out of my life!—that, you owe me. Beyond that, you owe me absolutely nothing. Zilch! You understand zilch, right?"

He nods. I have to hand it to the guy, he is hardy. What he did would have killed me, I think. *Would've killed anyone.* I tell myself I sure as hell don't feel sorry for him, though. He did this to himself. I look closer. On the messy floor beside him is a small drawstring bag, an empty gallon jug, a case of oil and a Mr. Cuckoo sandwich wrapper. I am stunned all over again as I pick up the wrapper.

There is only one Mr. Cuckoo in the world that specializes in pork chop sandwiches, and that is the one in the town in Kansas where I stopped for lunch on my way to the ball game.

Today is over one-hundred degrees, but at this moment, icy shivers travel up each of my arms to my shoulders, meeting at the back of my neck and cascading down my spine pooling, like a frozen pond, in the natural crevasse atop my ass. If I had a knife in my hands instead of a mid-iron, I believe I might have stabbed him. Paki-Boy points to the wrapper.

"When you went inside, Miss, I used my jimmy to let myself out, and I walked to a window. I got myself a Pork Chop Chubby and re-filled my water jug. I jimmied back into your car and ate my sandwich. It was delicious."

My brain works so hard and fast trying to digest all this ridiculousness that I don't even try to think. I am certain all the words spew out in less than ten seconds.

"Your jimmy? Your jimmy? I've got your jimmy! Why didn't you jimmy your way out again instead of letting yourself almost die? You been in my trunk since Kansas? You're stupid! You're a stowaway! Why did you get in my trunk? You should be dead. While you are weak and can't fight back, I'm hauling your sorry stalking ass to jail. Wait. You're Islamic for cryin out loud—*you* can't eat a Pork Chop Chubby!"

"I *can* eat a Pork Chop Chubby, Miss," he answered. "I am Coptic. Or, I should say my parents are Coptic."

"Get the hell out of my trunk!"

"Yes, Miss."

He tries to climb out, but he is too weak. Taking another huge gulp of air, I reach under his shoulder, past his armpit, and lift. Once standing, he staggers to the tree and sits at its base, with his back against the bark. "I am feeling ashamed, Miss… for the pissing of one's self."

"Hah! You're feeling ashamed of *that*? That's the least you should be feeling ashamed of. How about feeling ashamed of stalking me? Huh? How bout that? That's a major crime!"

He hangs his head, saying nothing. I open another bottle of water.

"Here… So you peed on yourself? There's no shame in that. Get over it. And turn around—I'm changing my shirt."

I strip off my t-shirt, which provokes honking and shouting from traffic on the bridge. I quickly pull on a dry shirt.

"You are calling whom, Miss?" he says in a weak voice with his head turned. "With the phone?"

"I'm calling 9-1-1. We're close to several towns over here. I want to find the nearest emergency room to drop you."

For a sick guy, he becomes energized, scrambling to his knees.

"No, no, Miss. Please! You are not doing this. Please no, Miss!"

"Heck yeah I am! You did this to yourself. I'm dropping you off with people who'll take care of you, cuz I've got to get on down the road. I am on a mission."

"Oh, so," he says, regaining his composure. "Drop me off somewhere if you must… but not the hospital! Please Miss, no hospital!"

I have no idea why I do it—it might have been the sight of the pitiful look on his face, but when the dispatcher asks, "what is your emergency?" I say, "I am sorry, Ma'am, but we are okay now. It was wrong to call, and we are sorry."

I make him get in the back seat. The smell is awful, and no matter where or how he positions himself, his pee-soaked pants touch my bags. I spread the morning's paper on the floor in case he barfs again.

"Thanking you, Miss," he groans as he lays his head back on the seat.

"Stop with all the thanking! You probably better *sip* that water and quit scarfing it."

I want to ask him why he is afraid of hospitals, but I catch myself. I don't want him to think I care, after he already thinks I saved his life. That's bad enough.

I don't know much about Pakistan. Almost nothing, really. Maybe it's like a tribal thing with them—like, you save a life—you are responsible for him forever... or worse—*you* can't get rid of *him* for the rest of your life! *Don't ask him anything. If I ask, he will answer, and then I will have information I don't require.*

I want to know nothing about this person beyond the obvious: he is a stalker of young women, he is dangerous, he must not be very bright and I have to dump him off as soon as possible. I glance in the rearview and notice he is recovering quickly, considering how I found him. He sits up, swaying a bit, but he is up.

He wants to avoid a hospital probably because hospitals mean authorities, who will have questions that will eventually lead to police with questions of their own. He will have to confess that he hid in my trunk to stalk me—with plans to assault and eventually kill me. All the more reason why I should drop him at an ER! A little jail time for the creep will put the kibosh on any future shadowing plans he might have.

These are my approximate thoughts as I wheel into the John 3:16 parking where *Siri* has directed me. "End of the road for you, Mister."

I hold my nose and help him out of the car, turning him to face a building. "In that door. Go ahead!"

I give him a slight shove to his back, a gentle push that would hardly budge a 3-year-old. He falls on his face.

Oh shit!

By the time I help him to his feet, he is bleeding from his mouth, nose and forehead.

"Man, I am sorry about that!" I exclaim.

Why am I apologizing to him? He's the stowaway!

I swipe his face with Kleenex.

"Thanking you, Miss."

"Yeah, yeah. Okay. Just go in that door right there. They will take care of you. Go on! I'm not touching you again. You can make it."

I sprint to my car, never looking back. I leave the parking lot turning left, eyes straight ahead as I speed down the street with the horn blaring. He will be at the door by now, and some person with a clipboard will greet him.

I need to turn onto a busy street, but I see no gap in the traffic. I jump out and shut the horn off. *What if he has fallen again and no one sees him out on the hot concrete? Tough luck; he shouldn't have been stalking me. Shouldn't have got in my trunk!* Volunteers at places like John 3:16 are tuned-in to their environment, so if he fell, they would eventually notice him lying out front.

As a police car cruises by, I wave. The officers don't wave back.

Okay. Okay! I will go back just to make sure he isn't in a heap in the parking lot. That's all. I'll only scoot by. Jodie would expect it of me.

What's her line: "Character is how you act when no one is watching?"

It won't be too much sweat off me to do a small thing like that. I make right-hand turns until I am back at the entrance. I scan the lot, and sure enough, he's still outside. What a dummy! He's standing next to a dipsy-dumpster as the police drive in on the other side. He sees them before they see him, and opening the side slot, he dives in head first.

Mother's Scent

Aqib lay utterly still and listened to the police car come to a stop. Doors opened and then closed. After an interminable, anxious wait, he heard laughter. Was good—the officers had only stopped for a rest, a break to relax in the shade of trees near the dumpster. He lay still and quiet.

He was immersed in filth. It was awful. To relieve the stench in his head, he tried to think of pleasant smells: flowers and favorite foods. He settled on his mother's scent, which is jasmine and amber, smoke of sandalwood and champa. He saw her shuffling back and forth in her preparation of the *badam ka halwa.*

He moved his elbow away from a box of used, blood-tainted syringes and into a puddle of oatmeal. *Ugh!*

Had his family learned of his disappearance? He wondered about their initial reaction if his parents had learned by now. Will they be worried, puzzled, afraid or angry? Of course they would be hesitant, but they would go to the authorities.

Aqib couldn't believe his relative good fortune. In one horrifying moment, he was resigned to dying an agonizing, suffocating death in the trunk, while in the next he was inhaling the delicious air of deliverance. He'd made the right choice with her. Obvious! She was his savior.

She had done what she thought was the right thing to do: bringing him to that place, but he had no intention of going in there. So if he could bear lying in this filth a short time longer, the police would leave, and he would be able to get out.

He had hoped that he would make it to a large city, but he would have to figure out a way to move on until he arrived at one. This did not looked like a large city. His plan called for a city with many people—crowds of people—throngs, herds of people of assorted colors and cultures. People of diversity!

Anybody's Dog

Anna, my Nanna, used to say I had the softest heart Jesus ever made.

Jodie laughed at that. "If there is ever a sore-eyed cat of a kid in a bunch, Sylvia is dead solid certain to cut her out of the herd and bring her home with her!"

Jodie said it started in kindergarten, when I swapped my lunch most days with Maria Menendez, until the teachers made us stop. I gave Maria my sandwich, apple, yogurt or cookie, while she gave me everything in her sack: a single tamale. I looked on it as a more-than-fair trade because I do love me some tamales!

In second grade, I asked if Nathan Brady could have a sleepover at our house.

"Why in the world?" Jodie asked.

When kids played catch, nobody threw to Nathan, and that didn't seem cool, so I began playing catch with him. He didn't have a glove, so I loaned him mine. I could catch bare handed since I was four. After we became friends, I went up in the attic and found one of William's old Rawlings mitts and gave it to Nathan.

When Jodie dug further into why I would want to ask a boy to a sleepover, I told her that Nathan smelled something awful, and since she never let me go to bed without taking a bath first, if Nathan came for a sleepover, he would get to take a bath.

All through grade school, I tended toward the out-of-favor side of the enrollment, making friends with the nose-pickers, lice heads, truants, anemics, gap-jawed mouth-breathers, the shiftless and other denizens of the unwashed.

It didn't get better in the teenage years. At my fourteenth birthday party, two Goth guys I invited stole Jodie's purse and jewelry box, but that was just the beginning. My first real "car date" was with Ronny Taylor, a good-looking, greasy guy who took shop half a day at Career Tech, but it didn't go well. It turned out that the car we drove to the movies was one that Ronny had hotwired at the mall. We got pulled over, Ronny went to jail, and later juvvie, and I got my first ride in a police car.

In junior year—since none of us had dates to the prom—my bunch staged our own "un-prom." We pooled our resources to rent the Forty & Eight Hall and to buy booze. When the cops showed up, roughly half—the quicker, more sober in our number ran into the woods and managed to escape. Those of us who stayed behind got hauled to the basement of the police station, where those who knew where our parents were could call them to come pick us up. The others had to wait until daylight, when they would be released on their own.

For some reason I can't remember, William came for me. He smiled, and he said only one thing to me on the ride home. "Little lady, you are either the worst judge of character in all the land, or you're just about anybody's dog that'll hunt with you."

Yeah, I guess I am. What the hell else would explain why, after the cops leave the John 3:16 parking lot, I help Aqib out the dumpster and back in my car.

Yes, my stowaway stalker now has a name: *Aqib.*

How a Bookish, Clinically Depressed Writer Got Messed Up With a Ballplayer in the First Place

The cigar box still sat on the coffee table where Jodie placed it four days ago. Jack had attempted to throw it in the trash, but she grabbed it out of his hands, triggering their last-ever fight.

She opened a sealed envelope and read the letter and put it back in the box. She fished out another envelope. She read half of the letter before she let it fall.

In college, Jodie landed in an association of people, known as The Group, who lived in a dilapidated motor court by the river. Members wrote stories, poems, essays and screenplays. Others painted and drew sketches. At last, she had found a bunch of bizarros like her! She fell in with them right away. She also fell for their leader, the charismatic Drury, of the curly dark hair.

Paul Demeter saw her for the first time in a bar. It was poetry night, when he and a couple of his teammates walked in. Realizing their mistake after about five minutes, his friends left. Paul looked at Jodie, sitting beside Drury. He stayed. Jodie noticed him, thinking him out of place, leaning on a bistro table alone and staring at her. As it happened, Drury chose that night to be unusually obtuse, so Jodie left the bar alone. Paul followed.

For six mornings he waited for her at the bottom step of her garage apartment to ask her to one of his games. Six times she told him that she hated baseball and the reasons why. Yet he persisted. On the seventh day, she relented—just so he would go away.

She could not have stood out more in the bleachers if she'd been a lumberjack at the opera. The only parts of her not protected from the sun were her hands. She wore an immense hat, straight out of Renoir, lashed to her head by a buttery bow. Around her sat co-ed cuties in tanks and halters and tiny shorts that left little to fancy. All seemed covered in lotion, paying attention to everything but the game.

Trying to be polite, she remained in the stands after. Paul Demeter, still in uniform and sweating, came to her. He had the nerve to duck under the wide brim of her hat and kiss her on her mouth before asking her if she loved Drury.

She told him that Drury was intelligent and dashing in a rogue-ish, handsome and narcissistic way.

"Not the question," he insisted.

"I am *probably* in love with Drury. Now will you go away?"'

"No."

"I think you have a brain, Paul Demeter. Don't get messed up with me."

"This happens to you a lot, I guess."

"Not so much in fact. Oh, they come on strong, but it fades under intensity."

"I won't fade."

"We'll see."

She explained that Drury was a magnetic man in their collection of misfits, and she was very attracted to him. He was kind to her and supported her writing. But she did not tell Paul that Drury had wandering eyes, or that whenever he came to the river and addressed them, pretty girls seemed to fall from the trees.

Drury was a natural leader, while she was in a position to be led. She had led herself to believe that the flirting would stop once the other girls realized he loved her, but this didn't happen, so along came Paul Demeter, this ballplayer, out of nowhere, and eventually she let him up her stairs.

Somehow Paul Demeter was good medicine. She didn't know the science. *He is better than I deserve.* She used him. She admitted it to herself. She had been on meds—strong ones—since middle school, but none of them could relieve the really bad auras—ones that turned her world blacker than Stalin's soul. For some crazy reason, and with no logic enforcing it, this Paul Demeter, this irritating ball player, helped her through the bad ones. He didn't quite make the pain go away, but his presence made it bearable.

In time, Paul told her he loved her… even if she never loved him back. He told her he had no claims on her, but he would be there always. That was not what she wanted to hear, so she thought she would shock him. She looked him straight in his face and told him she still went to the river sometimes.

The man never so much as flinched. He reacted as if she had mentioned that some mornings she put peanut butter on her bagel. He said it didn't make any difference to him.

Jodie closed the cigar box but left it on the small table.

Sylvia is going to find out my terrible mistake in the wrong way. Jodie knew she should have told her a long time ago. She wanted to do so on several occasions, each time telling herself that Sylvia was too young, or it was her time of the month, or it was too late, or that her daughter would be vindictive. Would it have changed anything about Sylvia? *Would I have changed?*

Land Of Lincoln

"Don't start thanking me," I tell him as soon as he gets back in my car.

"Yes Miss," Aqib says, not trying to stifle a yawn. "I am trying not to."

"On top of that urine reek, now you smell like garbage. That bag of yours? You have clothes in it?"

He nods.

"We'll stop at a 7-Eleven. While I get gas, you clean yourself up and change your clothes."

He doesn't say anything. Maybe I insulted him. So what? He *should* be insulted. "I don't know why I am doing this."

"I don't know either, but I knew you were the one." He makes a weak attempt to smile.

"Look, Buster, I can still turn around and drop you at the police station."

"I would not hurt you, Miss."

"Damn right you wouldn't! I got a big ole Colt .45 pistol under this seat," I bluff.

He doesn't laugh, but the slight flicker in his eye says, *Right… Sure you do.* "That morning you went back in the room after you ran, I let myself in the back of your car. I had with me the food I'd prepared. I had my jug I filled with water. I had experimented with many implements, and I constructed myself a tool, a jimmy, out of a jigsaw blade for which to open the trunk. I knew I could get out and back in whenever you stopped."

"So that's how you got to the ballgame…"

He nods. "When you didn't come out of the stadium, I thought I'd better go find you. Plus, I was very thirsty. You weren't supposed to catch me. When you stayed in the motel last night, I let myself out and slept on a bench. Just before dawn, I let myself back in. Where my plan went wrong this morning was, I must have dropped the tool in the parking lot. I could no longer let myself out, so I was trapped."

"Pretty dumb."

"One may think so."

"But not you?"

"I did what I had to do to carry out my plan."

"Your plan? Why didn't you just ask me for a ride?"

"Would you have taken me?"

"No." Then I have to laugh, remembering William's observation of long ago. "I don't know. Maybe I might've given you a ride a little ways."

"Especially if you knew my reason…"

"Stop. I don't want to know any more about your plan.

I stop for gas, and he changes clothes. The car smells better right away, so I let him in the front seat where I can see him. I don't like driving on a crowded inter-state, constantly looking in my mirror to see if he is making a move on me. He'd have to be sneaky-like, from the back seat, because I could probably kick his ass in a fair fight.

On the terrible night I was sexually assaulted, *raped, say it,* I tried to fight Kevin off, but he was too strong. My tears and pleas didn't stop him. If anything, they probably turned him on. Only my teeth crunching the IV and V metacarpals of his right hand finally got him off me. I look quickly at my stowaway leaning against the passenger door. No way this male is going to sneak up on me.

I drive with my left hand to the side, as if I am fingering a pistol that I can produce in seconds. He props his crow black-haired head on the side window, dabs his face with tissue and sips water. For a stalker, he isn't paying me much attention—no devious glares, no sneak peeks, no talk. He looks ahead, serious.

"Figured you'd be asleep by now," I say.

Looking directly at me for the first time, he smiles, which is also a first. I am practically blinded by two rows of the whitest teeth I've ever seen.

"No, Miss. I help you through traffic," he answers with a yawn.

"Fah. I don't need help. I'm a heck of a driver."

"Look out, Miss!"

I swerve to the inside median as the driver of a massive eighteen-wheeler, loaded with steel, thinks his horn will get him the lane easier than observing his yield sign. He is right, and he runs me off the highway. Moby fishtails in the gravel, and it is all I can do to bulldog him to a safe stop.

"Damn that was close!"

"He is crazy driver," Aqib agrees, looking back over his shoulder. "Now you can go, Miss. The way is clear, if you punch it. Now!"

I am back on the freeway and moving with the suffocating traffic. "Don't yell at me, Aqib. I know what I am doing. So don't yell."

"Yes, Miss."

I concentrate on the road, thinking about what he said. He knew I was the one? I was the one for what? Like this was planned? I focused. It *was* planned. He'd fashioned a tool for getting in and out a car trunk. That must have taken days. He had food and water ready. Frightening... What did he have planned for me? It couldn't be good, whatever it was. Still, he had made no move on me.

His face soaks up a third of a box of Kleenex before it stops bleeding.

"You know crap about baseball, right?"

"Yes, Miss. I am knowing crap from baseball."

"That's what I thought. You ever heard of Paul Demeter?"

"I may have, yes. I think I have heard his name spoken. I watch very much American television, especially *ESPN*, hoping to catch the soccer when it is on. He is like the Babe Ruth, this Paul Demeter?"

"Hah. Not even close to the Babe Ruth. He's just a guy, a player having a very good season, and a lot of the country is caught up in what he's doing. Oh, and he is my father."

"Ah, wonderful! Your Papa?"

"No. Not wonderful."

"No? But you are traveling now to join up with him. Yes?"

"Never mind. Sorry I brought it up. I'm done talking about him."

Aqib The Serious stays awake… to keep me company, he tells me. I would have felt more comfortable if he had gone to sleep. I tell him this, thinking this would insult him enough that he would drift off, just for spite.

"The Land of Lincoln is flat, Miss. Do you know Illinois is the only state that does not have a single mountain?"

I don't acknowledge his geography lesson. I try thinking only about Paul Demeter and the story I will write. I don't say another word until I stop beside the Sangamon. I reach for the mini-cooler.

"I'm going to eat now."

He is probably starving, so I expect him to ask if he can share my food, but he only nods and crosses the highway toward a convenience store. I am hungry, so I wolf down my food in minutes on the quilt that I spread on the grassy bank.

Hey! I think as I walk back to the car, *Leave his ass! Just take off.* He is much better now, so he'll be all right. Besides, I've helped enough, more than enough. Jodie would be satisfied.

It was not like I'd be abandoning him. We had stopped near a godly, Presbyterian or Methodist town with a church on every corner. Surely one would take him in and help him. Wouldn't they? What's Coptic? It's sort of Christian, right? Not exactly Episcopalian, but they would have to take him in, wouldn't they?

I take so long thinking about this (five minutes passes) that I miss a good opportunity. I look over the highway, and he is not in the store, but neither is he on his way across the road. He is standing by one of the gas pumps, looking my way. Damn! I honk. He starts over.

"I could've driven away, you know?" I say when he gets in the car.

"I know. That is why I gave you time… to make up your mind."

"And you're going to say you knew I wouldn't?"

"Yes."

"Fah. You are pretty sure of yourself."

"No, Miss. I am being sure of you. That is why I chose you."

"Well, lah dee freaking dah! Lucky me. You *chose* me." I sigh in sarcasm as I look over. "What? You are not hungry?"

"I *was*."

"Which means you aren't now? Just like that? Hungry one minute, not hungry a second later? Remind me to dial that thought up if ever I decide to go on a diet."

He casts famished eyes on the crust of my ham and cheese melt on the console.

"Let me guess, some redneck behind the counter over there at the *Stop N Hop* said something to you like, *We don't serve no ragheads in here*?"

He swallows once and stares straight ahead.

"People are just stupid. Here's an apple."

"Thank you, Miss."

In all my life, I have never seen a piece of fruit (or any other food item for that matter) attacked so viciously. He devours flesh, stem, seeds and core in four seconds, biting and chewing so savagely that tiny pieces of apple shrapnel spray the dash, and juice hazes the speedometer and the dead radio dial. Using only the tips of my fingers, I carefully hand him the remnants of my sandwich.

As I walk to a barrel to dump my lunch trash, a terrible thought comes to my mind. It is a horrid realization, and I am sickened by it. *Why hasn't this occurred to me before?* Aqib is so dang serious—too serious for a person his age. Deadly serious? There can be only one reason: Aqib is a lone wolf terrorist!

Shit! Of course! It's so obvious. What am I doing? He is on a mission to assassinate somebody or to blow something up and take a lot of people with him! He talks about a plan. What else can it be? I am a fool, and I've made it easy for him. He fits the profile perfectly—alone, secretive, prepared and filled with hatred. Right? His mission requires solemnity and singleness of purpose. He said he was not Coptic.

The Taliban or al-Qaeda radicalized him back home, grooming and training him, and the fervor worked him up enough to come to the USA? In America, he could only find work in a cheap motel. He couldn't understand American culture—females dressed so provocatively and shamelessly, and everything was so loud.

He hated being called names, hated being stared at. Disillusioned, he would join jihad against the great Satan. He was miserable, so he would martyr himself and go straight to heaven of the multiple virgins. Of course! I am so stupid! Oh, crap. I have been helping the guy. What have I done? I look for his bag, but of course he has it with him.

Don't panic. He hasn't done anything yet. It's not too late. I will definitely call the police. No fooling around this time. I might be the only one who can prevent a terrorist act, a massacre. I will be a heroine.

Let me think. No, no—I can't do that. That won't work. I would be on the *CNN* and *Fox News* twenty-four hour news cycle. It would have to be anonymous. The publicity would blow my cover and story.

I study him, slumped against the door of my car. Really? A terrorist? *This* guy? He is such a frail thing with skinny arms and tiny hands. A brisk wind would knock him over. Well, it doesn't take a lot of strength to pull a trigger or punch a cell phone. I must view him in a different light now. The eyes I once thought to be naïve and slow have become devious, his body lean and wolf-like. Even his wispy, once-Deppish facial hair has become jihadist. As soon as I get to Chicago, out on the corner he goes!

One More Thing

This one—this Miss—she is something special, he thought. Not only did she save him from a horrible death in the trunk of her car, she came back for him when he was in the garbage! Now if only she would take him far enough away! He wanted desperately to ask her destination, but she obviously did not feel comfortable conversing with him yet.

Certainly she had been highly perturbed when she first discovered him—one could not gainsay her that—but she was nice once she settled down. Well, "nice" is perhaps not the proper word, but at least she seemed to be making an effort to be not so annoyed with him. He must re-pay her in some fashion.

He once thought that he worked at the crummiest motel in the world, but somehow Miss found one even worse. She looked at the pool and dipped her toe in it. She then peeked in the office. When she yawned, he remembered how exhausted he was. He was tired, yet he was awed and glad they were far from Kansas. He was in Chicago. This was perfect for his plan. He would be hard to locate in such a big, tough city. He knew about Chicago. Chicago had gangsters and corruption and people of diversity. This was a place for his plan.

Miss came back to the parking lot and jerked her thumb in the direction of the office.

"He's one of your guys," she said.

"Yes? Meaning?"

"Meaning, the guy in the office? He's a homeboy. You said yourself you owe me, Mister, so before we say goodbye here, I need a favor."

"I see. You think he is Pakistani. If he thinks the room is for me, he will 'cut a deal?'"

"You got it. He'll drop the price for you, and then, you know, you can *jew* him down some more from there."

He frowned, tilting his head. "I am not Jew."

"Ooops! Shoot, I know that. Sorry It's not personal, Aqib. It's just an expression, y'know. And a pretty, damned lousy one too, I realize (now that I've heard myself say it aloud). Sorry—it means to haggle, to bargain. Anyway, go in there and work your magic for me."

She handed him three twenty-dollar bills.

"You are trusting me with your money? I can simply walk away."

She smiled, though not in a pleasant way.

"Maybe getting rid of you is *worth* sixty bucks."

He headed for the office and returned shortly, tossing the room cards and change to her. He was so tired that he could hardly hold up his head.

"So, here's how it goes. You listening to me? Look at me—I think I know what you are up to, and I don't want to be anywhere close when it goes down. You are planning something bad, so you have to go away from me—far away. You are going to have to go and leave me alone. I have been calling you dumb and stupid, and that was wrong of me, because you are not. You are probably intelligent—I mean you speak better English than me. I guess you're about my age, but if I was plopped down in Islamabad today, I couldn't learn your language if I lived to be a hundred. Surely you understand what I'm saying. Please try to keep your eyes open, Aqib!"

"Sorry, Miss," he said, yawning, barely awake.

"Now, I'm going to go up and take a shower and get ready to go to the game. And you are going to leave. Leave this place and leave me. And I don't mean go away for the night and sleep on a park bench and show up here in the morning, begging me to let you hang, either. You need money? I can give you money. Not much, but I can spare a little."

He yawned again and waved his hands. “No, Miss. I have money. Thank you.”

“Don’t thank me. I am giving you a head start. I am not calling the cops until I get out of the shower. Shouldn’t do it, but maybe this small favor might make you change your mind. Not all Americans are heartless. I gave you water and hauled you this far. That’s treating you okay, right? You can maybe think about giving up your plan, huh? So go. Go. Are you listening to me?”

He nodded, closing his eyes. “I am understanding,” he says, jolting awake violently. “I will go away, Miss. You have my word. I owe you so much. You have been a wonderful help. Please only one more thing, if you can, Miss?”

“No! No! No more things. Oh what is it, for cryin out loud?”

“Before I go, can I please wash up in the room? I have much filth.”

She threw up her hands. “No, no. Yes, yes—and hurry up. I’ve got a ball game to get to.” She put her hand in her huge handbag. “Just you remember, I’ve got this gun on me just in case I am on your list of infidels that need dispatching.”

He yawned, but he still managed to chuckle. “Yes, yes, Miss. Certainly. You make funny talk sometimes.”

Signed, Miss

Once in the unbelievably tiny room, I begin to regret this one more thing I am doing for a stowaway terrorist. The bed is tiny and the bathroom tiny. He sits at a tiny desk on the other side of the room, and yet he seems to loom over me. What a stupid thing I've done! Now he can attack me behind closed doors.

"You are showering first, Miss, yes?" he says, yawning again. "Khaleeq in office said hot water will not last. You should get nice water. I am Pashtun. My people withstand cold quite nicely."

"That's big of you." I groan as I grab a towel with the thickness of a worn-out bed sheet. "Remember—" I warn, patting my bag.

"Yes, Miss. I remember," he nods. "The gun."

I take the extra chair with me to the bathroom and triple-lock the door, jamming the chair, taut, against the knob.

The water feels wonderful on my face and bare shoulders. I am so tired. I shouldn't go to the ball game. I should stay in and sleep. No. I have to go to the game. I must make notes. The story matters above all else. I turn down the water pressure as I try to deal with my hair. My tangled mess could take up the hot water by itself. I rinse in the trickle, and then I finish my shower full throttle.

"Okay, I left you some hot water." I dislodge the chair and step out of the bathroom, fully-dressed. "Hey, Aqib…"

He is face down on the tiny desk, sitting on the chair with his arms around his head. His snores sound like a train roaring through a small town.

"Damn, you did this on purpose!"

I grab a pillow and give him a medium pop on the head, but he doesn't move.

"Hey, you! Wake up! Aqib, you can't sleep in here!"

I pick up the Gideon and whop him on his temple, but he only snores louder. His bag is on the floor next to his heel. Here's my chance to look in it. He has the drawstring looped around his shoe and ankle. Of course! Anybody trying to take it would wake him. Even better!

I jerk on the loop, and the bag comes away, though not cleanly. In fact, I may have sprained his ankle with the force. He doesn't stir an inch as I open the bag and find the soiled and urine-soaked clothes and a pack of condoms. Aagh. My blood turns cold. No weapons, no old flip-phone for detonating IEDs, nothing that looks remotely like bomb-making material. I am almost disappointed.

I should call the cops anyway. No—they will trace the call and bother me. I look at my watch. If I leave right now, get lucky catching the train, I might make first pitch. I try something with my hair, give up, and slam on a visor. I try to wake him one more time to no avail. The New Testament lands upside his head, though not in a holy manner.

Aqib is out. He is not faking it. He is dead asleep, so I scratch out a note on the pad I find on the desk.

Aqib, when you wake up, leave! I did you a favor. You gave me your word. You best be out of here when I get back!

Signed, Miss

Yeah, right! Like a jihadi who is going to blow himself up in a public place is going to care about breaking a promise to a stupid female he has duped!

Calamity

I have to settle for a seat deep in the center-field bleachers. I can't expect to get any closer—not with the White Sox sitting atop the standings in the American League Central. It doesn't help that this series is the last chance in the regular season for Chicago fans to see Paul Demeter in their home ballpark. It's okay. I have binoculars.

I hone in on his face as he steps to the plate. He doesn't look like a man the sports world is watching to fall on his face or make history. I catch the slightest wrinkle in his upper lip on the right side when the boos catch up with the cheers. I know this tic.

Most people who are delighted or amused grin wide or bust out laughing, but not my father. When he's tickled, he has this little lip twitch thing going. I saw it when Jodie smiled at him. I saw it when he came home from a road trip and let me jump into his arms. He must really enjoy this cascade of scorn from the Sox fans cause he's rocking that twitch right now. He steps out of the box. Which, naturally, makes the boos louder.

The Chicago pitcher, Ortega, steps off the mound and screams something at him. Because I have the binoculars, I can read lips. The hurler had not exactly invited Paul to join him for drinks after the game. He nods at the pitcher, which throws Ortega into a rage of cursing that doesn't stop when Demeter finally steps back in.

Ortega double pumps his arms in front of him and starts his ridiculously long windup, and he uncorks a throw of such cheese that I swear I can hear it break wind some four-hundred-seventy feet from home plate.

Demeter barely moves his head to avoid the high and tight pitch by inches. The home crowd buzzes. I peer in close for his reaction, and—swear to God—that little tic at the corner of his face is flipping around like a jitterbug in a frying pan. I wouldn't begrudge any ballplayer to piss himself after escaping a death-threatening pitch like that. Most, at the very least, would step out of the box and take a big suck of air before continuing, but not Paul Demeter. No sir. He keeps that little smirk firmly-planted on his mug as he takes a couple of practice swings in the batter's box with all the urgency of a man rising from his seat to open a window on a warm day. *Ballsy, I say.*

Ortega cusses into his glove as he stares at Paul Demeter again. He is known for a nasty little cutter that only moves about four inches, but the key is that it waits until it's right on the hitter's wrists before it breaks. He throws it inside to a right-handed hitter. It's his *out* pitch, but sometimes he throws it following a brushback. If I know this much, the Rangers advance scouts know it, and so Paul Demeter would know it.

He does. He starts his stride as Ortega's right hand is at nine o'clock, and it is too late to bring back. The ball comes in belt high, not as fast as the previous pitch, and just before it breaks, Paul Demeter's bat meets it in front of home plate with a righteous crack. The ball gets out of the playing field so fast the Sox left fielder neither looks up nor turns around as it screams over his head.

I am very tired, so what happens a few innings later when Paul Demeter comes to the plate again does not disappoint me. His homerun is the only extra base hit he has against Ortega in his career, so even the grandma slugging a Budweiser in the top row and I know what's coming next. Sure enough, the Sox hurler throws a fastball— not a brushback this time, but a for-real bean ball—straight at Paul Demeter's noggin. He goes to the dirt, but not for long. He rushes the mound and gets a bloody nose from Ortega for his troubles (back in Panama, Ortega was a Golden Gloves boxing champ).

The White Sox bench clears in support of their pitcher, but the only other Ranger on the field is William Kerrigan, who gets tackled by the first base coach before he can get to the mound. Paul Demeter and Ortega are thrown out of the game, while both managers are warned. When you think things have settled down, my grandfather jumps up, and throws every bat and helmet out of the dugout. He kicks over both Gatorade cans and berates the men sitting on the bench. For this little tantrum, he also gets the old heave-ho. With Paul Demeter expelled from the game, I am free to leave.

I fall asleep on the train and wake only after someone yells at me. The lot where Moby is parked is only two or three blocks from the station, but to me in my state of exhaustion, in the poor lighting it looks like a five-mile hike. I am even sleepier after the nap, and my shoulders and neck ache from all the driving and hunching over my laptop. I am also hungry, but all I think about is getting back to the motel and flopping onto the bed.

I am too drained to notice the set-up. The first guy approaches from the dark.

"Hey, how ya doin?"

And so, being the one hundred percent chump I am, I raise my hand slightly, and automatically answer the world's most rhetorical question. "Good. You?"

This is just enough so that the second guy, who I don't see behind me, is able to slip my bag off my shoulder, down my arm and past my wrist in one motion. It happens so fast I don't even have time to yell. I can't even take a breath. The first guy is already long gone across the avenue. The dude with my bag sprints the opposite direction, and after about a hundred yards, passes it off to a third guy, who runs a block and hands it to a fourth guy. *Damn, these guys are fast!* Stunned and mute, I watch as my bag is the baton in a sprint relay down a far avenue.

I slump against a stop sign. A bench is only fifteen feet farther, but I don't dare sit. I might not even try to stand back up. Mugged—this is what it feels like. Robbed! Damn!

Stupefied, scared and shattered, I try to sum it up. I have been totaled. Everything is gone—all of it—phone, the cash, Jodie's credit card, my notebooks and my laptop. My laptop! My notes! All my notes are gone! Tonight, I hammered out two more pages of top quality notes, now all gone

I have to re-start from scratch. How am I going to do that or anything without money? I look around. Nobody around to help. I see sparse traffic, two blocks away, feel hot tears on my cheeks.

Are you seriously going to slouch there on a street sign and bawl? I think I hear a voice. *Are you really feeling sorry for yourself?* Is that my mother? It has to be. Jodie, the mistress of misfortune, preaches:

"Calamitous things happen to people all the time. A person can choose how to act when calamity strikes: She can think, 'So what? Bring it!' or she can curl up in a ball."

Jodie had admitted that, for too long, she had opted for the latter choice, and only lately had she recognized the wisdom of the stiff upper lip.

So, now… this would rank as calamitous. With that bit of motherly wisdom supporting me, I bend over, put my face in my hands and cry like John Boehner. Ten minutes or an hour later, after I get it all out, I straighten up. I manage to push off from the metal post and schlep the remaining block to my car.

At first, Moby coughs and doesn't start.

"Don't you dare!" I hiss.

Another turn of the key, and he hacks to ignition and I begin to drive. Little about this mission so far surprises me anymore, so I am not cratered when I push open the motel room door and see Aqib slumped in the chair—in the same exact spot I'd left him four hours earlier. I kick off my shoes and trudge to the bed, falling, fully-dressed. I yank sheet and cover over my head and sleep the night through, and I dream.

PART II

The Interview

On the occasion of his 39th birthday, Paul Demeter told Berry Tramel in an exclusive interview with *The Oklahoman* that he was retiring from baseball at the end of the season. When asked how solid his decision was, Demeter said, "One-hundred percent."

Berry Tramel: You thought you would quit on a high note?

Paul Demeter: That's sure not a bad idea, but in fact I made up my mind in February—this would be the *last* year.

BT: You realize this will provide ammo to those wackier of detractors who say you are using a secret substance to enhance your performance? They'll say the drug, or whatever the substance, has a shelf life of say, nine to twelve months, and you're getting out before it wears off or MLB figures out how to detect it.

PD: (laughs) That's pretty wacky.

BT: (chuckles) If you don't mind me saying so, what you're doing this *season* is pretty wacky.

PD: Bingo.

BT: What are you going to do with yourself outside of baseball?

PD: I might teach school. My parents taught… still do. Mom—kindergarten, my dad—girls basketball—both for over twenty-five years. Teaching is what I would've done if baseball hadn't worked out. I have my degree. I can work on my alternative certification.

BT: Teacher? I'll be darned. What subject?

PD: Social studies—U.S. geography, especially. I've seen a lot of it in my career. Hah.

BT: You get along with kids?

PD: I'd better!

BT: Would you coach?

PD: Actually? I had an offer once, to help with school baseball in my hometown. During one of the really bad years when you thought I might be washed up, my old principal extended the offer. Who knows? I might take them up on it… if the offer's still good.

BT: Wouldn't teaching school be a big letdown after living a fairly high-profile existence as a Major League ballplayer?

PD: I thought it might be cool.

BT: I think it fair to say you have experienced unprecedented news coverage—probably the most intense scrutiny a sports figure has come under in the last decade. A lot of nosy people have entered your life, for good or ill. What's the dumbest question anyone has asked you?

PD: Let me think. (pause) I guess I would have to say: *Is it true that a Cheyenne shaman in Anadarko put special medicine on you to allow you to hit so well?*

BT: What do you think Ted Williams would say today about your quest for .400?

PD: He would probably say people shouldn't be so surprised. He'd say it's not such a mystery what Demeter is doing, tell em to watch him closely. He'd say it's obvious he is more patient, that he's waiting for the good pitch to hit, he's not fighting with the bad pitches he used to go after. Most importantly, it appears that his mind is uncluttered."

BT: He would *know* something like that?

PD: Ted Williams would. Yeah.

BT: How do you think he'd feel about his amazing mark being reached, not by a superstar, but frankly, by a pretty average ballplayer? No offense.

PD: None taken. I think he might get a kick out of it. He might say a lot of very good hitters have come and gone in the last seventy or so years and couldn't do it. Maybe it's fitting a regular Joe Six-pack kind of guy went out and had himself a miracle year.

BT: You think it's a miracle?

PD: No. No! That's a bad choice of a word. I shouldn't have used the word "*miracle.*"

BT: If it's not a miracle, why did you wait so long?

PD: (pause) It came when it came. I couldn't have done it earlier."

BT: Okay, so at the end of the day, here's the deal, Paul Demeter. The people want to know: are you a massive cheat, or are you a one-in-a-million phenomenon?

PD: I am not a cheat. Phenomenon? I don't know. I do know this: it is no hoax. The best pitchers in the world are trying their very damnedest to get me out, and for a half-dozen times out of ten, they do, but for the other four, I hit them safely.

BT: How? How are you doing it? It always comes back around to that, doesn't it?

PD: Yes, it does. I think I know how I am doing it.

BT: Please excuse me, Paul, but if you retire at the end of this season, you will never have to explain yourself. Isn't that about right? Isn't that what people will say?

PD: (nodding, smiling) You are excused.

BT: Good luck, Paul Demeter.

PD: Thank you.

Jodie Calls

Jodie tried to call Sylvia, but the call went straight to voicemail.

"*Talk, please,*" was her daughter's voicemail answer.

You'd think a talented writer like her would come up with a better recording! She'd told Sylvia to keep her phone charged and on at all times.

"Don't worry. I will be economical, and I will not call when you should be sleeping, unless it's an emergency, in which case you won't be able to get back to sleep anyway.

Sylvia likely stayed up late, working on her story, and planned to sleep in late, so she turned off her phone. *Nothing to worry about.*

Jodie called her father. "That was quite a little temper tantrum you allowed yourself in the dugout last night," she said when William answered. "Nicely done."

"I was pissed." "None of those bastards made a move to help Bud."

"I noticed. William, have you seen your granddaughter?"

"Yes, in Kansas City, and a breath of fresh air it was too."

"You will watch out for her?" She hoped to sound confident.

"You know better than to ask. We are supposed to meet for lunch. That is, if she makes it. Uh, sorry."

"I know."

They talked another five minutes—all around the subject of Paul Demeter until William sighed.

"Jodie. A funny thing happened. Yesterday, on the way to the ballpark, Bud asked the cabbie to drive by the neighborhood…"

Jodie was silent, allowing him to continue.

"… by the apartment."

"Yes, Dad!" she said more forcefully than she meant. "I *know* what neighborhood."

"Yeah, right. Sorry."

He was quiet. Then, "You haven't called me *Dad* since about sixth grade."

"Did he… uh, say anything?"

"Oh. Not much."

"*William!*"

"Well… Really, Jodie—he asked the driver to stop. Then all he said was, 'I should have done things different.'"

"He told you this?"

"Nope, he didn't. That's the bizarre thing. He told it to the driver. Leaned over the seat and spoke right in his ear, like I wasn't sitting next to him. The man looked at Bud like he was crazy—which I couldn't blame him—then at me like, 'What the hell is *this* all about?' All I did was shrug my shoulders. Then we just sat, and no one said anything for a while. It wasn't funny, actually. It was weird. It was macabre. Finally, I told the cabbie I'd give him a fifty dollar bill if he got us the hell outta there."

"Enough. Thank you, William. Later."

"Yes. Nice talking with you too, dear."

Taking Stock

When I awake, I am permitted two whole seconds to forget where I am and what has happened to me. Forget about being mugged—forget about the disaster that means the end to my trip, the end of the story. Misery was heaped on me nine, ten hours ago, and all I get is a lousy two ticks of consciousness to forget it all.

I check my watch. The morning is almost gone. I sit up and try to think. Jodie would send money, even if she has to take out a loan. I won't let her do that. She would send another credit card if I ask, but I won't ask.

I think of William Kerrigan, and it's not a pretty thought. I will have to go there for money. The very idea chastens me. He will do it. He's offered. I'll probably have to sit still and act like I am paying attention for a lecture and a bunch of advice I don't want, but at the end of the day, he will give me what I need. I think.

I look forward to going to him for help about like I'd look forward to pulling my own teeth with a pair of pliers. When I hear water splashing in the bathroom, I am further disgusted with the realization that I have a stowaway terrorist in my presence. Aqib. Right? Of course. The irrepressible Aqib, still in my miserable life, now cleans up for blowing up. *Sheesh.*

When the bathroom door flies open, I cover my eyes.

"You can look, Miss."

"No, I can't."

"I am fully-dressed, and I feel wonderful."

Feeling wonderful enough for jihad? I moan and drop my head into my hands.

"You have the hangover, Miss?"

"I wish I had the hangover. I ran into some bad customers last night."

"Did they hurt you?"

"No. No, they didn't—not physically, anyway."

When he coaxes the rest from me, I tell it in the opposite manner of one desiring to bring sympathy upon one's self. The last person I need to feel sorry for me is this guy. I spit the words out like a kid whose eye has been blackened on the playground, but she knows she would win a re-match. "Bastards can rob me. I ain't quittin!"

He picks up his bag, and places his other hand on the door knob. The focused look is back on his face.

"Uh, what are you doing, Aqib?

"I am keeping promise. I am going away from you. A thousand thanks to you, Miss, for all you have done for me. I will never forget you. I am missing your kindness already, and I am not even out the door."

I look around the tiny, sparsely-accented room and try to focus. It all gets away from me. The garish wallpaper does not fit together, pattern wise, and gaps, where sheets should mesh, expose ashy-textured dry wall. "Wait a sec," I say, walking to the door.

"Yes, Miss?" he asks, staring, intently in my face.

I close the door. "Aqib?" I say. I can't believe I'm doing it. "Can you stick around til I get back? Just for a little while? I have to meet somebody. Stay here in the room? You ask the maids to tell your boy down in the office not to give away the room? I will be staying another two nights, and I will pay him later today, okay?"

He shrugs and nods.

"And Aqib—you got five bucks?"

Lunch

William orders a beer in a frosted mug. *That sounds really good.*

"You, Miss?" the girl asks.

"Make that *dos cervezas, por favor.*"

"Can I see some ID, please?'

"Sure." I smile, handing over a card.

"Okay," says the girl, handing the card back to me. "Perfect, Heather, I'll have your order right out."

"Uh, hold on a minute, please," William calls to her, raising a finger. "I think maybe you'd better bring *Heather* a soda instead. She's taking medicine. Did you forget that, Heather?"

"Yeah, right… medicine. I guess I'll have a Sprite."

I can't decide if I should come right out and ask him, or I should wait until after we eat. *After we eat.*

"Some hissy fit you threw on the bench last night, Grandpa."

"Bastards!" he frowns.

"My dad's teammates haven't exactly supported him."

"Nope. Drop it. I got it outta my system." William rubs his chin. "Sylvia, I don't know if it makes a difference, but Bud was going to keep sending checks until after college."

"He doesn't have to do that."

"I told him that. So, your angle?" William asks, sipping his beer. "I mean, how do you see your story unfolding?"

"Of course he's cheating."

"You said your story would be from a different angle? I thought yours would be original? A lot of folks think he's cheating—including most of his teammates."

"Don't you?"

"No."

"You're his buddy."

"Even so. He told me he wasn't cheating."

"Like I said—buddies? You're around him. You haven't seen him taking?"

He chuckles, but there is no mirth in it. "If there is one culprit you can all mark off your list, it's drugs. All he ever takes is vitamin C. No steroids, no dope. He's clean. Paul has peed in more cups this summer than Secretariat."

My turn to laugh. "*Rolling Stone* wrote that he sold his soul to the Devil."

"Yeah, I saw that. That's pretty good."

When the food arrives, I realize I am starving. William has the chef salad. Me—the pork chops. I cover my plate, all of it—the chops, potatoes and carrots—in steak sauce and dig in. I choke down the Sprite, cramming another mouthful in.

"Take a breath," William says. "Bud tells the truth. He might be a lot of things: an imperfect mate, a flawed parent—how am I gonna talk?—or a blemished boyfriend, but one thing's for sure. He isn't a liar. Some guys'll lie if the truth is better, not Bud."

"So, tell me…"

"You're the journalist. You go find it out."

"Okay, I will."

"That's not the reason I won't tell you," he adds while pouring the dressing. "You'd laugh." He smiles. "I did. It was so preposterous what he told me that I fell out laughing, but he swears it's the reason. Anyway, if he manages .400 and tells you what he told me … how… I mean, you'll be a Pulitzer winner if you make a readable story out of it."

"Is that right?"

The smile is gone from his face. "Yes. It is. Because it is fiction."

"Thought you said he doesn't lie?"

"He's not lying. That's the sad part. Bud has lost his mind in a way. He *believes* what he told me. That accident with the bicycle did more to him than he knows."

He puts down his fork, pushing his bowl away. "I just lost my appetite."

He calls the girl over and asks for a whiskey. "Part of me doesn't want him to hit damn .400. That way somebody won't write a story that's gonna hound him the rest of his life."

"Even if that somebody is me? What accident?"

"*Especially* you! One night last winter, somebody ran over Bud with a bicycle. He's changed. What is it you're wanting from me today, Sylvia?"

"What makes you think I want anything? And it was *you,* William, that asked *me* to lunch. Remember?"

"You are your mama's child—makes me know you *needed* something the second you walked in here. What is it?

I take a gulp of Sprite and fold the napkin. With my fork, I maneuver a carrot around a potato slice as slick as Kane decking Mrazek. "William, I need money." In another gush, I tell him why. I needn't have, because he didn't ask. I could've made something up. I don't. I spit it out, giving him the colorful details. I steady for the lecture.

"You hurt?" the first words out his mouth.

"No. They were real gentlemen."

"Of course I will give you money."

"You will?"

"Sure. I'm your grandfather." He takes out his wallet. "How much?"

Aw! I've misjudged the man. He's got a heart, after all. I tell him. He doesn't balk.

"That's a lot for just getting back to Tulsa."

"I am not going back to Tulsa. Not yet, anyway."

He unfolds his wallet. "You are if I am giving you money. Three full tanks and maybe one more night hotel stay's worth I expect will do it. There you go."

The Trouble

William scolded himself after she left. *I'm getting to be a damned old Gran Torino!* He'd been hard on the kid. Down deep, he admired her spunk, her gumption. He knew he wouldn't have tried something so bold as what she was doing. He would have "teamed up" with a girl like her, though, if he'd run into one when he was that age—a girl who wasn't afraid to risk a lot, or better—who was scared, but going ahead and doing it anyway.

In truth, hearing about the mugging scared the hell out of him, but it was better for her that he didn't let on. *Be the hard-ass for Jodie's sake.* The kid didn't like him, but she'd be surprised if she knew a huge part of him felt like cleaning out his billfold for her. *Go after that story, girl*—that part of him wanted to say. She left his money sitting on the table.

Someone bumped him on the crowded sidewalk. He bumped back. Bud's mug was on the front page of a paper over there. William quit looking at that stuff in July. Things were getting all out of whack with the world. A man losing his freakin mind out on a ball diamond, doing something that hadn't been done in two generations. A kid, off on her own in a dangerous world, trying to track him down. What the hell? At times like this, he could've really used Anna's wisdom. She would have set him straight.

He grieved his wife still. The dull pain hadn't abated. There was no bottom to it. He thought about her about the same as he thought about the war, daily, but he made a point of *not* lingering on it.

AARP kept sending her magazines. He never got around to stopping the subscription, and threw them in the trash at first. Then he started doing the crosswords. Now he read the articles—but not the travel. Knocking around all his life, he was more impressed with sensible stuff, like reminding them at the cash register that you're a veteran, and how not to be a hoarder.

Damn, this sun is hot! At the Chicago River, he found a little shade and sat on a concrete bench. He should've drunk another beer instead of the Irish. He leaned back against a light post. He closed his eyes and let her come to him.

Anna was a perfect partner for a man like him. Besides her sweet love, she took care of the finances, and he was like, *God bless you!* A whiz at numbers, she filed their taxes in one sitting and took care of the bank, the investments, the retirement—the whole ball of wax, and he was tickled to death to let her have it. Their arrangement was that he would do baseball and send the money and come home when he could. She would do home, garden, manage the child's illness, and when she's too much, he would take time off to help her.

It worked. They weren't rich, but it was a good life. Anna wanted to visit Europe, so they did—even if he wasn't all that excited about it and tried his damnedest not to let it show. They ate well and purchased whatever they needed and wanted.

In Huntsville, William had a lot of time to think, and he realized there were signs he should have seen. The intracranial aneurism that ultimately killed Anna at age fifty-one dropped hints before it exploded her brain. Her perfect blood pressure suddenly went through the roof, she left the car running with the keys locked inside while she shopped at the H.E.B., she went for a walk and would have been gone over six hours if a neighbor hadn't noticed she'd lapped his block eight times and called 911. And apparently Anna had done some strange things with their money.

William was in for the shock of his life after he and Jodie took care of all the arrangements and scattered Anna's ashes in the Guadalupe. The bank called to tell him that his check to the funeral home bounced. *What the hell?* When he went to the bank to straighten it out, he found that Anna had withdrawn all but a couple hundred dollars.

With Jodie's help, he discovered that they were broke. Everything was gone. All they had worked for, saved and invested, gone! Over nine hundred and ten thousand dollars had vanished. Poor sick Anna had cashed in everything: the Roth IRA, the 401(k), the mutual funds and even the Krugerands. She had put all the money they had in an oil and natural gas company, traced to a clique of Austin attorneys.

This has got to be a huge mistake! William reasoned. How would conservative, innately suspicious Anna even know these people, let alone give them all their money? It got worse. The company failed. Apparently, the lawyers had lured Anna and hundreds of other investors (a lot of Asians, mostly Japanese) with the promise of high annual returns on working interests in oil and natural gas properties. It was similar to a Ponzi scheme, where the company paid existing obligations from new investments that it took in and had $170 million invested with it when it collapsed. The CEO maintained the company did nothing wrong and would resurrect itself and related holdings. Few investors had been repaid, though, apparently, the company had parted with very little of its own capital.

"Fellas, she made a mistake," William said to the men he'd caught in a meeting."

The girl out front tried to stop him, but he brushed past her as easily as Lou Brock streaking by a screaming first base coach. One man pressed a button. "Security."

Brian Smith, at the head of the table, held up a hand in protest.

"That won't be necessary, Larry."

William looked at faces. All were in their early forties, except for the wide-shouldered leader at the head of the table, who William knew to be fifty. They were stylishly dressed and well groomed. It was obvious that these men were accustomed to having the full attention of all in whatever room they happened to occupy.

William turned to speak to the senior partner, Brian Smith. "My wife would have never entered into this deal in her right mind, Smith," he said. "She was ill. Surely you could see she was at a disadvantage when presented the investment opportunity. If you can just cut a check for the biggest part of our money, I will get out of your way today."

From the corner of his eye, William saw a couple of the seated men smirk and exchange mocking glances with each other. Smith, with the jawbone of a leading man, raised a hand adorned with a diamond-encrusted national championship ring to censure the two without looking their way. He had not looked directly at William from the time he first entered the room, but his eyes held steady in the space just above his head. Now he leveled his gaze.

Smith's bio on Yahoo provided his statistics, and William filled in the rest, because he knew such men. Smith had lived a life of entitlement—a high school sports hero, with offers from all the SEC and Southwest Conference schools, while rich football boosters made sure he didn't hurt for cars, clothes or cash. His aura of authority didn't stop at the sorority house door, either. He went through flashy co-eds like he went through twelve-packs of beer, and when sated, he pissed them away.

He was popular among the Fellowship of Christian Athletes, always remarking humbly in post-game, "It was all in the hands of our Lord and Savior, Jesus Christ." He was all-conference, but too much of a "tweener"—not fast enough to play linebacker, though not quite big enough to play with his hand in the dirt - for the NFL.

Nonetheless, he was set for life. Alum judges made certain he got into law school, and when he graduated, other highly-placed supporters secured for him the best positions. Golf buddies at the Club knew about real estate deals that always domino-ed. The recent setback with the gas company was merely a blip on the screen for a man like Smith, a minor hurdle to overcome, as he had endured others on his race to wealth and status.

Smith's eyes indicated that he felt sorry for William. In Smith's mind, *Kerrigan had a right to be here.* In fact, Smith was glad he was there so he could know just how small a man he was and see exactly what he was up against.

Kerrigan was a nobody, a loser who couldn't keep a handle on his woman's financial dealings. Smith spoke in a cold voice, practiced in holding forth in front of momentous gatherings. "I'm very sorry about your loss, Kerrigan, but as I told Mrs. Kerrigan when she came to see us."

"Anna was here?" William asked, interrupting.

"She was," Smith answered, "she asked for her investment money back, and I tried my very best to explain the vagaries of the marketplace to her. I told her that it was out of our hands" Smith smiled and stood. "And anyway, my friend, a man of your experience shouldn't have to be told, here, that a card laid is a card played!"

He turned toward a man down the table.

"Now, Larry, *now* you may call Security."

Anna died the day after going to the law offices, and William grieved for the humiliation she must have felt. She had come to her senses, if only for a day, but it was too late, and he knew that knowledge helped kill her.

Jodie and the kid came down to stay a couple of months with William. Jodie snooped around the Hill Country with little Sylvia in tow, and she found out that Anna had met Brian Smith's wife at a gardening function, where Mrs. Smith was signing copies of her new book on Southwest American wildflowers, the proceeds of which would go to one of the Junior Social League's charities of course. When she reported this to her father, William dropped his head into his hands.

The author and Jodie's mother had hit it off immediately, since few lay persons in the country knew more about botany than Anna. Equipped with that knowledge, it didn't take much imagination for William to see how that meeting must have led to invitations for tea at the club or lunch at Uchi, where they discussed mountain laurels and yellow tack-stems. In the next step—though Mrs. Smith normally did not speak of the vulgarities of business—she would have invited her new friend to "get in on" her husband's wonderful business venture that all their special friends were getting in on.

In the immediate aftermath, William was contacted by a small group of swindled investors, represented by a firm of Japanese attorneys, who sought help from the legal system. *Would he care to join them?* He joined them, but as he suspected, Brian Smith was too well connected. After a tiresome wrangle, the courts friendly to such enterprises as Smith & Company allowed that what the Texas lawyers had done may have been unethical, but it wasn't illegal.

An Arrangement

Aqib sat on a cushion-less metal chaise lounge on the second level landing outside the room, bag on his lap.

I am in no mood for this, but I begin. "Taking on the big city?" I say, starting up the stairs. I wince. No need to be sarcastic, even to a terrorist.

"I think so, Miss."

"Fine. On your way out, would you tell Khaleeg I've changed my mind? I won't be staying here after all?"

Aqib rises. "Is not necessary. I paid."

"Wait… you did what?"

He holds out his hand. "Yes. You have no money. I pay for room."

I ignore the hand. "I'm not taking your money."

"Is done. Two nights more."

He is almost at the bottom of the stairs.

"I am paying this back!"

He turns, waves and smiles, the day's rays revealing rows of shiny teeth. "No you won't, Miss. We never see again. Us. Anyway, I owe to you."

"Hold on, Aqib. Hold on a minute. I'm thinking of something…" I climb to the ledge and lean over the iron rail, looking down. "You *didn't* do this thinking I would let you stay with me?"

He quits smiling. "Does it look to you as I am wanting to stay? I am ready to begin my plan. I need not stay with you to do that."

"Good!" I shake my head. For such a weakling, this kid's mighty damn confident. Where's he get off thinking he can pull off some big attack? He has no gun, no explosives—not even a knife. He sure is a cocky little so-and-so, in a pathetic way.

He holds up his hand, as unwavering as a flag in a lull. “You are on mission, a very serious quest. Same as me. I hope I am not impediment to your cause. Goodbye.”

There he goes. Fine.

“So Aqib,” I call to his back as he walks away. “If you were to stay. It’s gotta be the same sleeping arrangements as last night. Right? You know that, right? The desk and the chair?”

He turns and nods once.

“I mean. It *is* your money,” I conclude.

Stick

Not long after Jodie and Sylvia's visit, William did some snooping around of his own, and came up with information that Brian Smith and his associates liked to frolic on weekends with their families—and sometimes with ladies who *weren't* family—out at Smith's magnificent palatial house on Lake Travis.

He watched and waited, and when he was sure it was a day the attorneys would be there, and their families would not, he followed them to the lake. He waited until the men and their lady friends were on the dock in skimpy attire, drinking and watching servants, dressed in black and white, loading trays of ribs and steaks, coolers of ice cold beer and cases of wine and liquor onto Brian Smith's lake yacht.

They couldn't possibly have noticed William, with his fungo stick and a five-gallon bucket of new Major League baseballs, climbing up a fifteen-foot high platform on the next dock over, thirty yards down the private marina.

They didn't notice a thing until batted balls rained down on their scantily-clad bodies as coldly and accurately as bullets from a rifleman in a tower. Planting his stance firmly on the platform, William slapped line drives against bare bellies and knees, while the young ladies—who were not targeted—screamed as servants dropped their loads and ran for the big house.

When his victims realized what was happening, they panicked and tried to get away. Two dove into the lake, and William smacked each one hard on the ass with a ball. One paddled furiously on an air mattress, and he made it the nautical distance from home plate to second base before William knocked him into the water. One man climbed high in the branches of a live oak tree, and William plucked him as easily as dropping a squirrel with a .22. Each lawyer was hit at least three times, some more. All suffered broken bones, except for Brian Smith, who jumped in the captain's chair and frantically started the engine. William hit balls that cracked the windshields before he roared away, but he didn't hit Smith.

Sirens filled the air behind him. William held a baseball and laid the bat on his shoulder until he handed them to the first trooper on the scene. The attorneys groaned, the ladies wept, but Smith got away to the middle of the lake untouched.

In consideration of his exemplary military service, William didn't receive the maximum sentence for aggravated assault. The initial charge had been attempted murder, but even the prosecutor admitted—after watching the training tape submitted to the jury that showed William hitting infield to major league baseball players—that if Mr. Kerrigan had *attempted* to kill the men, he surely would *have*. Before the sentence was handed down, the judge asked William if he had anything to say to the court.

"Yes sir, your Honor, I do. I would like to say that I wish that one sonofabitch hadn't gotten away."

Sitting in a cell, William could not forget the image of Brian Smith's smiling face, and how he must have looked that day to Anna in the law office. Then he pictured Smith, standing unharmed and smirking, on the deck of his large boat as it trolled in deep water.

Smith is unreachable, William thought in misery.

Tulsa Time

Paul injured his foot in the All-Star Game, sliding into third, stretching a double into a triple. He missed eight games, then he tried to play on it again too soon, aggravating it further. He missed the rest of July. Was it an omen—a return of the injury that derailed his early career? Could he come back from it? Would he lose the sense of freedom that put him where he was today? He was 39, after all, and he had never been a quick healer.

Ted Williams had missed spring training, most of April, and parts of July due to injury in 1941. The layoffs had actually helped him hit .406. Williams laughed at the early absences.

"Nobody hits in the cold anyway," he quipped

Williams missed over 100 plate appearances, along with 147 walks, giving him fewer at-bats by which to divide hits. Of the twelve men hitting .400 in a season, his 456 at-bats that year was by far the lowest.

Paul knew that sitting out might not be a bad thing. He would be rusty on his return, but he was getting much needed rest in the middle of a long season and a respite from the spotlight. Percentage favored him. He would miss at least 70 at-bats. Idle, he was .402.

During the same string, the Rangers hadn't fared so well. Without Paul, the Rangers lost 13 of 16 games and dropped from second place in the AL West all the way to last. They missed his bat and glove more than most of his teammates wanted to admit.

He could do rehab exercises anywhere, so he thought to get away from Texas for a few days. He wanted to go see his parents, so he hopped in the car and headed due north, feeling guilty, though he was content because he felt himself relaxing. Northward, he continued past Marietta, Ardmore,

Paul's Valley, Wayne, Payne and through OKC. At a key crossroads in Edmond, he veered east on impulse. An hour later, he crossed the Arkansas and took the Peoria/Riverside exit ramp.

A fender-bender ahead stalled him in traffic. He idled fifteen minutes next to a daycare playground, where out his window, a little girl, probably a kindergartener, held court on the highest rung of a set of tall monkey bars.

Cute kid. Cute kids often made him think of Sylvia.

He and Sylvia had a park thing going in Chicago—actually, in various towns. She hounded him to roll her to the park, and he moaned back at her, but he considered it a hoot to take her. It was a load off. Baseball wasn't even in his psychological zip code at the park. Squeals, shouts, and giddy ruled the day.

Sylvia had been this monkey bar child with other kids: self-confident, a born leader, in charge of that tiny universe, but not bossy. She organized kickball, positioning the tiny fielders just so while coaching them. When they shied away from structured activities, she made up games for them, always in charge.

Sylvia was a daredevil too, and he forced himself to look away when she was high on jungle gyms. When she did crazy stunts that were inappropriate for her size and age, he wanted to yell at her, but if she wasn't scared, he would shut up and turn around as she shouted.

"Look at me, Paul Demeter! Look at me!"

At that instant, the kid executed a back somersault from her rung of the monkey bars to a lower rung, flying in the hot air and righting herself like a saki monkey. *Whoo!*

How had Sylvia turned out? She's probably a bright little number, ready to take on college by now. No probably about it! What kind of person has she turned out to be? Is she popular? She would have boyfriends, right? Is she sexually active now? That's a hell of a thing to wonder.

Is she stunning like her mother? Has that beautiful, crazy hair ever lost its curl? Is she a good friend? What is her answer when people ask about her father? What father? You mean the loser who left me and my mom? Does she have enemies? How do they strategize against her? Does she still like sports?

Probably not, because sports has Paul Demeter in it. She is likely so consumed with friends and activities that she probably doesn't even know about the season he is having. If she happens by chance to hear the name *Paul Demeter*, what thoughts, if any, does the name invoke? Does she hate him? Is his relationship with her such a trivial segment of her life that she hasn't the gumption for such an emotion? Does she even think about him?

Probably not. By now, she probably doesn't even remember him. He could've insisted on seeing her. He had the love equity for it—except for road trips with the team, they were almost never apart. When at home, she was with him more than with her mother.

They could have worked something out—if not on regular visitation times, at least a weekend now and then, or holidays and birthdays? He hadn't tried very hard. He told himself Jodie wouldn't have gone for it. He figured that for her, like him, everything was too painful, and she probably wanted a clean break.

So he wouldn't miss her. She wasn't his child, after all. Who the hell was he kidding, thinking he could raise somebody else's kid? He didn't have a kid of his own, so what did he really know about parenting? For a while after he left, he teared-up any time Sylvia came to mind, but the thoughts gradually stung less and less until they mutated into a dull ache.

Writing letters to Sylvia was lame. He never heard back from her. It was a total waste of time, ink and paper. Who wrote letters anymore, anyway? She probably never read them. She wouldn't even know what a letter was. If a kid got a message that wasn't on a smart phone or computer, she wouldn't know what the darn thing was. She'd probably think letters were like hieroglyphics or runes from history books.

He turned onto their street and instantly felt goofy driving slowly by with the window down in broad daylight. *What are you, sixteen years old?* A family returning from church approached behind him. They were practically on his bumper. They honked at him, but no one waved. When they turned into a driveway, the father looked hard twice at Paul, who nodded in the rearview. The father did not nod back.

Paul had an explanation ready in case Jodie took that moment to catch him out there: he was just driving by to see what condition the old house was in. *Weak!.* He had not seen her in over two years. *Was she with the same man?* She hadn't ever married. This guy was at least the third that had a lasting relationship with her—not that anyone was counting. What was this guy like? What was it to him?

Two years ago, Paul had called her because he was finally getting rid of the apartment in Chicago. He'd rented it out all these years. He didn't know why he bothered, since he didn't need the money, and it wasn't like he was ever going to use it. Jodie's name was on the property, so she would have to sign papers before it could be sold. When he asked her on the phone if she could meet him, she said she could and asked where.

"I'm in town. I could come by the house," he offered.

"I don't think that is such a good idea," she answered

She thinks or someone else thinks? Paul wondered.

"Okay. Wherever."

She named her bank, where they could use a meeting room. He thought she might bring Sylvia with her, so he tried to prepare himself. She didn't. She brought the man—Jack.

Paul was not prepared for how sensational Jodie looked. The meeting took place thirty minutes after Paul called, so he knew she didn't have time for makeup or even a shower. She'd come just as she was: in baggy Lee jeans and a long-sleeved flannel shirt, and he had trouble yanking his eyes off her.

They hugged, hardly touching. Jack shook hands and excused himself, saying he'd be in the lobby. They had small talk as he showed her where to sign.

"I forgot my name was even on here," she said.

"How's Sylvia doing?"

"Oh, fine, fine. She is a handful, that girl!"

He wrote out a check.

"Here's your part."

"No. I can't take that," she protested, pushing it away.

"Sure you can. The place was part yours."

"I'll put it another way, Paul. I *won't* take it—not a thing from that awful place!"

"Okay? Maybe you could put it in Sylvia's college fund?"

"No! I will find a way for her college, Paul."

"It's none of my business, but I know you don't make much teaching school. I read only Mississippi and Arkansas pay their teachers less than Oklahoma."

"You're right."

"Yes?"

"It's none of your business. Thank you for trying, though."

They quit talking and looked into each other's eyes until it was uncomfortable.

"So we had to do this, I guess," she said, breaking the silence.

"Yeah, I'll go now."

"All right. Are you going to play more?"

"Excuse me?"

"Baseball. Are you going to play more?"

"Oh, yeah… probably… at least one season, maybe two."

A knock on the door. Jack opened it from outside, peeking in.

"Everything okay in here?"

The man is jealous, Paul thought, *but who could blame him?*

"We were just wrapping up," Jodie said, standing.

She and Paul hugged again before she moved to Jack's side.

Paul parked under a mulberry tree in front of their house. He looked at the home, which was in very good shape for a place built in the twenties. They don't make them like that anymore. Two cars were parked under the carport: an old white Buick that didn't look driveable and a yellow slug bug. Yeah, a VW would be perfect for Jodie. Through the hedge, he saw a pickup in the alley parking spot. That would be a man's vehicle.

He knew now for certain what he was going to do at season's end, and it involved another trip to Tulsa. He had already consulted a CPA and informed his lawyer of the plans. The attorney, at the time, was Elizabeth, and to her credit, she didn't try to dissuade him. He now had a new attorney. The man had taken it all in, and he assured Paul he would be able to tidy up all the details.

A Healthy Dose

"I told you I'm not worth it," Jodie said one night to Paul in the garage apartment in Austin. "You won't listen, so I will tell you things that will make you want to run from me like your hair's on fire. My parents knew little about the problem when I was small. By the time I saw a psychologist, I'd experienced headaches and spells of emptiness, lasting three or four days. I thought I would die, or best case—stay crazy and be sent back wherever they found me."

"You're fine now," he said.

She shook her head. "Anna and William tried to find my birth parents for a history, but they had no luck. Today, with the internet, it would be easy. I'm not interested."

"You seem wonderful to me."

"Medicine helped in high school. By then, this happened…" she said, pointing ballet hands toward herself. "And guys started hitting on me. However, word got out fast that I was too smart or crazy and I could make for a confusing date."

"It's not working," Paul smiled.

"Maybe this will. I jumped out of my classroom window junior year. I thought three stories would kill me, but all it did was mess up my ankles. I cut an artery going through the glass. Ironically, I almost bled out before my teacher staunched the flow."

"I'm not going anywhere."

"Staying with the meds and exercising have been key in college. Actually, running landed me in The Group—literally. That's how I found them. I jogged the river and straight into one of their readings. I fell in with them, and then with Drury."

"Again, here I remain," Paul said, undaunted.

Her garage apartment was tiny. The kitchen and living area were the same room. The ironing board unfolded out of the pantry, its front leg propped on the sofa. Paul choked down a mug of green tea as she ironed a scarf.

When they made love the first time, they got to the sofa, where their clothes fell on the floor.

"A thousand thoughts creased my brain," he said to her, "and the most insistent was that a man could die from this!"

Moments later, he held her with the tips of his fingers.

"Your hands are strong," she said.

"I don't want to hurt you."

"You can't. You should go."

They lay, not speaking, as Paul caressed her skin.

"I'm ripe," she joked, "You can quit poking me. That's funny."

"Funny? You sounded pretty damn serious a few minutes ago."

She jabbed his ribs.

"Not ha-ha funny, but *curious* funny. It is funny that I don't have a headache. I had a terrible one last night, and a little while ago I felt another coming on when… ya know… this happened."

"I can always get aspirin."

"I don't have those kinds of headaches."

"Maybe a healthy dose of me makes you feel better?"

"Don't say that!" She rose on her elbow.

"It might be true."

"That is what I am afraid of," she sighed as she turned to face him. "If you are not going away like you should, can we do that again?

Windy City

I accept money from Aqib for train fare and a bleacher seat for the night's game. My plan—the big picture—has devolved to day-to-day, like Scarlett O'Hara's.

Tomorrow's going to have to wait until tomorrow.

After lunch with William, I find an elementary school not far from the motel that's got a large playground. I figure one lap is a half mile, so I do four, working up a good sweat. I feel decent, considering. Oh, yeah—I gave up cigarettes this morning. They say it's the hardest thing to do. Guess the people who say that never had a parent leave them. It wasn't like an epiphany or anything, or a goal I set. It was just me lighting up after I peed, and it tasted like shit. So I stubbed it out in the toilet. No big deal.

I arrive early to watch batting practice. Paul Demeter sprays line drives in gaps between third and short, between short and second, second and first. None of these screamers would have been caught in a game. Then he hits long. Kids and a few adults scramble after and tussle over shots he hits into the stands—even the foul balls—historic souvenirs, all of them

He swings the bat with such ease, something he hasn't done in the last dozen years. *What are you doing, Paul Demeter? Really, what are you doing?*

William told me, among the other things, about the batting cage and the machine that Paul Demeter had tricked up in the winter. I picture him hitting ball hour after hour, day-in day-out, in a barren, frozen Kansas batting cage, icicles hanging from his ears and nose. I see snow settle in the creases of bulky sweats and the folds of a stocking cap. *What was he thinking?* What was his plan? Did he have a plan? Could he have possibly seen this coming? How's he going to explain this? I can't wait until he reveals it all to me.

He hits safely once in four at-bats tonight and makes three good plays at third base—nothing dramatic like last night. He is back over .400. This is just mind boggling! I write notes on the flimsy motel tablet and fill it up quickly. Back in the room, after Aqib saw me tuck it in my back pocket, he went to the office and came back with four more. I look at my notes again. This story is going to be solid.

I find the Citi Field crowd every bit as interesting as the action on the field. It's a blast. The fans are truly torn. They don't know which way is up. Paul Demeter is the enemy, so he is hated. His performance on the field is incredible and impossible, so he is due adulation. He could be cheating, so people don't know how to feel. They boo when his name is announced. They cheer when he hits the double and runs it out. They jeer when he settles in at second base. Talk about a quandary!

Naturally, I am a little spooked getting off the train late tonight. Nobody exits with me. The doors open and slam shut, meaning: *Hurry. Get out!* I plant a heel and do a three-sixty look-a-round. *Shouldn't there be better light in public places?* It was creepy in daylight, but now shadows loom. A dark figure hunches over, back against the brick wall. I stop walking. I am quiet. Then I remember. *Why? I don't have anything. Go ahead and rob me!*

The figure moves. "Hello, Miss."

I jump sideways, like I've been poked with a cattle prod. "Dang, Aqib. This is stupid! You scared the crud outta me!"

"I am sorry for frightening you. I didn't mean to do this."

"Well, you did! What are you doing here?"

"Oh, nothing." he says while looking down at the concrete.

"You came down here to wait for me, that's it! You didn't know what train I would be on. How long you been here?"

"I have not been here long." He shrugs.

A burly security guard turns the corner.

Where the hell were you last night when you could have been some help?

"What are you doing here, fella?" The guy says, pointing his stick at Aqib. "I run you outta here two hours ago. If I see you again, Mister, I'm bustin your chops!"

"Yes, sir," Aqib mumbles as we walk away.

"Not here long, huh?" I say.

Seigi

William had waited until he had been in Japan three weeks with the SoftBank Hawks before he called Hideki. Hideki had been in the group of attorneys who, more than three years earlier, represented the investors swindled by Smith & Company. After one drawn-out legal proceeding in Austin, Hideki had politely approached William outside the courtroom and told him he knew William was a baseball man.

"Cardinals, right, Mr. Fungo?" Hideki had told him and shook his hand. "I'm a big fan of American baseball, especially of the San Francisco Giants."

"Well, we won't hold that against you," William said.

On a couple of nights, after long court sessions, William and Hideki drank beer at Madigan's and talked baseball. Hideki turned out not to be an average baseball fan; he knew his baseball, his stats, and his players and teams. His favorite all-time player was Bobby Richardson. "I played a mean second base for my school team," Hideki bragged.

William had enjoyed his company—Hideki did most of the talking—and with Anna no longer waiting for him. William was glad to have an excuse not to go home early.

It hadn't taken very many courtroom sessions for William to become skeptical of the group's chances to win their case against Brian Smith and the other lawyers. He was blunt with Hideki.

"This is fruitless, isn't it?" William said one night at Madigan's. He and Hideki watched a muted re-play of the 1960 Yankees-Pirates World Series finale on the bar's big-screen TV. "I mean this court's not going to touch Smith and them, is it."

Hideki put his beer down and shook his head. "I fear not," he said quietly. "I suppose we are here now only on principle. I'm afraid I may have let you and the others down.

My specialty is criminal law, and I may be slightly out of my league here. My regrets about your money."

"Oh, it's not so much the money," William said. "I gave up on that some time ago. I'm not that big on principle either." Then he told Hideki about Anna.

"Now I am even more disappointed that I have been no help." Hideki said. "I am so sorry for your loss, and I apologize for my futile attempt to bring seigi, justice."

William nodded. "Thank you," he said. The two fell silent as both turned to watch Mazeroski's mad jaunt around the bases to win the game and the Series.

"I guess there won't ever be a way to get at Smith legally," William said with a weary voice. "I would sure like to, though. It's a damn shame."

Hideki had not said more; he only shook his head in slow agreement.

A week later, the court handed down its ruling, and Hideki and the other attorneys went back to Japan. Before he left, Hideki said goodbye to William, thanked him for the times they had at Madigan's, and told him that if he should come to Japan in the future, to please look him up.

"Oh, thank you, Hideki, but I don't think that will ever happen," William said. "Not to be impolite, but I had my one trip to Asia, and that's probably going to be plenty for me."

Of course, back then, how could William have known that he would be spending more than two years in prison, or that when he was free, the only baseball job he could find would be in Japan?

Hideki was glad William called him. "When your team comes to my city, I will attend your game," he said on the phone.

"Good, Hideki," William said. "I have a little something I need to talk with you about."

"You look good, sir," Hideki said to William when they met after the first SoftBank Hawk game in Osaka. "Confinement did not wear on you too much, I see."

"You don't have to be polite," William said. "I know I look like crap. I maybe had too much time to think. It might've worn on me."

Hideki laid his hands on the bar, palms up. "You are still bitter. You think seigi has not been served."

William shrugged. "It hasn't."

"It's been a long time."

William shrugged. "I found out I was coming over here before I left prison," he began slowly. "They had a decent library in there, and I did some studying up on Japan. Y'know, reading about your people, the culture, stuff like that. I was surprised how many books they had. Then when I got out, I found more information at the public library."

Hideki paused before he spoke. Then carefully, he said, frowning. "My country is rich in bunka, Mr. Fungo." He set his beer mug down on the table. "This is not about immersing yourself in our culture?"

"No." William drank from his beer.

"I know people whose reach are great."

"I didn't even know if you would help me. You owe me nothing."

"You cannot let it go," Hideki said. It was not a question.

William didn't say anything for a moment. As the two men looked in each other's eyes, William wondered if he had gone too far. They were not really friends, after all. He said, "I don't want anybody hurt. I *have* let that go. If that's all I wanted, if I wanted a hit man, I could have found half a dozen knuckleheads playing pool in Ft. Worth bars who would give it a go for fifty bucks. Anyway, if so much as a hair on Brian Smith's head is hurt, the laws will come straight for me."

Hideki dropped his gaze. He said, "I will introduce you. Only that."

William nodded. "I wouldn't want more."

A month later, Hideki interpreted the introduction in the Tokyo office.

"Thank you for seeing me, Mr. Akihiro," William said to the well-dressed, gray haired man behind the desk.

William was surprised by the airy, well-appointed office, which he expected to be dingy and dark. It could have been a modern corporate office in any American city. Akihiro was formal, rising as he poured sake into three cups.

"To you, Mr. Kerrigan!"

When the man lifted his cup, William noticed that he was missing part of the little finger on his left hand.

"And to you, sir," William said, raising his cup.

Sipping, he felt a nice burn. Akihiro across from him drained his cup. Hideki did not lift his cup. Looking at William, Akihiro spoke to Hideki in slow, terse sentences, which Hideki interpreted.

"Texas is a long way," William said to Hideki, after he heard what Akihiro had to say.

Hearing this, Akihiro smiled slightly, waved his hands as though shooing a fly. "Poof."

No interpretation needed.

An hour or so later, when Akihiro rose from behind his desk, William knew the meeting had come to a close.

Hideki rose also. "'We always look for new ventures—intriguing, challenging business opportunities.' This is how Mr. Akihiro phrase it."

William stood. He said, "You tell Mr. Akihiro… No, Hideki! You *ask* him how I would go about returning this great favor he would have done for me!"

Akihiro shook his head at Hideki and he spoke to William in perfect English.

"We won't worry about that right now, Mr. Kerrigan."

Then he smiled for the first time.

William stayed as busy as he'd ever been in his life. In the first season, the SoftBank Hawks won the pennant and the Japanese version of the World Series. Then the next season the team got off to a great start, and William was named interim manager when the old skipper suffered a stroke.

William guided the Hawks to another pennant, but they lost the Series. William felt good and satisfied that he had done a decent job. He'd even been able for the first time in years to put the memory of Anna and her experience with Brian Smith out of his mind for long stretches. The only negative aspect of the remainder of his time in Japan was that he saw no more of Hideki. The attorney didn't come to anymore SoftBank Hawk ball games, and William's phone calls to him went unanswered.

Then, as he was preparing his return to America, William received a large envelope in the mail from Paul Demeter. William opened one end and shook out the contents. There was no letter of explanation from Bud, not even a card. He shook the envelope again, and a dozen newspaper clippings tumbled out.

He unfolded each and spread them on the floor. They were articles from the business sections of papers from Houston, Dallas, New York, San Francisco, OKC and Austin. At first, he didn't realize what he was reading. Then upon focusing, he realized the subject of the articles—all of them—was Brian Smith.

There were pictures, too. Fungo scanned the pages and re-read the articles. It seemed Mr. Smith's various businesses were not doing well, not well at all, and that he had lost his largest venture, another energy company in a hostile corporate takeover by a group of Asian businessmen.

Touching Home

Jodie didn't recognize the number. Then she saw *Illinois* on the screen, and she breathed again. "Yes?"

"Hey, Jodie."

"Sylvia. How nice of you to call!" She hoped her daughter didn't hear the edge to her voice.

"Sorry about that. I, uh, I sort of lost my phone."

"Oh. That is dangerous these days, especially while traveling. What happened?

"Uh. I dropped it in the lake?"

"You should see your grandfather. Ask him to buy you a new one and tell him I will pay him back."

"Yeah. Okay, I might do that."

"Which means you have no intention whatsoever to do that. I wish you would try harder. Your grandfather loves you, you know? How are you getting along, dear?"

"Great, Mom. Great—couldn't be better."

"What's wrong, Sylvia?"

"Does something have to be wrong, Jodie? I'm only checking in, touching home."

"I don't know. You sound stressed. Have you seen your father?"

"Nope—not up-close and personal anyway. I am saving that for the end, I think."

"And he doesn't know?"

"Not unless William told him. I asked him not to."

"Then he hasn't. How is it coming, anyway? Your story?"

"The story is going to be deliciously nasty. I had a bit of a setback, but I am back on track. I hope you like it."

"Will I?"

"Depends on your stomach."

"I'm going to Texas," Jodie said.

"Oh good—we can go to the games together."

"We'll see about that. The reason I am coming to Texas is to tell you a few things you should know."

"What's wrong with right now? Save yourself a trip… though it's fine if you do come, of course. I'd love to see you."

Jodie paused. "Syl, what I have to tell you—what I have for you—needs a location. We need to be some place together, not over two phones."

"Okay, whatever Jodie. I really gotta run. I'll talk with you soon."

"Do that. Yes, and please try to call more often.

Jodie really meant: *You have me worried mindless, and I wish you would come home.*

Exactly How Far

The spring Paul and Jodie first spent together became summer before he could blink. He had his degree, he signed with the White Sox organization, and he was hopelessly far gone over a woman for the first time in his life. He knew she didn't feel the same way about him, but he was okay with that—*that's* how far. Also, he knew about her occasional return visits to the river.

Exactly how far!

He also knew she was pregnant. She tried to hide her tiny bump, jumping up and slipping on a kimono after making love. Usually she would lie in his arms long enough to fall asleep and sometimes to make love again. She flushed the john and ran the faucet and shower at the same time to muffle her morning sickness.

One week before he was to leave for Rookie Ball, he found her naked on the bathroom floor. At first, he thought she was dead and shouted.

"Please don't," she moaned. "Please don't say more."

He jumped to the floor with the medicine bottles.

"Can't take those now," she mouthed silently.

"Right!"

He ran for a sheet, and then ice. He covered her and sat flat on the floor, cradling her head in his lap. He rocked her back and forth, rubbing her neck, forehead and temples with ice, using one cube after another as they melted onto his jeans.

After a while, she fell asleep. He snuck his nose in the juncture of her neck and shoulder, inhaling the scent of soap and sex. He rubbed the bump. He held her so long that his legs grew numb, but he would have amputated them before he moved her.

He fell asleep at some point in the night, and he awoke on the floor with a folded towel under his head. Jodie sat on the toilet, wearing one of his jerseys. She wrote in a notebook under a Beatles night light.

"You snore," she said.

"I like it when you smile," he said. "You don't smile enough. What makes you sad?"

"Everything—everything apparently, besides you."

"How are you feeling?"

"Pretty good, I guess. Anyway, my head doesn't hurt. You want to go to bed?"

"Ah, I don't think I'm sleepy anymore."

"Me either, stupid," she said.

Do You Know Who I Am?

When I finally face Paul Demeter, I am not sure what I am going to say. I haven't rehearsed. You'd think that would be the first item I'd have nailed down, since I've planned for it most of the summer and have fantasized the moment for years.

I don't have an opening statement yet. I don't even have something written down that I can practice. I have writer's block of the most serious kind over this. I will have to get serious about coming up with a greeting soon.

Do you know who I am? Lame.

Where have you been? Needy.

Guess who? Trite.

Why do I have to be the one who talks? Maybe I present myself, stand there, and let him come up with something? He throws the first pitch, so to speak?

Today is Thursday, an off day for the Rangers, a travel day, and I am driving to Milwaukee. I reach for a smoke in the console, but then I remember I don't do that anymore. Aqib is in the car with me. *I know.* I did not plan it this way. He hasn't blown anything up yet. He hasn't attacked anyone—anyone that I know of anyway.

I attended the third game against the White Sox, filling two more tablets with story material. I do not know what Aqib did during the day. He probably scouted potential targets, but he met me again at the train at night. He irritated me, but I was okay with him being there. I spent a third night in the lousy motel, and for a third night, Aqib slept at the desk.

I'm feeling desperate. In Milwaukee, I will try the old man again. I will put on my *good granddaughter* face, play nice, and make promises. I am not so proud I won't grovel for money. Not saying I will, I'm just saying I might think about it. Then, if none of that works, I'll go for the deal breaker. I'll show my story to him.

This morning on the way out of town, I stopped Moby on Michigan Avenue. I jotted down Jodie's address and gave it to Aqib. "If you're not in jail, you write me to let me know where I can send the money I owe you. I really appreciate it, and before I let you out on this corner, could you do me one last favor and let me have enough money for a tank of gas to Milwaukee?"

He showed me those teeth, reached into his pockets, told me to hold out my hands, and then he dumped a lot more cash in them than was needed for gasoline.

"What is this, young man?"

"For you. You need it more than I."

"Is a lot. You don't have to. I think I know a way to get myself money when I get to Milwaukee. I'm hoping anyway."

"A dishonorable way?"

"Naw. Naw. Nothing like that. It might be uncomfortable, but not shameful."

"Then take my money, Miss. I know now I can carry out my plan without money. It will be more difficult, but I can do it. Please take. I owe you much."

Sheesh! What's a person supposed to do with that? I so did not want this person, probably a terrorist, with me for a single minute more. But how do you kick a guy to the curb when he's given you everything he has in the world? And, hasn't asked a thing from you in return except for a ride and a shower?

Into the Desert

Jodie was clearly showing when he arrived at the encampment at the base of the New Mexican mesa. Instinctively, she kept one hand curled beneath her stomach when she moved. The movement that morning, with the other women, was mixing the mud that would be the walls of The Group's new shelters. She rested by leaning on the hoe as she watched him walk through the pinon, mesquite and sagebrush. She knew it was him when he was still a mile away.

Exhausted, she was glad for the few moments' rest. The work was hard and every day. The sickness of the early months of pregnancy had not eased. Every afternoon, and sometimes twice a day, she threw up anything in her stomach. Her co-workers didn't seem to notice, or if they did, they were too tired to care.

This utopia was hard living. The never-ending heat and glare of the day and dust, and the fitful sleeping on the ground in the chilly nights, took a toll. The food was awful and plain and didn't provide enough calories or protein for the hard work they did. And after the first couple of weeks of bliss, Drury had been less than attentive to her needs.

He acted like she didn't exist, to be blunt. She tried to convince herself he was busy in the wider worries that burdened him as leader, but in her gut she knew his cold shoulder was suspiciously well tailored to coincide with his discovery that she was with child.

One of the worst headaches of her life had struck the day Paul Demeter left for Rookie Ball. The apartment's living space crowded her like a vault, and it took all her will to resist clawing at the door. If she ran outside, the sunlight would have killed her. She was caught betwixt and between, desperately in need of space, but that meant facing light, which would ratchet her pain.

She clutched her bump and lay flat on the kitchen floor, easing her burning cheek to the cool tile. Larger movement meant lightning bolts through her temple. She heard a terrible scream, only later realizing it was hers.

She knew she'd made a terrible mistake going away with Drury, but she couldn't go home now. Anna and William had rushed to the river and tried to reason with her, but she wouldn't listen. She knew what she was doing. She begged her father not to smack Drury.

She was too ashamed to face them now because she had been so wrong. Drury was a charlatan, a quack and a pretender. The hard life she endured was her atonement. She deserved all that was coming to her, including whatever she had coming from the man walking into the desert.

"I tried to warn you," she said when Paul Demeter was close enough.

He wasn't dressed for the terrain. He wore cutoff Levi's and sandals. His legs and ankles bled from thorn and cactus. You'd think a ball player wouldn't have to be told to wear a hat out in the blazing sun, but there he stood, bareheaded.

"I told you I wasn't worth it," she said.

He stopped walking. "Yeah. You did. I guess you are to me... worth it."

"Shouldn't you be playing baseball?"

"I heard you were gone."

"The team must be upset."

He only shrugged.

"Look at me!" Jodie shrieked.

"That's what I'm *doing*. You are amazing."

"Tell me you are not sorry you found me." She spoke in an undertone.

"No way!" He laughed.

What in hell does this crazy man have to laugh about?

He laughed again, and then he settled into a smile that affected his eyes.

"Look, I have to tell you that I don't really know…" Jodie said, her hands on her stomach. "I mean I don't know *who…*"

He finally quit that stupid smile. *Okay*, she thought, *here it is. This information will turn him around and make him walk right back out of this desert.*

Paul held out his hands. "I know."

"You do?" Jodie asked, realizing it was the stupidest thing she could have said.

"Yeah. I kinda had it figured out."

Exasperated tears burned Jodie's eyes and trailed onto her cheeks. "Then what's wrong with you? I don't understand you. You are not like any man I have ever known. Don't you ever give up?"

"Not on you. I love you," he said, covering her stomach with his hands. "Why don't you and this kid come with me? I am going back to play ball, and you can stay with me… y'know… as long we don't get in each other's way."

Weeping, she swung her head in wide loops. "I don't love you, Paul. I'm fond of you. You are good to me and for me. I care for you, but I can't help it; I don't love you."

"I've thought about that," he said. "It doesn't matter."

She dropped the hoe.

That first winter was hard. They had only Paul's signing bonus to live on—plus the little bit of money Jodie's father slipped Paul from time to time that she wasn't supposed to know about. She was sick right into her ninth month. Paul force-fed her Gatorade and his own recipe of hand-crafted power milkshakes to replace electrolytes, potassium, iron, sodium and whatever other nutrients she was losing every afternoon.

She had to give the man credit: he was relentless and resilient, staying and caring for a woman who didn't love him, and who carried a child that might not be his. He was beyond kind to her, and she was grateful.

She knew she didn't deserve the treatment she received. He rubbed her swollen feet, cleaned up her sickness and held her hands when she sat or stood. He even hauled her across the snow to Braum's in a red wagon on New Year's Eve, all trussed up like a show heifer going to the county fair, because she had to have a hot fudge caramel sundae.

On the next day, when Sylvia was born, the first thing he saw was her mop of curly black hair. He took her from the nurse and kissed her on the nose.

"I saw you," Jodie said, dumbstruck, her eyes drowning in tears.

"What?" he said. "Isn't she beautiful?"

"I saw you!" she gasped. "You never blinked an eye or balked. *I saw you.*"

"You ever been to Arizona?" Paul asked her in February. He lay the sleeping Sylvia on the bed next to the bag he was packing for himself.

"Yes," Jodie answered. "Once. My father thought he'd take my mother and me to spring training one year. Disaster! We never went again."

"C'mon, go with me," Paul said. "Give it another try. You don't like it, you can always catch a plane back."

Jodie leaned over to kiss Sylvia. "We'll see… we'll see."

After spring training in the desert, A-Ball in Florida was a short, relatively mild summer, during which Jodie regained strength and health and spent precious time with her baby. Paul talked her out of working, though he barely made enough money to rent a duplex, two miles from the ocean. He pushed baby Sylvia on the beach in a big yellow stroller that he bought for fifty bucks at a yard sale. Jodie had few episodes and generally felt better than she ever had.

In September, the White Sox traded Paul to Texas for his first stint with the Rangers organization, and he was disappointed at first until he found out it was a promotion. They were sending him to Tulsa—Double-A.

"It's all dust, oil, and cattle, isn't it?" Jodie asked when Paul gave her the news.

"Don't forget football. It's like a smaller Texas. You'll feel right at home. So will the Scamp."

They rented a house near Riverside, so Jodie and Sylvia could spend time in the parks along the Arkansas. Jodie was able to take classes at TU because the Driller's manager had teenage twin girls who watched Sylvia. The girls were helpful when Jodie had an episode, because their aunt was felled often by the same headaches. They knew what to do and what not to do.

In Tulsa, Paul hit .335. His career was on the rise. During the following year, the Rangers sent him to OKC, Triple-A, just down the turnpike.

"We kind of like it here," Jodie told him. Her classes and a gig reading at a bar on Cherry Street gave her chances to get out, while Sylvia hung with the girls who loved her.

"Stay then. I'll drive back every other night or so when we're on a home stand," he explained, looking into her eyes. "If you think I ought to."

"That'll be okay. The Scamp thinks you are her personal night light."

Jodie and Sylvia stayed in Tulsa, while Paul shared an apartment in Bricktown with two other 89ers, driving back to Tulsa every two or three nights and on off days. Her studies, poetry and Sylvia kept Jodie so busy, well and content that she went all summer with only two dark periods.

On one serene day in the river park with Sylvia, she considered her situation. If a pollster had shown up here in the sandbox with a clipboard, and one of the questions was: *What kind of life would you say you are living?* And if the only other choices were *Miserable* and *So-So,* she would have had to check *Happy*. Yeah, she was fine.

She definitely couldn't check *Miserable*. How could she possibly assign *So-so* to the daily joys and minor crises of keeping up with Sylvia—to the respect and affection from a man who adored her? Compared to years of purgatory? Yeah, has to be *Happy*.

Paul hit .324 at OKC, and incredibly, he made only one error all summer at third base, which created attention in both major leagues. When the White Sox bought him back, he stood a good chance of making the big team in spring training.

Another move. A big move this time. Time to re-evaluate. Would Jodie move again? Paul knew that a campus was a target-rich environment for a beauty with no ring on her finger. Men would be hitting on her like mosquitos on a fat man. He asked her again to go with him.

"This is so unfair to you," she said.

"If it's okay, I will decide what's fair to me," Paul said.

"You have been almost everything for us."

"Almost.

"Yes, and that's not fair to you."

"Again? Okay if I decide that?"

"You are so strong for me. You are my prescription, and the Scamp thinks you hung the sun *and* the moon."

"All the more reason we should take her with us." He grinned.

"I'm being serious, Paul."

"Me too. That's why it's the same deal as ever. Never a lock on any door! Every town we've been has had an airport or bus station, and I know you keep a bag packed under the bed."

"Then you have to make me one promise." She sighed.

"Okay. Anything!"

"You have to stop telling me you love me." She looked away, nodding her head as tears burned her cheeks. "Hearing you say it leaves me in a bad way."

"I don't know, Jodie."

"That's the deal."

"That will be hard to do. You sure?"

"Yes," she nodded, weeping.

"Okay," Paul said. "I promise."

Crazy American Female

She thinks I'm a terrorist. This was funny. She tossed awful glances at him if he made a sudden move, and she maintained the idiot ruse that she had a pistol ready to blast him should he try anything funny against her person.

"You think is safe?" he'd asked her this morning when he saw her in tight shorts.

"To run?" she said. "I run anywhere."

"Like *that*?"

She whirled her head and fixed him with an intense stare. "What the hell are you talking about? My *clothes*? How dare you? I'll dress any damn way I please, buddy."

"I am sorry, Miss. I will be quiet."

"Yes. You should do that."

When she'd asked him for gas money, he had shoved all his money to her. He let it spill out of his pockets into her hands, as if he were Croesus. He didn't think about the act. He had acted on impulse, but when he thought about it an hour later, he still didn't regret it, as he knew it was the right thing to do. He assumed she would then cast him adrift in downtown Chicago. He was actually fine with it because it was part of his plan. It wasn't that he was fearless or that he looked forward to living on the street. It was more a case of his wanting, tentatively, to test his mettle—to see if he could cut it in one of USA's toughest towns. Considering the odds stacked against him, if he was ever going to carry out his plan, living for a while like a bum would be the least of hardships to overcome.

She shocked him. Instead of kicking him to the curb, Miss announced they were driving to Milwaukee. "They" meaning "*we.*" He was coming with her. *Okay; Milwaukee is a large city, too, and has many people.*

Up the highway, they stopped and went into a market, a store, where one packed one's own items in sacks. People cut quick glances at them. Aqib was amused. *They think we are couple.* They bought a loaf of bread, some faux-looking meat and a large bottle of Pepsi. Then they stopped beside a river and ate lunch at a concrete table.

Miss didn't speak during their meal. When she finished eating, she stared at the river, apparently deep in thought.

He did not know what he should think of this girl… this woman—this young woman who was single minded and with her own plan.

"Will you like to talk, Miss?"

"Not particularly."

"I will talk."

Miss threw a rock into the river. "Knock yourself out, Aqib."

"Miss?"

"Means suit yourself. Do whatever you want. I don't care. Meh."

"Fine. I will then. You are not crazy American female," he said. "Not that I am expert. I am not novice even, chained as I am to motel desk. All I know about American females, I know from the cable television. By this measure, you might well be crazy, but you are not typical American girl obsessed with fashion, boys, popularity and number of friends on Facebook."

"How insightful, Aqib."

"You are serious person. On mission. I hope not to be in your way."

"Well, you haven't slowed me much so far. And I appreciate the money."

In Milwaukee Miss easily found a motel in the *dumpy* category, to which she had, apparently, become accustomed. It was a dump that also employed another of Aqib's countrymen to watch the front desk. *Is this all Americans think we can do?*

She handed him some of his money. "You go in first."

"I see a pattern unfolding, Miss." He chuckled.

In the new room, she handed him the other card and pointed to the table and chair. Then she left the room to go call her mother on a pay phone, while he went back down to talk to Ibrahim in the office.

Ca` Phe` Den

The little nothing of a house that William rented in a leafy Eisenhowerian neighborhood was close enough that he could walk to a restaurant, a grocery store, the library, or even the ballpark, if he wanted to leave early. He made sure the house did not have a lawn. Where neighbors had fescue or Bermuda, William had gravel. They had geraniums, he had sage; they forsythia, he cactus, decorative brick, boulders, and so forth.

William walked the wide, white-brick street, dressed for August. He wore a pair of faded Levi's, a plain white t-shirt that exposed the anchor & globe tattoo on his left forearm, huarache sandals and a boonie hat on his short-cropped hair. The Rangers had just returned from a long road trip to the west coast, and his day was open. He thought he might spend the afternoon in the library where it was cool.

He limped noticeably today, his feet rising ever so slightly, straight up, as if he were walking barefoot on broken glass. Twenty-seven months on polished cement in a jailhouse laundry wasn't good for a man's feet. He could've jailed easier, as they say.

First thing he got settled in, the deputy warden asked him if he wanted to coach the baseball team, but William declined. He wasn't interested in hobbies or activities. He preferred to sit and think with his time, he told the man. If it was all the same to him. Man said it was, but it wasn't. Pissed off, he made sure William got the worst job he could think of.

He stopped walking at Ca` Phe` Den, taking a table under a palm frond and bamboo arbor. Mamasan, whose family owned the place, brought midnight dark coffee without being asked. She also served him a ban mi.

"Très bien, merci, madam," William said, nodding.

"*Pas de quoi*," Quan said as she spread a white cloth over the table beside him. "*A votre santé, monsieur*."

William had helped Quan come to America in 1975. Her son, Thanh, was a friend of his. He would have helped Thanh also, but his friend never made it out of the re-education camps. He had been far too helpful to William and his countrymen.

William ate the small sandwich and savored the coffee. He had come late in life to coffee. One might think that after four years in the Crotch and a quarter century in professional baseball that he would've taken it up a lot earlier, but it wasn't until Japan that he did. Starbucks was the only place where English was spoken when he first arrived.

He saw them in the parking lot. They were probably up from Houston, he surmised. Three broad Asian-looking men in expensive dark suits walked across the gravel toward him. In spite of the ninety-three degree morning, the men looked impressive in their Hollywood shades, dark pin-striped suits and long-sleeved, high-collared shirts with ties.

"Konnichiwa, Mr. Kerrigan," said one of the men, bowing.

"Konnichiwa."

William shook hands with all three men, then he turned back to the leader. Years of participation in male-oriented activities was not a criteria for recognizing the alpha dog in a group, but neither was it an impediment. The other two men were roughly the same size and demeanor, but this man was the leader. He was first to speak.

"Mr. Kerrigan, would you want a ride back to your home?"

It wasn't really a question. He waved a hand toward a massive black Cadillac Escalade with darkened windows. Like the other two men, he was missing the first joint of the pinky finger on his left hand.

William took a deep breath as he sunk into the plush upholstery of the back seat. The men were not a total surprise. They came on behalf of Akihiro, the man who helped provide seigi for William. It was understood that they could come to see him anytime for a return indulgence but William had allowed this knowledge to lapse into the further regions of his mind. He thought such people would never have need of anything from him. This didn't make much sense. What could he possibly do to help influential people so far away?

The leader was seated next to him. The other two men sat in front, never once turning around. When the car pulled onto the street in the direction of William's house, and rolled to a stop at his curb a minute later, he decided to get right to it.

"I owe you."

"You are direct, sir. First, may I say we hope you are well, Mr. Kerrigan."

"Me? I'm just fine and dandy, myself."

"Your team, Ranger, is having a magnificent season."

"Look," said William, beginning to sweat, though the Escalade's a/c was going strong enough that the driver shivered. "I am grateful. I appreciate what your associates did on my behalf. It was a big deal. Thing is, I can't possibly see how I might be in a position to help you, which without saying, would be my honor to do."

The big man smiled, showing no teeth. His massive hands had fingers so thick that his three rings looked like tiny metal tourniquets. The men were so huge that they seemed to hog the oxygen inside the large car.

"Your friend, Paul Demeter, is having a sensational season. An incredible season!"

William nodded, saying nothing.

"Inharmoniously sensational," the man beside him added.

"Yeah, very," William nodded, thinking he might know where the conversation was heading and what help he might be to the gentlemen.

On the Road Again

Using Aqib's money for gasoline, cheap motel rooms, baloney, bread, potato chips and soda at grocery stores—plus bleacher seats at ballgames—I follow Paul Demeter and the Texas Rangers through the American Midwest on the last road trip of the season. Through it all: at highway rest stops, in city parks, on the banks of rivers, in cheap motel rooms, wherever—I scribble notes and fill tablets of paper.

I miss my laptop, but I write ferociously, as if the paper itself has dealt me wrong, and I am getting back at it. With the tip of my tongue at one corner of my mouth, I go long stretches during which I forget to breathe as I attack the paper with short, staccato sentences. The story is developing.

I stop mid-sentence and look from the pad to Aqib, who is staring at me. "What?"

"I enjoy watching you write."

"That's goofy."

"I do. It is like you are angry."

"Maybe I am."

"You stab the punctuation, using your pen like a dagger. Your papa, he is faltering, no?"

"No! Don't call him my papa. But yes, Paul Demeter's going through a dry spell—a slump it's called in baseball. He went O for Detroit and Cleveland so far, and he only got a bloop single in Milwaukee."

"Do you think you are the bad luck for him? You have put like the *mojo* on him?"

"Hah! What do you know about mojo?" I frown. "I don't know. Maybe?"

Aqib nods at my notebook.

"Would you like me to look?"

"You mean read what I have?"

"Certainly."

"Fah. Remember? You know crap from baseball?"

"Ah, but Miss. I believe you are writing about more than merely a sport."

"Look at you, Mr. literary critic!"

"Still."

"Okay, maybe a little bit it's more than merely a sport."

"Anyway, I would be happy to read it."

"No way. I don't let anyone read my stuff until I'm sure."

"Okay."

"Thanks for being interested."

"You are welcome."

Aqib leans back, but he keeps looking at me. It is irritating.

"Okay, now what?"

When Aqib smiles, I have to shade my eyes from the sun's rays ricocheting off his spectacularly white teeth.

"Has it occurred to you, Miss," he says, "as it has to me—that having covered so much territory together, the two of us—we are becoming like a team?"

"No. No, it certainly has not occurred to me. That's stupid." I wave my fingers like a gunslinger, loosening up.

Where in the World?

William hadn't slept three hours any night since the men from Houston came up to pay him a visit a couple of weeks earlier. It was such a small thing—the vial the big man gave him in the dark Cadillac.

"It is nothing to hurt him," the leader had said." It will be out of his system in a week, perhaps two. The contents' effect will merely slow him a step, take some of the snap from his swing. He won't feel it. He will know only that he isn't hitting the ball quite as well. You and Paul Demeter are very close physically each day. You would have no trouble placing it in his drink or on his food, yes?"

William went to the back porch and sat in the deck chair where he liked to position fielders in his head. *It's a hell of a thing to expect a man to do to a friend, if in fact I actually have to do it. I won't have to do it.* The next day they would start the last road trip, a long one: KC, Chicago, Milwaukee, Detroit and Cleveland. It was going to wear everybody down. It was still insufferably hot; with the added tension of what was becoming a pennant race. Paul couldn't keep hitting like he was. Could he? Surely, the pressure would finally get to him. Wouldn't it?

The man in the backseat of the Escalade had admitted as much. "History is on our side, Mr. Kerrigan. The overwhelming odds are Demeter will not continue his magnificent performance, and therefore you will not be asked to do a thing for us."

"Sure, you don't need me," William agreed.

Smiling for the first time, the leader continued. "With you, Mr. Kerrigan, we are merely insuring the odds."

The man didn't say why it was so important to their organization that Paul Demeter should fail to hit .400, and William didn't ask, though he believed he could make a pretty good guess. No doubt the importance was in the many, many millions of dollars being wagered.

William couldn't keep down anything more than a couple of crackers the first few days after accepting the vial. He'd dug a hole in the yard and covered the little bottle with gravel, putting birdbath over it. When he did sleep, he was fitful and had bad dreams. To stop the nightmares, he dressed, went outside and walked in the dark until daylight.

"You look like shit, Kerrigan," Lavernicus Thibodaux told him. "You on the bottle again?"

"I never got off it."

"Shoot, you gotta quit worrying," the manager said.

"What the hell are you talking about?"

"Hell, you fuss and fret like a little ole lady ever time he gets to the plate anymore. I know you and him are close'n all, but damn, you jarhead, lighten up! Do like I do—just sit back and enjoy the ride. He's either going to hit .400, or he ain't. We're either gonna win the fuckin pennant, or we fuckin ain't."

Fungo laughed for the first time in days.

"Enjoy, hell! You used to be a two-pack a day man, Vern. What are you up to now? At least three, I'm sure."

Thibodaux mumbled under his breath.

"What's that?"

'Four," said the manager. "I'm up to four fuckin packs a day."

That night, William sat on the deck chair with a bottle of Nyquil and a glass of Jameson, staring at the moon. He took a few sips of syrup while avoiding looking in the direction of the bird bath. He took a drink of the Irish, put up his feet, and the next thing he knew, was the sunlight awakening him.

Where in the civilized world would I be out of the reach of these people? If they could reach across the planet and touch a powerful man like Brian Smith— a man who had done nothing to them personally—to ruin him financially in less than two years, imagine how far they could reach someone who actually betrayed *them*?

He could run to Africa or hide himself in South America. He would have to go deep into the mountains or jungle, though. He once knew how to get by in such places, and maybe he hadn't lost the knack.

Could he make contact with the *flecheiros* of the Amazon? He'd watched a piece about them on *Nat Geo*. They were poison arrow-shooting natives so wild and isolated by jungle they had almost no contact with the outside world. They thought jet planes were big, loud silver birds. If the Indians didn't shoot him full of arrows or beat him to death with clubs, their jungle might be the only place on the planet he would be safe, if somehow Paul Demeter managed to hit .400.

"You might give it a test run, Mr. Kerrigan," the leader concluded, nodding.

When the sun rose above the live oaks that marked the eastern boundary of his yard, William went to the *porte cochere* and found the shovel.

Slump

Paul Demeter was officially in a slump. In a week, his batting average fell to .389, the lowest it had been since April. The consensus of talk radio comments was expected and summed up in the words of one host.

"See, there he goes. We knew it! Say 'Bye Bye' to .400, Paul *Fraud* Demeter!"

He was not hitting safely, and he was not hitting the ball hard. It started with 1-for-4 against Milwaukee on three weak grounders and a bloop single. No ball left the infield. After the game, William sat at the other end of the dugout.

"I saw the ball fine tonight, Fungo," Paul said. "I thought I could pull the trigger on all those pitches I swung on. I don't know what happened. Just one of those nights, I guess."

"Aw, you're fine, Bud" William said, gravely studying the ground crew pulling the tarp on the infield. "You are probably tired. It's hot, we're all hot."

"Nope. That's not it. I feel fine, and you know me—the hotter the better."

In three games, he managed the one pitiful single. The Rangers won those games and three more games after that; games in which Paul went hitless.

Even though Demeter stopped hitting during the team win streak, he contributed to the team in a positive way. Playing third base with the bases loaded and one man out in the bottom of the ninth, he made a sensational unassisted double play to save a win against the Tigers.

The next night, though hitless in four times at the plate, on his fifth at-bat he punched a fly to short center field to score the Rangers' lone run in a 1-0 victory over the Indians. In the next game, he started a team-record-fifth third-to-second-to-first double play—each time with runners on, and each time foiling Cleveland rallies. Twice in the five-game stretch, he ignored a hit-away sign with a man on first base and laid down a perfect sacrifice bunt for his first and second time all season to move runners forward.

I'll get through this. Don't get so down on yourself you hurt the team.

He didn't. His selflessness for the team in the face of a personal bad stretch was not lost on his teammates. Neither was his attitude. Unlike other players, who mired in a slump, exhibited outrageous public behavior, he didn't break any bats, throw helmets or sulk, letting the negative string affect other parts of his game or bring his teammates down. He was never a rah-rah guy in the dugout and not one to whistle and lead cheers, but neither did he whine about his misfortune; and when the team made a big play or won, he was in the middle of the fist-bump line.

Baseball players, the most notoriously superstitious athletes, treat a slump like the plague and avoid the poor victim at all costs. Strangely, something in the air snapped, and the Rangers, who had not exactly been in Paul Demeter's corner all season, broke the pattern with him.

"You got this, Slugger!" teammates called, urging him before his at-bats and high-fiving him.

The right-fielder tossed him an ice cold Gatorade when he came back to the dugout after popping up to the catcher, and while most of the season, he had been unnoticed and left to sit with Kerrigan at the end of the bench, now his teammates left seats to walk down, pat his back.

"Don't sweat it, Dem; you'll snap out of it."

The crowds were acting differently as well. Slowly, the cheers caught up, surpassing the boos. Fans did not wait for his name to be announced before they began to applaud and whistle. Whereas before he touched the bill of his cap to show his appreciation, now he lifted the hat from his head. He didn't wave it, but it cleared his straw-gold hair.

Paul plopped down beside William after striking out against a pitcher he'd hit two home runs off in May.

"See anything?" he asked.

"Nah, nah," William answered, looking away. "I'm not seeing a thing. You look fine up there. Don't change a thing. It's gonna wear off soon."

"It is going to *what?*"

"It's gonna *end* soon, I mean. The slump ain't gonna last."

"Man, I hope so! I don't know what's going on. I feel fine, I think. Where you going?" he asked when his old friend stood and walked away.

William waved his hand. "Ah, I gotta go to the head. I'm not feeling so good."

The Texas win-streak reached eight, and the team climbed from fourth in the AL West standings to second place. In the ninth game, they trailed Cleveland 10-0 in the top of the eighth, with two outs and nobody on. The win-streak was certain to end, as the game seemed all but over. Probably because Paul Demeter had batted .500 against him for the season (including 2 homeruns) the Indian pitcher knocked Paul Demeter down with a pitch—up and inside—even though Paul hadn't hit safely once in the three-game set.

Four Rangers, along with Demeter, and five Indians and their manager were ejected as a result of the bench-clearing melee that ensued. When the Ranger pitcher knocked the Cleveland leadoff man down with the first pitch thrown in the bottom of the inning, Vern Thibodaux also got thrown out.

Everything Changes

Jodie was almost packed. She would check the one big bag. She would carry the cigar box. The windows were open in the quiet house, and a breeze moved the curtains. It was not exactly fall, except on the calendar, though the awful swelter had abated some. The drought departed with the flash flood that over-topped an Arkansas levee, busted three state park dams and drowned thirteen people.

She would go to Texas to come clean with Sylvia. William sounded tickled when she called and asked if she could stay with him. Despite what she told Sylvia, she had no intention of going to games.

The wait on the tarmac lasted longer than the actual air time from Tulsa to DFW. After her eyes hurt reading a paperback, she looked out the tiny window at the ground crew hustling like roaches, ducking and merging and breaking away under silver wings. The cabin air grew stale and chemical. Claustrophobia crept up, but she resisted it by concentrating on Paul Demeter. *Wasn't he the one responsible for all of this?* She would, probably, find it necessary to face him this trip. Since he was already on her mind, she went ahead and considered the day everything changed between them.

It had been a travel day for the team. Paul's bag leaned against the door in the Chicago living room. When he walked out of the bedroom, she looked at him. Then he smiled. Suddenly choked-up, she swallowed as portals within her brain and heart shifted. *Can a girl get a warning here? What just happened? Did he do something different?*

After he picked up Sylvia, carrying her in his arms toward her and kissing them both, she asked him a question. After she did not receive the response she wanted, she asked a second question. "Will you watch the Scamp?"

"Love to…" Paul said, smiling again, "but not for long. I gotta go."

She looked at him once more to make sure she wasn't seeing something new, something different about him. No. It wasn't about him; it was about *her. It was her!*

She walked fast along the street, not quite like a power walker, but she was really moving along. The only parts moving faster than her feet were her brain and heart. She swung her arms as she stomped through the wide, shady streets. The sand at the lake stopped her.

She re-thought the action of the morning. *What had he done?* He had just woken from the night's slumber, sandy hair all over the place, lopsided grin.

She hunched over, hands on thighs, at the sidewalk, gasping, attempting to put the morning in its proper sequence: *Okay, he walks out of the bedroom, like he always does—no shirt—in boxer briefs; he lifts Sylvia in his arms, and then he comes over to me with the kiss on the mouth--yawning n the middle of it with the not-really-stale morning breath that I still haven't gotten used to. Same-O, same-O…*

Then what was it?

"Did you feel that?" she had demanded of him.

He yawned again as he arranged the wriggling Sylvia on his lap

"Feel what?" he asked.

And that is when she bolted.

"You okay, young lady?" one of three ladies walking the path asked.

"No, ma'am. No—I am most definitely not *okay*."

She was smiling so wide that she thought her lips might crack. Her skin tingled.

"Lot of people struggling in this heat," the lady said. "We saw you here and thought we'd come over and check on you."

"Thank you. Thanks a lot. I'm fine—more than fine, actually. I'm good now."

"Be careful," the lady called out.

She counted the stair steps to their floor while overhearing Sylvia tell Paul his scrambles sucked and the toast was burnt. At the door, she saw him whack Sylvia on her heinie with the rubber spatula. The little girl cartwheeled out of the kitchen as he shouted.

"Never diss the chef, Missy!"

Jodie walked up to him, her chin bumping his bare chest.

"I love you," she said.

Sylvia saw Jodie at that very instant and screamed. "I love you, too, Jo-Dee! Paul Demeter's a lousy cook. Can you make me scrambles?"

Paul laughed and shook the spatula at Sylvia. He handed a bottle of cold water to Jodie and kissed her mouth. "What were you saying?" he asked. "I couldn't hear you for all the racket Princess Di was making."

Jodie felt her face blush. She sipped the water and smiled in his face. "Thank you," she said, still with the achy, wide open smile. "It was nothing, really."

"You sure?"

She smiled as he grabbed Sylvia in one arm, kissed her on the top of her mop of curls and tossed her on to the sofa.

"I need to tell you something," Jodie said to him.

"Okay," he said, grinning. "But make it snappy; I'm running late."

"Don't go," she said.

"What?"

She held him tightly, around his waist. "Stay."

"Hah, crazy woman!"

"I mean it."

Paul stopped smiling. "I know you do. I can feel it. Uh, you know I got to, right? We're going to Baltimore? You feeling a bad one coming on?"

Actually, a terrible one had begun advancing, but when he had appeared this morning, and everything changed inside her, it left. She shook her head and moved her hips against him. "The opposite," she said.

"Cuz if you are sick, I'll stay—that's the only way I can miss a team flight without a fine, and the way I am going at the plate, even *that* might not save me."

She kissed him long and deep. "Go, then. Come back soon. I am fine. Really fine."

"Let him go, Jo-Dee," Sylvia screamed from the sofa. "We don't need him around. He's a lousy cook."

She squealed as Paul threw a small pillow at her. She fired it back at him, and it slammed against the door as he ran out.

Jodie cracked two eggs at the stove, stirred them in a cup with a tablespoon of cream and sprinkles of shredded cheese before she poured them into the skillet. She hesitated, thinking about the words she might have spoken to Paul Demeter:

I love you, I am in love with you, I don't know how it happened, I never saw it coming, so *I can't explain it. It is not like an arranged marriage, where the couple meets each other on their wedding day and grow affectionate for each other over time. I don't know if I am ready for it, but it feels wonderful and scary. I don't know what it means. I can't even think straight right now, I am so sorry, I am so-so sorry for how I treated you. I feel wonderful. Anyway, I love you now… and I'm having your baby,* she might have added.

Charlotte

"We can go with you," she had said when he told her the White Sox were sending him down to Charlotte, Triple-A. "Not for long," they said—just until he got his swing back. An All-Star for two consecutive years, he had gotten off to a terrible start at the plate this season, and by July, it hadn't gotten better.

"I need you," Jodie added.

"*Sylvia* needs me, you mean?" he asked.

"Me, I mean. I'm not doing well."

Paul touched the side of her neck with the backs of his fingers. He never tired of touching her and could not imagine a time when he would. He spoke low and tried to laugh, but he failed. "It won't be long till I start hitting again."

"This apartment is a cell," Jodie said without emotion. "The walls choke me."

"You have Shelley."

Two weeks earlier, he'd arranged for Shelley, an RN who lived in their building, to come by and check on Jodie and Sylvia. She was single with no kids, so she also took Sylvia out to play at times."

Jody had not been appreciative. "You would tell me about this when?" she asked.

"Soon. Today," Paul said. "She's nice," he added.

"I know she's nice. I don't like the idea of being *checked on*."

"I worry about you and Sylvia."

"You shouldn't worry about her. I can take care of my child!"

"Of course. I didn't mean it like that."

"I want to be with you," she said, measuring his reaction.

He looked away, and then he sat, listening to the soft hum of appliances in the apartment and to the beat of her heart that seemed to move her blouse. "You don't have to say stuff. We've gotten by for five years without it, okay? You don't have to say things you don't believe."

"We should go with you. We always go with you."

They looked at each other. In that stretch, his own heart filled his ears. "You don't have to say the words. In Charlotte, I'll start hitting again and the Sox'll want me back. I call Sylvia every night, and in no time, we're family again."

"No," she insisted, climbing onto his lap. "You don't understand me. A change has taken place inside me. Haven't you felt it?"

"Honest? It has always been sublime for me, but then I'm goddamned selfish. I surrendered a long time ago wishing that you might care for me. Only I couldn't give you up. I figured my part would have to do for both of us… the three of us."

Silence hung in the small space, like an uninvited guest. Neither moved or spoke for minutes.

"Tell me you love me," Jodie said.

"How's that again?" Paul said, frowning.

"You know what I said."

"You told me *not* to."

"I know what I said. Now is different, Paul. Everything is different. Tell me."

"It was a promise."

"Promises can be broken."

"Not mine, Jodie."

"Oh, my," Jodie said, wincing as she touched her ear.

He laid his head between her breasts.

"Bad?"

She nodded, taking his hands and put them in her hair, smiling. "Irony sucks. You've loved and cared for us blindly, never looking back. I treated you like dirt. Worse! No matter, you stuck with us, dragging us behind you. Now, here I am in the bucket with you, and you say we can't come along. You won't tell me you love me."

"It won't be long," he said, pulling away. "I'm sure of it. I'm getting your meds, now."

As he handed her the tiny bottles with the big medicine, she looked up, but not at him. "Nope, I don't want those," she said to the refrigerator, dropping the bottles.

One cap spun off, throwing pink pills across the floor.

"*You* are the prescription, Paul. We could stay in a hotel!" she pleaded, honing in on the pix of Sylvia on the freezer door.

"Can't do it," he explained as he picked up the bottles and swept the pills into a pile. "Nailing that spot for the Scamp in Pre-K was a piece of good fortune, and she's happy as a clam there. We can't disrupt her sweet deal at school—not when we're only talking about maybe a month if things work out, or two tops, if they don't right away."

He held out his hand. "Here we are. Now open wide. Down with the dope."

As he wiggled two tablets between his fingers, she took his hands again, looking at him with the eyes that still turned his breath shallow. Kissing his hands, she protested.

"Don't want the medicine. I mean I *want* them, yeah. Oh, I *want* them, but I can't."

"Yeah, you can. You have to. They bring you back."

"Shsssh," she said, placing a single finger to his lips.

"Oh…" He glanced down, thinking that he could make sense of what she was trying to say if he wasn't looking at her. He circled the sofa, picked up a book on the end table, opened it, flipped a few pages, read a caption and replaced it. "Sure, no-no on the feel-goods? They haul your narrow, sweet behind back from the abyss, so of course you can't take them. What?"

"Come here," she smiled, nodding.

"Let me think," he grinned. "I'm concentrating."

He lifted her blouse and kissed her belly. "Is this your way of letting me know I hit the lottery?"

"I like that way of putting it," she laughed through the agony.

"I'm crazy about this new kid already," he said.

"I know. I know," she winced. "No medicine for me now. I can manage, I think."

He kissed her belly again before his face went blank. You're going to be okay, okay?"

"I will manage, I think," she nodded "Please hurry back."

In his first game in Carolina, he went 0 for 4, and made an error at third base that cost the game. That dropped the Knights out of first place for the only time since May. He was glad he didn't know his teammates. They wouldn't drop by and say encouraging things to him. They were free to do as they felt, which was scowl and look disgusted at this jerk intruder.

Sylvia answered the phone. "Hey, Paul Demeter."

"You on your computer?"

"Yup, and I'm good."

"Did Miss Shelley come by today?"

"Oh, yeah! We went for ice cream. She's cool. You want me to wake up Jo-Dee? She's here on the sofa.

"No, no! Let your mama sleep. I know you are taking care of her. The door is locked, right? And you've got Shelley's number on Jodie's phone? Good. How long has Mama been asleep—just a little while or a long time?"

"Just a little while. Just since I been home. Paul Demeter, I'm hungry!"

"Since you've been home? Crap, it's almost eleven! You get home at three-thirty!"

"You yelled at me, Paul Demeter."

"Sorry, Scamp. Cut the computer, put a mac'n cheese in the mike, two minutes thirty secs, max, you know how, right? Okay, I know you are not a baby. After you eat, get a blanket, and you lie on the sofa with Jo-Dee. Okay? And go to sleep.

You call me if you need me, right? Good girl. I'll be listening."

Damn!. He listened to the sound of the word echoing off the bare walls.

He went eight games without a hit. His ass was in Carolina, but his head and heart were in Illinois. He didn't sleep. He tried to read, but his head was full. He called each night and talked to Sylvia and Jodie, but he lacked energy. He lugged three other humans around in his body parts. His bat speed was slow motion. He was swinging in water up to his neck.

When Jodie said it was too early to know if it was boy or girl, he said he didn't care what came out. Was raising your own child different? He didn't think he could love a child more than he loved Sylvia, but he wondered. His mind strayed, and when he should have been thinking about the pitch he would get in a 2-2 count with a man on second, and when he was creeping down the line on the quick left-handed hitter, known for bunts down the line. Instead of focusing, he imagined all the cool stuff he would do with a new child—*their* child.

When his mind wasn't on the baby, he worried about Jodie. Did she think she had to act like she loved him now? Why now? Wasn't it obvious he was in it for the long haul?

It was hard enough hitting major league—check that—Triple A pitching unfettered, let alone with other things on your mind. After striking out the second time in a game, he risked the wrath of the manager, who was already pissed at him, by ducking into the clubhouse and sneaking the cell phone. Jodie did not answer. He went hitless, and the team lost. He called again. When Jodie answered, he was determined.

"It's not working out down here," he blurted. "I'm playing sorry. I'm worried."

He told her he was quitting and coming to pick them up on his way back to Tulsa or to Texas. He would give up baseball and go find a job so he could look after his family.

But she surprised him, saying nothing at first. He could only hear the sound of deep breathing, like she was speaking from the bottom of a well.

"Not on me, brother," she said with a force he had never heard from her. "I won't let you. You will *not* quit baseball. Am I blind or something? I don't see how you love the game? You think I've just been along for the ride?"

"Not exactly the reaction I was expecting," he said.

"You may be goddamned selfish, but then again, so am I. Come back to us, I'd like that, but I'm not signing up for blame, seven years hence, when you find yourself in a bank, showroom or cubicle, desperate, in some despised labor you've taken on. And each time you look at me and Sylvia, I'd wonder, Does he loathe a little of us?"

"Seven years hence?"

"Well, it's a number."

In the next game, he came out of his slump like gangbusters, smacking two doubles, driving in three runs, and making a spectacular, game-saving catch at third. Knights win. The team hit the road for an eight-game swing, and Paul hit for the cycle in the first game, went 3 for 4 in the next, and 5 for 5 in the last of a three-game set in Charleston. Four teammates asked him to go have beers.

In the second game in Mobile, he hit 2 homers—one a grand slam, and the Knights were back in first, riding a five-game win streak. They won the two remaining games in that city by scores of 4-3 and 5-4, with both margins of victory coming on late-inning RBI singles by Paul. The manager took him to dinner.

Back in Charlotte, his streak continued, and so did the Knights'. He went yard 3 times in one game, had a 10 RBI game, hitting for the cycle again. On the road again, he hit 4 doubles in a game in Savannah to move his consecutive hit streak to 15 games. In that stretch, his average was over .600. He was the first Triple A player who wasn't a pitching prospect to make *Sports Center.*

It was an exciting time. He was jacked like a kid heading into summer with season passes to both Whitewater Bay *and* Frontier City. It was heady stuff. He was hitting well. He hadn't connected with the ball so well since kid ball. Plus, he was going all Brooks Robinson, at the hot corner. It was all right. He felt great, fired up. He looked forward to going to the ballpark each day. He was going to be a dad… again.

Masking his energy and excitement for Jodie's sake, he told her how well he had been doing, and he said that if he kept it up, the White Sox were sure to haul him home early.

"That's good," she whispered on the phone, weeping. "That's good."

Back in Charlotte, the Knights hosted the second place team for a four-game stand and split two-two, losing their first game in 15 starts. Paul kept hitting. The Sox did not seem likely to wait the three weeks left in the Triple-A season to bring him back. Sure enough, the next night, after a Charlotte win in which Paul knocked in the winning run with a sac fly in the bottom of the 13th inning, the Knights manager told him to come see him the next day before B.P.

Paul called Jodie with the news.

"I told you. They want me back in Chicago."

"Are you sure?"

"Sure I'm sure. Only two reasons a skipper wants you in his office. One's to tell you you're going up to the big club, and the other's to tell you you're going down to Paducah or Gotebo, and the way I'm hitting, I know it's not the other."

"That's wonderful, Paul," Jodie gasped. "And not only for me and Sylvia—it's wonderful for you. I hear it in your voice. "She coughed, trying to muffle a groan.

"You're not okay," Paul asked, concerned.

"I will be—now that you are coming home. I love you, Paul."

He was quiet on his end.

"Paul?"

"I'm here. I don't even know what I am thinking right now."

"Don't think then. Just come home to us... to me."

Paul could hardly sleep that night, with Jodie's words murmuring in his head, like the sweetest of music. After six hours of fighting covers and fluffing pillows, with only brief stretches of uneasy slumber, he gave up and quit the bed, feeling as fresh as if he had slept fifteen hours.

"They want you back in the Windy City, young man," the manager said before Paul sat down. "We appreciate all the help you been to us down here."

"You're welcome, skipper," Paul smiled. "Glad I could help."

"You helped us a ton. Really happy for you, Paul—getting called back up!"

He paused to put a pinch of tobacco in his lip and pushed the can toward Paul, who declined.

"Paul, I'd like to run a little idea by you. See what you think about it. Don't say anything right away. Just listen. The White Sox are twenty games out and are certainly not going to get even a sniff of the playoffs." He paused and spit in a styrofoam cup. "But down here, we're in first place by a half-game and fighting desperately for a pennant. We, the organization—meaning us and the White Sox, I mean, we have been talking."

Paul thought he saw where this was going. He apologized for interrupting, but he explained his family situation back in Chicago.

"Paul, we are mindful of your concerns, but have you ever thought you might never get another chance to play for a title? Any kind of title? A pennant? At any level? Any league? If you are not a New York Yankee, it's harder than you think. What do you think of your chances are of ever hitting like this again? Not to bruise any egos, Paul, but I can *Yahoo* like the next man, and I looked you up. What you're doing right now is unconscious. Think you might wanna ride that pony a little longer while she's running good and stay on with us?"

Paul stared at the floor, thinking. Skipper made sense. What if he never got it going like this again? He was a hero down here. Guys looked him in the eye as he stood on deck. He would start a rally or win the game for them. It felt good hitting so well.

"Chicago says it's up to you," the manager said, now standing. "Told me to let the young man decide on his own. So I put it out there for you, Paul. I need you to let me know by four, so I'll know whether to get you a plane ticket or write you in tonight's line-up."

"Four more weeks is all," he said to Jodie early that afternoon on the phone.

"Oh," is all she said.

"The skipper is right. I may never hit like this again, Jodie... or play for a winner. This could change my career forever, and give me a confidence that I can take anywhere."

"I understand."

"You do?"

"No."

"C'mon, girl. You'll be fine. We'll be fine. Hang in there for me. You can do it."

A Team

In Ohio, Aqib offers to drive. I almost careen off the highway.

"I got a fat picture of that," I say when I regain control of the car. "Aqib, if you were to try driving, you might as well throw a kaffiyeh over your head and hold a sign out the window that says: PLZ PROFILE ME, PULL ME OVER!"

Aqib lowers his eyes. "I would never wear a kaffiyeh. Anyway, I did not think of you as one who would be thinking in those hateful terms."

"Not me. I meant the *cops*. You wouldn't get five miles." I drive on a few miles without speaking again. We are both silent. I say, "I can't believe it! You see me as prejudiced? Well, you are wrong. I am not. Most people would look at you, and… Dammit, okay—I probably am. Prejudiced, I mean, a little... maybe. I don't want to be a bigot, and I tell myself I'm not… I definitely was not raised like that, but I have to admit—when I am on the block and see a black guy in a hoodie and baggy drawers, I cross to the other side, and when I see an Asian guy like… well, like you in an airport, I get uncomfortable. I try to work on it. Thank you for offering to drive."

"You are welcome. I believe you, Miss." He nods. "And you are probably correct about the inadvisability of me driving your automobile."

"I like to drive," I say, frowning at him. "Quit pouting, Aqib. Don't feel bad. Look, this traffic is about to gag me, though. If you wanna help, you could be like my lookout, y'know, and let me know what's happening in the lanes behind me and in my blind spot? Tell me what's going on? Just don't yell at me."

"I would be like your co-pilot?" he says, excited.

"No. No, you would not. You would be like my *lookout*."

And so he becomes my lookout. He tells me when I can move into the left lane and he lets me know if someone is coming up the ramp or whether I can beat the car or I should yield.

He is adept at it. He synchs in with my speed and predicts our moves almost perfectly. He keeps his head on a swivel, but he mostly looks behind and speaks only in a soft, firm voice.

"Left, Miss. Right, Miss. Clear, Miss," or, "No, Miss. Go, Miss."

I have great reflexes, and I react instantly to his directions. We are coordinated. We are in rhythm, like a well-maintained motor. We are like, uh well, a team, I realize.

To Err

When the aura descended, walls skulked in on Jodie like a *film noir* moving doors. She'd been down how long? Based on the angle of light coming in the lone window, her first guess was "three hours?" The glow was the wrong color. Perforce the engine idled in her ears. Sylvia was where? With Shelley? She couldn't be sure.

She tasted caked bile and felt flecks of mucous on her chin. She should rise. It required various stages: first, hands and knees, then, a foot flat and a hand to the table—something that took a minute or more. Five minutes later, give or take what seemed forever, both feet were planted and both hands seized the table.

Standing, her fingers and toes were cold and numb despite the small window air conditioning unit being turned off and the day's high promised to reach ninety. She shivered, as if she had just stepped naked out of Lake Michigan on New Year's Day. She tried to let go of the table, but the waves of nausea rocked her. Frantic, she re-clutched wood, squeezing minute slivers from the table edge.

Paul's last transmission sounded disorderly, but her auras had brought auditory hallucinations before. She heard things—gobbledygook words and garbled phrases. Did he say he was this far from coming home? Was she losing her mind? *Who* would leave Charlotte?

She heard Carolina was nice. It would be nice if Paul were home. He would know what to do. *I love you, Paul Demeter. There, I said it.* It is not so hard. Why was he so afraid of *I love you?* It was but a simple declarative—only words lined up in sequence. He had the opportunity to leave Charlotte, and he didn't take it? He could have been with her right now. What was he thinking? What, for that matter, was she thinking?

She concentrated on her steps. *I will get there.* As she reached for the fridge, her perception became murky. Ice cubes fell to the floor. She hung onto a half-dozen, though she dropped a couple more. One fell inside her shirt. She pressed a handful against the side of her head, feeling the lumps on her scalp, and yet she could not feel the cold of the ice. It was not enough… not, nearly enough.

She re-directed for the cabinet. Funny, their doors already gaped wide, and medicine bottles lay strewn on the counter—on their sides and opened. *Open? Why? Well?* She had to think about the bottles for a minute. *Why were they already open?* She reached for a vial, fumbling. It popped out of her hands, into the air and tumbled to the floor. Pills ricocheted off counter tiles and into pantry creases and gas jet openings. A fork would prize them, though that was not necessary. Later for those.

This being one and done! Right? Think! Just this one dose wouldn't hurt anything? Correct? Had she said those words earlier? She couldn't remember. *Think. Think.* A single pink tablet rested on an edge, teetering.

"Stay!" she demanded.

She fielded another other bottle, removing the lid, twisting, but it didn't come open. *Kids and old folks, right!* She raised the pepper mill to strike it, but she missed. She missed again. On the third try, she lifted the weapon shoulder high and smashed the vial. Plastic shards and capsules flew across the stove top. Almost blind from the pressure in her head, she flicked a piece of plastic from a blue pill with a fingernail, but she also spotted the pink one, and she crammed both in her mouth, swallowed them down with a gulp from last night's milk.

Aqib's Plan

He hadn't missed his family yet, but he knew that this emotion lay just over the horizon. He wondered where they were and what they were doing. They would not have wanted to, but they probably went to the police and provided them information required to find him. Were they frustrated at their lack of success in finding him? Would they give up when their money ran out? What were his little brothers thinking? He knew that, wherever she was, his mother was frantic with grief and worry. His father would be worried also, and disappointed, but he would be angry. Very angry!

He stole a look at Miss. She told him to call her Sylvia, but that seemed too familiar for him. He had not earned her friendship yet, though he had tried, so he would continue to be as formal with her as possible. Also, and show her respect.

She certainly loved her baseball. He saw the passion in her face when she prepared to go to the games and when she wrote in the notebooks after the games, but he did not understand her fixation on the Paul Demeter player. He was her father, but they were obviously estranged. Maybe one day she would explain to him this enmity she carried in her heart.

She was strangely ambivalent with Paul Demeter's sudden decline in hitting the ball and referred to it as "a slump." He had the impression she wanted her father to fail, but she acted quite irritated in the mornings in Milwaukee and Detroit after Paul Demeter failed to hit the ball well. Aqib made a point of not being in the room when she returned. He stayed away, walking the streets and avoiding police until he was sure she had finished writing her story notes, and she was in the bed.

Miss was not a talker—at least she was not a talker with him. When the traffic thinned in the countryside, she put on headphones and listened to a radio. This was rude, but he would never tell her such a thing. It wasn't that he just had to talk. He was okay with silence—now that he wasn't lonely.

He had been lonely for almost two years. One might think that, working a place where people came and went constantly, a person working there would never be lonely, but the comings and goings were exactly what intensified his loneliness. People, exhausted from the road, didn't want to visit with a mere desk boy. They only wanted to flop on a bed.

In the mornings, they wanted only to get on the road again, to get away from the shabby place where they spent the night, and they were too much in a hurry to linger, much less converse. Couples wanting a room only for sex were generally mute and preferred to make the transaction as briefly and silently as possible.

He was not lonely in her company, even though she did not trust him completely and was actually not very friendly with him. Though she didn't say much to him, he felt comfortable with her.

He didn't know what he could possibly do to make her realize he didn't want to ravage her body or carry a bomb into a crowded market. He would like it if they could become friends, but he knew that was probably not going to happen. Of course, he also knew he was along for the ride for only as long as his money held out, but at any rate, he was still free in this country, and he was enjoying the trip.

That night in Cleveland, Miss announced they were changing from one terrible room to another terrible room in the terrible motel.

In this room, there were two beds. When Aqib glanced over at her, she only shrugged.

"I feel bad using your money and then you have to sleep sitting up."

Aqib smiled slightly, sitting up in the chair. "Oh, I am used to chair and table, yes? I sleep like that going on two years now."

"You are serious?"

"Yes. I worked my motel always. I had to be ready at the desk day and night, when someone came looking for a room. I learned to be quite comfortable sitting up."

"I guess you caught up on your sleep on your days off."

"Hah. Days off are for rich persons! My family are poor. I take no days off."

"How many people helped you at the motel?"

"No one helps me. I do it all."

"Don't act crazy, man. There're child labor laws in this country, preventing that stuff. What did your folks, your parents, think about how you were treated at the motel?"

Aqib smiled full on and shook his head. "Is their idea. To survive in America, we run three motels—one by my father, one by my mother and small brothers, and one by me."

"You're only seventeen, for cryin out loud!" she said, crawling to the end of one bed.

"I am eighteen," he countered, puffing out his chest. "Yesterday!"

"Nice for you! Happy birthday, Aqib! So tell me—what in hell are you really up to?"

"You are actually wanting to know?"

"Yeah," she nodded. "I guess I do… but not if your plan includes hurting people. Then I'd have to turn you in—even if it means I might not get my story."

Aqib sat tall, clearing his throat. "I considered long and hard about what I have done, because it frightens me and makes me sad. But it strengthens me, too, because I would do it over again a thousand times. My parents moved our family to America because we were treated very badly at home. Copts suffer greatly in my country, and I personally suffered intimidation for other reasons. We were persecuted. My family was lucky. We lost only our home. Others—our friends—lost everything," he sighed, narrowing his eyes. "You understand *everything*, Miss?"

"I think so."

"We were treated so severely that we and others received special refugee status to come to this country. We were lucky in this way. I was so glad for this—the coming to America. No more broken glass and fire in the night, no more open threats when we went to market or worship, no more threats and name calling to me, I thought. I was happy to come to USA. More than happy, I was overjoyed.

"But after three years here, my parents are unhappy. They want to go back home. As bad as it was back home, they believe it is worse here. They do not find worship close to us in Kansas. They don't speak language as I do, and they say the name-calling and graffiti and the torment abuse is worse for them than the physical threat in Pakistan. They are desperate to go home, but I am not. I love America. In spite of the difficulties I have had to face here, I want to stay. There is so much freedom to be the person who you are. You can do anything here."

"Like hide in somebody's car?"

Aqib frowned. "I had to. My parents sold the motels—all three of them. I begged them to let me keep running my motel so I can stay in America. 'No,' they say. 'We are family. We live together. We work together. We go home together.' We were to fly home the next week. So I went away. I formed a plan and I escaped. You have helped."

Miss shook her head.

"Some *plan*, man! You almost died a slow, terrible death!"

"It was worth it. I hoarded money from the cash register a little at a time, for months, and I waited for the right person to come along. You were that person. I had a good feeling about you. You would have to admit my plan worked out nicely. I am not in Kansas anymore, heh heh."

"Whew. So you really are not on *jihad?*"

"Hah hah. You are very funny sometimes." He paused, his face becoming serious. "I will never be able to pay you back, my friend."

"I don't think we are friends. Sorry to be rude. You can forget about paying me back, and I am definitely returning this money of yours that we're using."

"Never!" Aqib protested, shaking his head. "I am not permitted to forget."

"What about your family? They must be going out of their minds."

"Yes, this is the part unfortunate. My family will try to find me, but their resources are limited, so they will probably be unsuccessful. I feel very badly about that, but I will make it up to them in the future. My plan is to blend in with the common people of this great country and make sure the police do not have a reason to talk with me. I feel very terrible for stealing the money from my family, but I had to do it. I will pay them back some day. I will do the American Dream, no? I will be a—how do you call it— an American success story?"

"Yes."

"I will live the way homeless persons live starting out. Even a homeless person in this country has it better than the life I lived in Pakistan. My plan is to be a gradual success in USA, and to live the way I want to live and need to live. I am not afraid of work. When I am making it successful, I will send much money to my family, and they will be proud of me and will want to come back and live with me."

Miss left the bed, and picking up the pillow from the desk, she tossed it at Aqib.

"You got a set of balls on you, Aqib, you know that?" she said. "I gotta give it up to you. I thought *I* was on a mission, but my stuff is awful weak compared to yours. We'd better get some sleep. We're heading back to Texas tomorrow, and there's no telling what's in store for us down the road."

Aqib stood, and walking to the bed, he sat, taking off only his shoes.

On My Watch

When we reach the outskirts of Ft. Worth, I remove my headphones.

"Would you like to talk?" Aqib says.

"Not particularly," I answer, shaking my head, eyeing the crazy traffic.

"Left, Miss."

"I gotta pee. I'm about to bust. Will you do the gas?"

I pull into a Quik Trip, and Aqib gets out.

After I use the ladies' room and go to pay for the gas, the lady at the register is excited, glancing out the window.

"Better look out there. Trouble on five!"

When I look, two locals, with bare arms like bricklayers, have Aqib by the neck. His feet flail in the air, like a man running in space beneath the gallows.

"What's a camel jock doing riding in a car with a white girl?" I hear one of them say as I get closer.

Aqib told me stuff like this happened to him a lot—not just when he was with a white girl, or any girl, of course—but at times when he's been alone, as he always was, and cornered with scant chance for escape. He said he learned when he couldn't run, he took the affable, humorous, self-effacing route, and that usually spared him the bloodshed… but not *every* time.

I guess he's taking that route now, because I hear him.

"That is very funny, my friends, for I think there are few camels left in Pakistan today. Hah hah."

"Not your friends, Abdullah," one of the men says. "You blow up any cars today or other shit? Hah hah."

"No, hah hah," Aqib says, smiling. "None blowing up so far today, hey, hey but there is always tomorrow, right?"

"Wrong!" the other man says.

He bats the handle of the hose out of Aqib's hand, but the lever catches on his ring and doesn't shut off. The nozzle dances out-of-control on Aqib's hand, like an iron-headed serpent, gushing gasoline onto the fronts of the brick layers' shirts and pants before they can snatch the snout and cut off the flow. They are soaked… and pissed.

"Goddamn it!"

"Hold him still, Wayne," one says, hopping from foot to foot as fuel drips from his crotch. "Now turn him this way, and I'll see if I can't separate some of the boy's teeth from the rest of his head."

The man holds his nose and cocks his fist.

"What seems to be the issue, gentlemen?" I ask helpfully, arriving on the scene with what I hope seems like the earnestness of a grocer asking a patron if she needs assistance with the cauliflower.

"Me and Lloyd are just helping you out, young lady…" the one holding Aqib in the air says. "… helping get Kareem off your hands for you. We were only going to hit him a couple times and let him go, but then the dumb shit got us drenched in gasoline, so now we're going to mess him up good. Step aside, girl. Go on, have your go, Lloyd."

"Fine. Go ahead," I mumble, keys in my mouth, as I fumble in the car console like I'm looking for something very important. "He's only a hitch hiker I felt sorry for, but I was starting to think he might cut my throat if he got half the chance, so be my guest. Wail away. Before you beat him up, though? One of you fellas got a light? Can't find my lighter, and I'm about to have a nicotine fit. I keep my lighter right here in my car, but I'm having a time finding it. I've got to have a smoke in the worst way and right this second. Oh, here's my lighter!"

The heavy metal lighter clangs open in my hand and my thumb scratches out a reliable bright, four-inch flame from it. I drop it to the pavement. "Ooops!" I say, and then I scoop it up, holding it up before the men, daring them.

Flashing terrified eyes, the one drops Aqib like he is suddenly radioactive, and he almost knocks his buddy to the pavement as he crawfishes away from the crazy, clumsy girl with fire in her fingers.

"Don't! Girl, Please!" the other whispers, walking backward in a hurry.

After we are miles down the road, I look over at Aqib. "Well, that was fun. Assholes like that need to be taught a lesson!"

Aqib remains mute several more miles. He shivers on the passenger side, and then he takes a deep, ragged breath. "You needn't have risked yourself for me like that, Miss. I have been beat up before."

I look at him level and shake my head. "Not on my watch you haven't!"

PART III

Texas

"This is perfect!" Aqib says as I turn into the parking lot.

"What do you mean, 'perfect?' It's only another dump of a motel."

"We are somewhere between the Dallas and Ft. Worth, Texas, yes? Two large cities nearby is perfect. I will leave you now, Miss. It is my time. It is my place… and you are nearing the end of your mission."

"I don't see any reason why our sleeping arrangement has to end," I tell him. "You are not that big of a bother anymore."

"Thank you very much, Miss, but if I am going to carry out my plan, I had better start getting out on my own and begin making my way

"Sleeping on a concrete bench is going to help you make your way?"

"It is a start, Miss. One needs to be independent."

"Like a lone wolf?"

"Hah, Miss. You are funny."

"Okay, that's fine, if you are sure. If you change your mind, this is where I'll be. See you around, Aqib."

"Yes, Miss. Later."

I watch him go, and I feel… I don't know what I feel exactly. He is not my friend, but we have been through a lot of stuff in a short period of time. Oh well, I've got other business to think about.

Jodie is going to be staying with William Kerrigan. I am to pick up my mother at the airport tomorrow. She told me she had important things to tell me? Fine, I have stuff to tell her too.

Meanwhile Paul Demeter's personal bad streak ended with a bang at home against the Angels, when he hit a walk-off grand slam home run to win 5-3. He knocked two singles and a run-scoring double earlier in the game. He hit safely each at-bat in the three games of the home stand, all of which the Rangers won.

I witnessed each game from the bleachers. I am writing strong, and I feel ready to begin putting all my notes into a cohesive, powerful story. I need only the finale.

Heading into the last three-game set at home, the Rangers are tied with the Astros for first place in the division, with the Astros coming to town. Paul Demeter's slump is definitely over, and his batting average stands at .4017.

Jodie in Texas

She dreaded seeing the condition her daughter would be in after travelling in an old car, state to state, sleeping in hovels and eating god knows what!

In the terminal, mother and daughter hugged. Jodie held her tightly in her arms and then backed to have a good look at her. To her amazement, Sylvia didn't merely look all right—she looked amazing! Living out of an automobile and on the road apparently hadn't been overly difficult for her daughter. She'd expected baggy eyes, a poor complexion, unkempt hair—well, her hair would always look a mess. Its wildness was also its splendor. Jodie expected overall road weariness and unhealthiness. Instead, Sylvia's eyes were clear and sparkly, her skin looked as smooth as a silk pillow slip and her hair was clean, though unkempt, but dazzling.

Jodie pulled her close again. "Oh, I missed you high to sky."

"Me too—high to sky," Sylvia said, using the greeting they'd used with each other forever.

Jodie shivered in the sultry heat as Sylvia guided her old clunker onto a long industrial stretch, with intersecting roads full of men walking not only on the sidewalks, but in the street itself, like in a bad, redundant zombie movie. Between the half-hearted factories stood "left-for-dead' buildings and store-fronts with boarded up and broken windows. The landscape reminded Jodie of news clips from Fallujah. Despite the morning's warmth, she wore a sweater. "Is this the only route you know?" she asked.

"Only one I know on the way to your father's place."

"Syl," Jodie began. "We have to talk about something..

"Fine. Talk," Sylvia said, slowing the car. "Hey, stop that!" she yelled out the window toward an alley. "Hey, what's going on?"

Jodie looked where Sylvia pointed and saw a young, haggardly-dressed man being accosted by three other men near trash bins in an alley, not fifty feet from the car. "They are beating that man!" she said.

"Right. Hang on!"

Sylvia yanked the steering wheel sharply and sped the car into the opening between buildings, crashing so hard into the trash barrels that they scattered like bowling pins—as did the men who were beating the young man. They were knocked far enough off balance by the tumbling barrels that the boy—and Jodie then realized how young he was—was able to scramble to the car and jump through the door Jodie held open for him.

"Queer!" one of the men yelled.

Despite the suddenly overcrowded front seat, Sylvia was able to maintain her grip on the steering wheel. Instead of stopping to shift into reverse, she capitalized on her car's forward momentum and kept going, straight over the bins and through the startled attackers, on a direct shot toward the far exit of the alley.

"Great move, Syl," Jodie screamed in a muffled cry beneath the boy.

"Thanks, Jodie.

"Once again, you have rescued me, Miss," the kid said, a lot more cheerfully than Jodie would have expected.

"You guys know each other?"

Neither responded.

They traveled another block, and the only sound was the kid's coarse breathing.

Then, "No biggie, Aqib," Sylvia said and shrugged. "You okay?"

"I am okay," the kid said "A bit frightened, but I am fine. Thank you so much!"

"I got terrible manners," Sylvia said. "Jodie, this Aqib. Aqib—my mother, Jodie."

"Pleased, I'm sure, Aqib " Jodie said.

"I am being so honored to meet Miss' mother?" Aqib said as he executed a neat backward roll off of Jodie and fell into the back seat. When he smiled, Jodie was bewildered at how a street person could have such splendid teeth.

"I see you're livin the life out here, old son," Sylvia said to Aqib.

"I am quite fine, Miss. I have learned something very valuable. One has to keep moving. As long as one keeps moving, persons leave you be. It is when one tarries that trouble finds you."

"Ah, right. I guess you must have tarried a bit too much back in that alley."

He frowned. "Yes, I chanced a diversion, and it proved disastrous."

Jodie opened her bag, pulled out cash, counted it, then thrusted it over the seat back toward the boy.

"Here," she said, "take this, uh, Aqib."

"Oh no, mother! Thanking you." Aqib pushed her hand away and opened the back door, jumping to the curb. Sylvia had stopped at a red light at least a half-mile away from the alley.

"What are you doing?" Jodie barked

"Thanking you once again, Miss," Aqib said. "And to you, mother."

"Hey come back," Jodie shouted, but he had already jogged away toward a forlorn-looking city park, overrun by mesquite bushes and down-in-the-mouth elm trees.

"What's he doing? You can't let him go like that. You have to go back and get him."

The light turned green, and Sylvia turned right.

"Why are you leaving your friend like that?" Jodie asked incredulously.

"We're not friends."

Jodie's brow narrowed over her sun glasses. She shook her head slowly. "I think he thinks differently. How can you leave anybody like that? He wouldn't take the money."

"He'll be fine."

"He's just a kid."

"He might be a terrorist. You wouldn't believe how we *know* each other."

Jodie laughed. "That boy? Hah. He is no terrorist."

"You are probably right."

"Can't you tell?"

"Yeah, I guess."

"You might have saved his life back there."

"He's been through a lot." Sylvia shrugged. "He's tough."

Jodie turned to look for Aqib. Found him briefly as he glided through a park that had no children on its playground.

Getting Close

"You made it. I wouldn't have given you two bits for your chances."

"Nice to see you, too. Now answer my question, please."

"Sure. I can get you close," William said. "Just holler. How's that story coming?"

"It's coming," Sylvia said.

"Thanks for picking up your mother. I would've done it, but she said she wanted you to pick her up. There was something she had to tell you—something personal."

"Well, she hasn't gotten around to that yet."

"I expect she will."

"He's going to get it done, isn't he?"

William shook his head. "Oh, I don't know about that. He doesn't hit Astro pitching too well. Vegas is against him four to one."

"I have a good feeling about it."

"I thought you wanted him to fall on his face?"

"Never said that. Said I wouldn't be disappointed if he failed. Now I know my story is better if he makes it. It will make the sting sweeter."

"Uh-huh…"

William looked at his granddaughter and coughed. "Excuse me, Sylvia, but I was wondering something. I don't know how much you remember, but are you *aware* of how Bud treated you and your mother when you were together?"

Sylvia returned his look, eye to eye, her curls jiggling in a hot gust of wind. "Splendidly, from what I hear," she said. "And the part I can remember myself was, well… warm. Why, you got more to add?"

"No. No, not really. I just wanted to hear it from out of your own mouth."

Coming Clean

"Sweetheart, will you pull over somewhere quiet?" They drove along a corridor stacked with big box stores and fast food joints. Jodie had fibbed to Sylvia about wanting to go to a florist in order to get out of William's house.

"What's wrong, Jodie?"

"Nothing. I mean, something *is* wrong—very wrong. It is a wrong I need to put right… finally! Stop the car when you can?"

"Okay."

Sylvia drove another ten minutes, during which neither she nor her mother spoke. She pulled into the lot of a small post office. Beyond the parking flowed a flood-ravaged stream. She parked close to the edge. A small live oak's roots were exposed, and the tree tilted so radically, its uppermost branches almost reached the water.

"Before you go to him?"

"Yes?"

"Your father…"

"Yes."

"I mean before you do it—there is something you have to know. You have to know some things I've been keeping from you—deeds of which I am not proud. You have to know my dirty little secrets, Sylvia."

"Aw, Jodie! Do I *have* to?"

"No, I mean it. It is going to be a pretty nasty little surprise. You will discover that your mother is a wretched person."

"C'mon—you know I will never think that."

"That I am a liar and a terrible mother…"

"You are a *great* mother."

"Oh yeah?"

She shoved a box toward Sylvia.

"What's this?"

"It's a cigar box. Open it," Jodie said, resolute in keeping a dry face.

Sylvia accepted the box, lifted the lid and poked at the envelopes, some of which were opened.

"What are you trying to do here, Jodie?"

"Just look…"

Sylvia sifted through the envelopes, taking a handful and sorting through it. All the letters were addressed to her. She read a return address out loud… then another, and another. "Missouri, Illinois, Kansas. Huh. Why did you give this to me?" she asked her mother.

Jodie shook her head as she watched people walk up the sidewalks with packages.

"I lied to you. Paul Demeter wrote letters to you."

"I see that." Sylvia picked at one of the unopened envelopes with her thumbnail. The edges of the old, slightly-grayed paper didn't come away cleanly, ripping in gashes. From the envelope, she withdrew two pages of notebook paper. She unfolded them and read.

Dear Scamp:

I hope you like your new school. I didn't think much of junior high (guess you call it middle school now) myself, but I wasn't as smart as you or as popular as I am sure you are. I kind of struggled (sports saved me), but I'll bet you'll breeze right through it.

As I've written you many times before, if you ever need anything, let me know, and I will get it for you. I really mean it. I guess you've got everything a girl could ever want since I never hear from you. But, that's okay, I'm not upset that much by it. I know you have your reasons.

She stopped reading, though she was only halfway down page one. "How many are there? Twenty? Thirty?"

"In the box? I don't know. Only about two years' worth, I think. For the first five years or so, I threw them in the trash—probably about fifty in all. I don't know why I quit trashing them. I don't know why I began keeping them. He finally gave up."

"I don't know what to say."

"Neither do I… and I won't expect you to forgive me."

"That's good."

Jodie stared through the windshield at the stream. She realized the water flowed on three sides of Sylvia's car, as they rested on a peninsula. She was surprised that, for an urban stream that had recently flooded, it held such clear water. As she listened to Sylvia rustle through the box and tear open envelopes, she watched a gum wrapper twirl in an eddy atop a tiny waterfall, doing a complete pirouette before it shot over the edge. She grabbed the letters out of Sylvia's hands and stuffed them back in the cigar box.

"This is not the worst, Sylvia."

"It's pretty *bad*," her daughter acknowledged.

"When we lived in Chicago…"

Sylvia held a hand in the air. "I don't want to hear about Chicago, Jodie."

"So, I'm sorry," she said, stiff. "You're going to hear it."

Why did I pick the front seat of an old car for this? How am I sweating and shivering at the same time? Gawd, Texas is awful. Here goes nothing…

'When we lived in Chicago," Jodie started. "I was pregnant. We hadn't told you yet. We wanted to surprise you. Then Paul was sent down to Triple A. Charlotte."

She paused and swallowed. The gulp sounded like someone wearing a heavy mitten, pounding once on a metal door. "I was ill, really sick—worse than I had ever been. I barely took care of myself, let alone looked after you. I think I sent you off to Shelley; I really don't know. I can't remember. It was miserable, and I got careless. I didn't mean to, but I got careless with my medicines. I took a chance and messed up horribly."

Jodie moaned, covering her eyes with both hands, rocking her body in the seat. "Syl, I am so sorry." She didn't know how long she rocked. She didn't make more sounds.

When Jodie finally stopped moving, Sylvia spoke. "That's *it,* Mom?"

"What?" Jodie said and looked up with disbelieving eyes. "What can you mean?"

Sylvia repeated, "That's it?"

"*That's it?* Yes, that is it, young lady. That is only everything! *That* is why Paul Demeter left me. That is why we are no longer a family. *That* is why I never wanted to marry again. Yes, that is it. That is *everything.*"

"You don't have to get mad at me."

"You don't get it."

Sylvia placed the box beneath her seat, putting her hand on Jodie's bare knee and squeezing. "Look here, Mom. Listen. Sorry, Jodie, but *you* don't get it. *That's* the nasty little secret, so awful, you've been keeping from me?"

"Yes, and I am so unbelievably sorry… and ashamed."

"Cuz if it *is,*" Sylvia said behind the mere hint of a smile. "Cuz if it is;" she repeated, "I knew about that a long time ago."

The stillness was shattered when a gigantic dumpster fell off the lifter tines of a trash truck about five feet above the blacktop and landed like a bomb. The impact rattled Moby Dick's frame, causing him to shudder from tires to roof. Instinctively Jodie and Sylvia grabbed each other's arms.

"How could you possibly know?" Jodie asked. Her mouth popped open like a gag toy, making a little noise and forming a perfect *O.*

Sylvia squeezed Jodie's knee again and left her hand in place. She shrugged. "So. I knew. Sure. Yeah. I knew what happened to you. When it actually happened? No! No, of course not. I had no clue. I only saw you on the floor in all the blood. Of course I knew nothing about those things. I only knew I was scared to death and thought you were going to die. But over the years—yeah, I pieced it all together, and I kind of figured it out."

"What are you saying to me, child?"

Sylvia pulled Jodie across the console into her arms. "I guess what I'm saying is that if you have been carrying around all this shit for my sake, then you've been worrying yourself to sickness all this time for nothing."

"Oh, my gawd!"

Sylvia gently rocked her mother. "Nothing's changed, Jodie. I still hate Paul Demeter. The letters make him a little less of a jerk—I admit that, but he never should have left us. You were very sick."

"I never blamed him."

"I know. You were such a sap. Sorry, Mom."

Sanctum

"How did you get in here?"

"My grandfather."

"You know you are not supposed to be here."

"A lot of places I'm not supposed to be. So you know me?"

"Of *course* I know you. This is a shock."

"I'll bet it is."

"It is nice to see you."

"Is it?"

"Yes. Look, I'm in a towel. I was going to the training room."

"Doesn't bother me."

"Does me!"

"You hurt?"

"Nah. Just sore. Old age, y'know…"

"No, I don't know. You don't look old."

"Thanks."

"It wasn't a compliment."

"You are really cute."

"That is really inappropriate."

"I apologize. I don't know what else to say. How long?"

"Almost a month."

"Fungo?"

"Yep."

"The sonofabitch!"

"Wouldn't blame him too much. I asked him not to tell. I figured he'd blab anyway, since he doesn't much care for me. That he didn't must've meant he thought it might mess with your head."

"He's right. And you've been *studying* me?"

"You might say. Look, before you embarrass yourself by asking if I'm after money, I should let you know I'm doing a story on you."

"Story?"

"A story. I'm writing your story."

"Like everybody else?"

"Like *nobody* else."

"This is uncomfortable, Scamp."

"Good. Please don't call me that."

"Hey, you! What the hell is that chick doing in here?"

"It's okay, Vern; she's a friend.

"I can see that. And no—it ain't okay. Get her the hell outta my clubhouse!"

"Sure thing, Skip. Don't worry about him. So you are a writer? Of *course* I'll talk to you. Give you all the stuff you need."

"I don't *need* to talk to you. I have all I need."

"Then what are you doing here?"

"I don't know, but look at me closely, Paul Demeter. I am not shaking anymore. I am no longer nervous. I am not about to wet my dress out of fear or apprehension. I have been living this scene in my head for years now, playing it over and over, like a stupid, unfunny joke you keep re-telling to people who are sick of hearing it. But like not being able to look away from a car crash, they can't keep from listening until you get to the punch line. I did not know what I was going to do when I saw you, if I saw you. I did not know how I was going to act if I met you. And here I am. You wrote to me."

"You never wrote me back."

"Today. Jodie gave them to me. I didn't know about the letters. Today. I read them. Just today."

"Would it have changed anything if you had read them… you know, earlier?"

"Yes. No. Maybe. I know why you left us, too."

"Yeah…"

"Don't look down, Paul Demeter. I've tried to understand how you felt when Jodie made such a terrible mistake. I really tried to think like I was in your mind. I even made up a script in my head, where I acted out how the two of you would talk it through and work things out. I played both roles. Pretty goofy, huh?"

"No. You are so bright."

"You think so? I could've won a Tony playing Jodie. You, I would've got booed off the stage."

"So, we ought to, I don't know, get together somewhere... somewhere not a locker room?"

"I think this might be enough."

"You sure?"

"No. But probably."

"I would like to read your story."

"Probably not."

"Do you like baseball?"

"I freaking *love* it!

"So you still know it?"

"I know a lot."

"Then how do you like my odds?"

"A little while ago? Not so much. Now, though, I think you've got a shot."

"Really?"

"Really... though you haven't hit Astro pitching very well."

"*Tell* me about it! Are you like a lot of the people, and you think I'm cheating?"

"Yes. I *was* positive you were a fake."

"Now?"

"Now? No. I don't believe in miracles, so god is out. I do believe in karma, though, and she has been all over your ass the last decade or so. For some reason, this crazy season, she has backed off, giving you a little breathing room for the natural talent you showed at the start of your career."

"Well. Not bad. That's as good as the crazy stuff people have been making up out of the pure, blue sky. How is your mom?"

"There are a lot of questions I would let you ask me, Paul Demeter. That is not one of them. If we *are* going to do any talking—and I don't really see a point to it—there will be ground rules. Ground rule #1: No more discussion of Jodie. Ground rule #2: No more discussion of me. This is business. This is my job."

"Do you hate me?"

"Out of line. See rule #2. I don't want to confuse you or mislead you. I'm here to make money off you and not *from* you. That's all. You are public property. I'm here today because… I don't know why I'm here today... exactly. When I started out, I planned not to meet you at all. Why did I change my mind?"

"You are decent and wanted to give me a heads up?"

"I doubt it. I'm sentimental, but not overly."

"You watched all summer?"

"All career."

"I see. Are you a good writer?"

"Guess you can judge for yourself when the story comes out."

"I bet you're good."

"Don't condescend. I don't need it. I am leaving now."

"Breakfast in the morning?"

"I don't eat breakfast… usually."

"We could talk."

"Like I said, I don't need anything more from you."

"Borrow your pen a sec? And that card? This is the place I go for breakfast. People leave you alone in there."

"I'm probably not showing."

"I will be there."

"Suit yourself."

"Look, I don't think I'm going to worry about what you're going say about me."

"Maybe you should."

"Well, I don't. You seem like a tough gal."

"I have my soft spots."

"But you try very hard not to let them show, I'll bet. I want you to know I am glad to see you."

"Ground rules?"

"Right. See you tomorrow."

"I doubt it. How do I get out of here?"

Breakfast For Three?

"Don't get up," Jodie murmured to Paul Demeter at a table in the restaurant.

He saw her first and waved. Had it been the other way around, would she have walked back out the door? Now close to him, she wondered if her words had tumbled out in the correct order.

He rose and pulled a chair for her, speaking in a voice just above a whisper. "Sit?"

She stepped closer. Too close. She smelled him, remembering Zest and loamy soil. It caught her off guard. "I suppose I could," she muttered. "Thank you."

"You are welcome."

He didn't sit right away. He stood unmoving, looking at her until it was rude. She returned his stare, forcing herself to not blink.

"So… Hello."

"Hi," he said before frowning and sitting.

She removed her hands from the table and placed them on her lap. She wondered if he noticed that they quivered. "I'm guessing this is not an accident?" she said.

When he smiled, a corner of his upper lip didn't move with the rest of his mouth. She remembered once thinking that a lot of women would find this twitch attractive.

"We've been set up, looks like," he said. "Would you like to stay and have something to eat… since we're probably waiting for the same person?"

"Yes. I suppose I would. That *is* the reason I came."

"Gotta warn you. Food here is pretty greasy. I like it, but I have an iron gut."

Jodie chuckled, and before she thought, she blurted out, "I remember. That egg and sausage and peppers thing you used to sling together was abominable!"

"Hey now!" He laughed. "That was the breakfast of champions."

They both laughed and then fell silent.

"Maybe she won't show," Paul said after a minute.

"She'll be here," Jodie replied, glancing toward the door. "I am surprised you are in a public place. Shouldn't you be in disguise to avoid all the people fighting to get next to you?"

As he smiled again, Jodie felt one tiny layer of uneasiness fall away.

"As you can probably guess by now, people who come in here must not care for baseball," he said. "A quirk of demographics, I guess. Now if I were a Cowboy or a Horned Frog, they might get all hot and bothered and try to swarm me."

She watched his face as he talked. "My. My," was all she managed to say. *Weak*!

"You look amazing."

She frowned and said, "You look like a .400 hitter."

"Today. At least."

"Why do you look at me like you expect me to explode?"

"I do? Sorry," he said

"I watched," she admitted.

"You did?" His face showed no emotion.

"I was curious. I wanted to see what effect all the hoopla, all the *everything* had on you."

"And?"

"*Pfft.* Nothing... It hasn't touched you."

"Hah. What is it they say about the tip of the iceberg?"

The waitress took their orders and left a pot of coffee.

"We are some conversationalists, the two of us," Jodie said.

"As ever."

"Ah, not exactly as ever. We used to talk. Well anyway, you did. You talked. You talked a lot to me," she recalled, suddenly finding that a button had come loose on the middle of her blouse.

"Yeah," he chuckled. "I guess I did. I was a blabbermouth sometimes. You should have told me to zip it."

"Oh, it was all right."

"I didn't expect to see you."

"So… me either," she fibbed.

He filled their cups. "Are you going to be home later this fall? That's dumb; of course you'll be home. Because I was going to stop in Tulsa when the playoffs are over…"

She opened a mini cup of creamer and tipped it into her cup. Stirred. She'd never liked cream in her coffee. She sipped. *Ugh.* "Well, come by if you are in town," she said.

He smiled again. "I will. We could meet in that bank again… if Jack would be uncomfortable with me in your home."

"Jack is no longer in my home."

"Oh."

Jodie felt a presence at her shoulder.

"Ah!" Paul said, standing again. "Here's our third now."

Sylvia sat and gave her order to the waitress straight away. "I need eggs—over easy, sausage, hash browns, and grits with biscuits and gravy… only, could I have toast instead of biscuits? And a short stack?"

Then she acknowledged Paul and Jodie. "Yes?"

"Thought you didn't like breakfast?" Paul said.

"Said I didn't *eat* breakfast… *usually*. But when I do eat it, I love it."

"Do you think it a bit early in the day for stunts, young lady?" Jodie asked.

"Nope," Sylvia answered. "How are you two doing? Catching up on old times?"

"We just got here."

"Surprised?" Sylvia asked.

"Somewhat off-balance," Paul said, "until you arrived."

"You've been hiding in the wings and watching us?" Jodie asked.

"No, but I wish I had thought of it."

"About to wrap your story up?" Paul asked.

"Just about."

"Maybe these last three games will sew everything up for you," Paul suggested.

"*Counting* on it," Sylvia said, glancing up.

Pre-Game

Hours before the first pitch, the edge was set in the Rangers clubhouse. Not much talk, mostly whispers. When Felix Sandoval strolled in, un-attuned to the present vibe, and he laughed out loud at his *Beats,* four men whirled on him to *shut the fuck up!* The usual latecomers were already at lockers, in the training room, in the stalls.

Not much of anything substantive going on. It was male athletes mostly moping uneasily back and forth in cluttered spaces, like travelers waiting for repairs on a damaged plane. The clubhouse guys were tetchy and cursed back at players whose jerseys and shoes were in the wrong lockers. In his office, Lavernicus Thibodaux sat at the desk, glum, staring at nothing and sucking on a Pepto Bismol milkshake. Seated on the sofa, William Kerrigan contemplated the Astros starting lineup.

It was a dead- even tie with Texas and Houston atop the American League West. Three games to go. Both teams were guaranteed spots in the post-season playoffs (the series winner would wind up Division champ, the loser a Wild Card) so some of the drama was gone, but not much. Bragging rights, incentive bonuses, job stability and home field advantage were still at stake.

Not exactly an afterthought was Paul Demeter. The ball club had cordoned off an entire thirty-acre section of parking for all the news vans and satellite trucks. *CBS* beat *ESPN* for the national coverage, and next to the Super Bowl, Paul Demeter's hitting campaign and this series would be TV's most widely covered domestic sporting event of the year. Crews from Mexico, Venezuela, Panama, Japan and the Netherlands stood ready to broadcast coverage back to their homelands.

Paul sat at his locker wearing only a jock strap, reading a book. He was surprised that the butterflies had not arrived. They soon would; in a massive swarm. His average sat at .402, rounded-up, but the road ahead looked steep and rocky. Tonight, he would face Houston's ace, Badu Bryant, who he hadn't hit this season in seven at-bats.

Paul's mind saw the huge right-hander who led the league in wins, ERA and hit batsmen. His name was already etched on the Cy Young Award. He stood six-foot-seven with the wing span of Kevin Durant. He always took a full wind up against Paul, so it seemed he was throwing from third base, and he ended every pitch with a grunt that would make a lady tennis player proud.

Tomorrow was no smoother. They'd be sending the league's second-winningest pitcher, another big right-hander that Paul hadn't touched his entire career. And Sunday, if the teams were still tied, for Houston it would be pitcher-by-committee, when everybody was on call and they would throw the whole staff, including the bullpen, if they had to.

William Kerrigan stepped into the locker room. He looked down at Paul. "What's the book, Bud?"

"A biography. Tamerlane. Interesting guy."

"I'll take your word for it. Never seen you read so many books."

Paul looked up. "Had to. Quit looking at newspapers in June and stopped TV after the All-Star break. I've read more books this summer than in all of college.

William sat beside him. "The kid finally showed herself."

"Yeah. My daughter. *Daughter*—the word feels strange in my mouth."

"I shoulda told you. She's writing a story."

"It's okay. Kinda feisty, isn't she?"

"Kinda? Smart too."

"Already knew that. At four years old, she grabs the box scores out my hand and says, 'I think I got this,' and she just takes off, reading herself."

"The two of you were thick," Fungo said, nodding.

A teammate walked past, causing a shadow to cross Paul's eyes. He blinked. When it became clear Paul wasn't going to say more, William left without further comment and went about his business.

Slowly, Paul pulled on his uniform. It was ritual for him—conducted thousands of times since PeeWees. Still got a kick. Long, tight, sliding shorts first, and then the long sleeves (no matter how hot the day), then the white sanitary socks and the stirrups just so, before he stepped into the tight pants. He wouldn't button the game jersey until just before heading for the dugout—a quirk. He sat again and replaced the strings in both shoes. Then he grooved a lyric in his head and rubbed a couple of his bats down with a cherry Crush bottle, awaiting the Lepidoptera.

Aqib and David

Aqib met someone. He felt extremely hesitant and nervous, but didn't it always feel that way initially? He wasn't sure. He was thrilled but cautious. He was in virgin territory here in Texas… literally. He had made one feeble, hapless effort with a boy back home who he thought was interested; but all he got for the attempt was a bad beating from the boy's friends. They beat him so badly that he couldn't go to school for a week. He was lucky he was not killed. If adults had found out, he would've been.

He was not sure if he was proceeding properly. He'd reassured himself *ad infinitum* that when the time was right, when the person was right, nature would take over and guide him. Now that the opportunity loomed, he wasn't as certain.

He'd met David at a farmer's market. They were both looking for tomatoes that hadn't burned up in the heat. No luck on finding those, but it was a conversation starter. David was not exactly handsome, though his physique was pleasing, if not spectacular. The important thing was his pleasantness. Aqib liked that David asked personal questions and then seemed genuinely interested in his answers.

He also appreciated that David hadn't said a word about how unclean he was or how he must have smelled. David was older, about 23, Aqib guessed, and he was a travel agent.

They left the market together and stopped in a shop for a coffee. Then they began walking, covering over eight miles, gabbing the entire distance. When they finally squared back to the market, David told Aqib that he might be thinking that it was hurrying matters, but he didn't mind Aqib staying at his house for "a few nights, or whatever."

He promised he would not try to rush him, offering friendship, if that was the only thing required. He said that his house was very small—tiny actually, but it probably beat sleeping in the park, which is what Aqib eventually got around to telling David he had been doing since he and his female confederate had reached Texas.

Speaking of Miss, he saw her again the previous day. She told him she now had money from her mother, and that if he came to the motel, she would pay him back all that he had given her on their road trip. That was where he was headed now, walking to the motel, *with a bounce to his step.* He'd always thought that was a banal adage until he found himself ricocheting off the sidewalk in the morning.

He also felt refreshed from the shower in David's small bathroom. David was amused that Aqib pronounced his name *Dah-veed.* He had told David that *Yes*—he thought it might be hurrying matters just a little if he stayed at David's house right away, but he was grateful, and if he didn't mind, he asked to avail himself of David's shower once in a while as they both thought over the arrangement.

Aqib felt one slight damper on his day. He was saddened when again he thought of his parents. He wondered if they had given up finding him and had left for home. He hoped they had, because he knew they wanted to go home. They suffered in America as he had not.

The things they saw as hopeless obstacles were things he saw as challenges. The wrongs done to him only made him stronger and more determined. He hoped his mother would not continue to be sad, but he knew that was impossible. He knew his father was still angry with him, broken-hearted: furious that he abandoned the motel, and saddened at the true secret that he had revealed to him and Ammi.

Papa would never be able to understand, and he would forever blame himself for the way his eldest son turned out. But Aqib would show them... somehow. After he did what he had to do, he would write to them. Well, he would do that before. To wait until then to contact them would be cruel. He would reach them soon, but now was not the exact time.

Snatched

Moving to the door to answer Aqib's knock, I lecture myself.

You did your part. You could have done no more. Anything further would have to be on the two of them. What did you expect? A brawl? They fall into each other's arms? A Mexican standoff? What?

I really don't have a clue what I expected between Jodie and Paul Demeter. I am not sure I know what I want. I throw the door wide open. "C'mon in, Aqib."

Aqib is not there. Two men are. Two enormous dark men, whose bulk blocks the sun's light in the doorway, stand before me… but not for long. They move with surprising quickness for such large humans. Before I speak a word or have time to be alarmed, one backhands the door hard and loud against the wall, while the other swoops me up like I'm a cotton swab, and gently but firmly carries me out the door.

I kick the air and try to wriggle out of his arms, but it is as if my body is wrapped in steel cables. When I realize any practical movement is impossible, I go limp. Quickly, though trying to appear unhurried, the men whisk me across the otherwise deserted motel parking area and deposit me, sitting properly in the backseat of a large luxury automobile.

I am sitting beside a third large dark man in sunglasses; and next to him, Aqib squirms in the seat with a petrified look on his face.

"Ah, there you are," I say to him. "About time!"

"Yes, Miss. I fear I am being detained." Aqib's entire body shakes as he speaks.

"You too?"

"For a short time, yes," says the man in the seat between us. He speaks in the lowest, deepest, most action movie-like voice I have ever heard. "You will be our guest. It has become necessary for your friend here to come along with us, also, as his inconvenient presence at your door proved untimely."

"Wrong place, wrong time, huh, Aqib?" I say.

I consider the situation. I am not frightened. The reason I'm not has more to do with the impossibility of such a situation happening than any logical explanation. Why in the world would these men grab me? It is clearly an abduction gone awry. It is a crazy mistake. *Wrong girl.* I open the car door.

Like a rattlesnake striking, the man's arm shoots toward the door handle in one fast motion, slamming it shut just before my foot cleared the opening. His fist, the size and texture of the business end of a sledge hammer, lands on the door lock with a pop.

"Just testing." I say, smiling.

"You should relax, Miss Kerrigan," says the man in the bottomless voice.

"You know my name. Should that worry me?"

"No. That in itself should not."

"So that means *itself* paired with another *thing* should?"

"You are perceptive," he says as he blindfolds me with a scarf.

Game One

Texas beat Houston 2-1 in game one of the series. Paul Demeter was a major part of the victory, but he had not helped his chances for .400. He went hitless at the plate against Badu Bryant, with 2 strike outs, but he drove in the winning run, with a long sac fly to center field. On his first at-bat, he gave himself up on a bunt to move a runner to second base, and the man later scored the initial run. At third base, he made two extra-base killing catches of line drives, with runners on base.

At the post-game celebratory gathering at the pitcher's mound, an unusual moment happened, notable for its emotion and spontaneity. After the Rangers bumped fists and gave high fives to teammates all around; they circled Paul on the mound, and then, one by one, teammates stepped up and shook hands with him until Paul was left alone on the mound. He stood for a standing ovation from the delirious crowd who, for the large part, had not exited.

His batting average had dropped to .3974, with no round up to .400. Two games to go.

It was hard to believe it had happened, but Paul realized as the shower jets pounded his aching shoulders, that his concentration had wandered during the game. He didn't blame his hitless performance on lack of focus, but it might have been a factor.

In a sport often decided by inches and split-seconds, one small seemingly innocuous thing—a momentary lapse, a quick look the wrong way, a blink of an eye—might make a significant difference in the outcome of a single play or an entire game.

The box seats he reserved for Sylvia (and Jodie?), just behind the Rangers on-deck circle and four rows up were not occupied at first pitch. When the third inning came and passed and no one sat in them, Paul asked a clubhouse guy to check Will Call. Nobody had picked the tickets up.

Maybe Sylvia was too proud to use them. She had refused them outright when he first brought the offer up at the restaurant. She preferred to sit in the cheap seats, as maybe more distance gave her the perspective she was after? Whatever the case, Jodie might be with her. He told himself that it didn't matter, but he was thinking of the empty seats in the seventh inning and not concentrating on the hard slider that painted the corner on a 2-2 count. *Bear down*!

Jodie had looked wonderful that morning, even in a piqued state. Did she ever change? They had sipped coffee quietly as they watched Sylvia inhale her breakfast. He tried to steal a look in Jodie's eyes, but she caught him.

"Sorry," he said.

"Why?" she asked.

"Your eyes have not changed. I have wondered."

"Hand me one of those slabs of butter?" Sylvia asked in a voice louder than necessary.

"Don't," Jodie said to Paul as she handed a saucer to her daughter.

"Right…" Paul said, looking down at his hands. "Have you thought about coming to a game?" he asked Jodie.

"I have."

"Good."

"I don't want to jinx you."

Sylvia exaggerated an intentional cough.

Paul chuckled. "I think I'm whammy-proof now. I'll leave seats."

He looked toward Sylvia, who stared back at him as she poured syrup.

"Two," he added.

Stashed

When "Sumo" removes the scarves, I see that we are not being stuffed in a dank, dark, dusty warehouse on the metro's industrial extremities, but we are standing in front a Bastille-like palace. It is not a mansion, but a *palace*, plopped down in the middle of nowhere. There are no other buildings or dwellings in sight, no trees, no water, no hills, nothing. No roads. The *road* we must have driven up on isn't even a road. It is merely a set of automobile tracks across dead grass.

Only the man from the back seat, who is obviously boss and whom I have mentally dubbed "Sumo," accompanies us into the foyer or grand entrance to a cavernous domicile of marble, glass and stonework. He does not remove his dark glasses, and they become mirrors to anyone looking straight into them.

He speaks Japanese to three women who appear in black, servant-style uniforms and who bow and skip away to other rooms. Almost immediately, they re-appear with trays of drinks and dishes of food they place on a baroque dining table.

"Please enjoy yourself," Sumo says, waving his hand at the food on the table. "I will leave you to your meal."

"What happens to us, Miss?" Aqib says when Sumo leaves. Aqib's body still twitches with the heebie-jeebies.

"Hah!" I smile. "Someone is going to a lot of trouble to create this elaborate joke on me. A person is trying to scare me, but it's not working. Could you send that soy sauce my way, please?"

"Then please let me in on the trick, Miss, because frankly, it is working on me."

"It's Paul Demeter."

"The person constructing this scenario is your *father*?"

"One and the same… and because these goons happen to be Japanese… and because he doesn't like me, my grandfather is somehow in on it too. William Kerrigan spent two years in Japan. The two of them have put their heads together and come up with this tactic. I think my old man is worried I am going to do a *Daddy Dearest* on him in my story, so he's arranged with William to enlist exotic bogeyman friends to scare me—ergo the Three Oriental Stooges. I gotta hand it to those two. They are elaborate."

"Oh," Aqib whispers. With a chopstick, he pushes rice around on his plate.

"Relax, Aqib," I reassure as I take a bite of ahi. "It's a prank."

Aqib looks doubtful. He sniffs at a tiny morsel of food on the end of his stick. "Miss, I do not believe these are prank-playing persons. Did you see their little fingers? Or what's left of them?"

"Spooky. Might be they're in some kind of cult. A fraternity. Couldn't be a coincidence."

"I think these are very serious, determined men."

"C'mon. Lighten up. Nobody's hurt us, and they're feeding us good."

"What is this?"

"Eel. It's good. Eat up."

"My appetite has vanished."

The women appear again and take away the plates. Sumo returns. "And you are feeling, Miss Kerrigan?" he asks in a polite voice.

"Captive."

"You will be our guest for three days."

"Why three days?" And then I think about the Rangers/Astros three-game set.

"You will see."

"Then you will let me... let *us* go?"

"Hopefully," the man says.

"Hopefully?"

"Hopefully."

"You don't know?"

Sumo shakes his trashcan-sized head.

"If you don't know, who does?"

"William Kerrigan knows," Sumo says.

"Told ya!" I slap the table and look at Aqib before turning back to face Sumo.

"I have already got this little party of yours all figured out, so now that we're all in on the joke, sir, you can just let us go. Thanks for the sushi. It was delicious. Now you can give us a ride back in that fancy car of yours."

Sumo frowns. "This is very much the opposite of a joke, Miss Kerrigan." He frowns again and leaves the room. I stick my tongue out at his back.

"Mr. Grumpy Pants!"

"Miss, I fear you are making too much the light of this," Aqib pleads. "I think seriousness is in order for our situation."

I hear Sumo intone low commands in a room, and then in a rush of pounding and the sound of flesh hitting wood violently, a man enters the hall behind six snarling pit bulls on a single leash. Though the man is the size of an NFL lineman and strains with all his might at the end of the leash, the monsters yank him across the marble floor as if he were a child behind a water-ski rope. One dog nips at my knee but misses, and his fangs slam shut on each other, making a sickening clack.

I jump back quickly and push Aqib in front of me. "I'm not real fond of dogs."

Aqib feels behind himself for my hands. They pinch his flesh. He holds them while they grip him. He has stopped shaking. "Steady, Miss."

"Guess they must be the reason he is not bothering to tie us up."

"Yes, they would make short work of us if we tried to run, I'm sure."

"What the heck kinda dogs don't bark, Aqib?"

"Single-minded dogs, I should think, Miss. Steady," he whispers.

"Got that right. Don't let them get me."

Sumo gives another order, and the man with the dogs leaves the room, again dragged behind the straining, snapping dogs.

"Would you care to watch the baseball game?" Sumo says to me as casually as if he were asking me if I wanted dessert.

"Seriously?"

"Seriously!"

I look at Aqib, who shrugs.

"Yeah, I guess so. Looks like we got nothing else to do."

The dogs have shaken me. It is very unnecessary and over-the-line cruel of Paul Demeter and William to include them. They are aware of my life-long fear of canines.

"Come this way."

We follow Sumo up a broad Tara-like staircase and through at least a dozen rooms, finally arriving at a spacious chamber, fitted out like a movie theatre, with plush leather reclining chairs, large enough for two normal-sized adults or one giant Japanese. The chairs face a screen that covers the entire wall. Sumo points to two chairs in the first row, and sits behind us. When he punches the remote, *Family Guy* pops up on the screen.

"Hmmph!" Sumo mutters, slapping at the remote repeatedly with his enormous hands until the Rangers/Astros game appears.

"Isn't this comfy?" I say, slinking down in the chair, trying for a good face to overcome my creeping unease.

Even held against my will, and watching the game from a macabre vantage point, I feel the buzz from Globe Life Park through the big screen. It feels like post-season baseball. Every Ranger batter receives a standing ovation on his first time at-bat, and Paul Demeter gets three minutes worth, which ends only when he steps into the batter's box and the umpire orders the pitcher to throw the ball.

Every defensive play ending in an Astros out brings a roar from the crowd. Every time a Ranger makes contact with bat against ball, the fans jolt to standing positions. When a Texas run scores, delirium reigns.

Tonight, the Rangers are outstanding, but Paul Demeter is brilliant in personal failure. I wish I had my notes. He contributed to the win, but his chances at .400 dimmed slightly. He struggled against Bryant, striking out twice. He went hitless for the game.

Sumo must have been a fan. He watched intently for the two and a half hours the game lasted, eating popcorn and drinking soda, never rising from his seat once. He sat still and mostly stoic, except for the crunch of popcorn.

The only words he spoke were during Paul Demeter's turns at the plate, when he sat up and muttered an unintelligible monologue throughout the at-bat and ended in a satisfied grunt when Demeter failed to hit safely. Okay. *For some reason, he is not a fan of Paul Demeter.* Maybe Paul isn't paying him enough.

When the game is over, Sumo leads us back through the succession of rooms and hallways, down the stairway, and to the palace's grand entrance way. Strangely, or perhaps *aptly*, servants are covering the entire floor with wide sheets of clear plastic—the kind you'd see on construction sites. Thick plastic layers overlap every inch of marble and carpet. Even chairs and sofas are synthetically wrapped and then secured with duct tape. Sumo grunts appreciatively, making a point of his captives witnessing the bizarre scene.

"Okay, Mister." I say as I step on the slick floor and suddenly slide six feet forward. "You've successfully shaken me and terrified my friend. I know this is a joke to scare me off, and I admit, it has, a little bit; but this has gone far enough. The prank's over now. You let us to hell out of this place right now, or I might just have to include a sidebar of you, Larry and Curly along with my story, and then we'll see if the authorities see the humor in what you have tried to do to us."

Sumo pads across the floor, his big shoes crackling with every step.

I half expect him to break out into a big, silly grin and pop off, *"Hah, hah. Pranked! Go ahead, admit it, we had you worried there for a while, didn't we?"*

As Sumo nears me, I realize he has no neck. His massive head seems to tip sympathetically on his shoulders. "It is my sincere hope no harm comes to you in this matter, Miss Kerrigan. You may continue to believe this a hoax if you wish. It is as nothing to me." He points at the staircase. "You may return upstairs. You will find any number of sleeping rooms above, so help yourself," he says. "Sleep well."

When I stop on the second floor landing, Aqib is following so closely that he bumps me. I listen for Sumo's heavy tread below. They grow faint and vanish. *If this isn't a joke, then what the hell is it?*

A cold spot in my throat has settled in my gut. Paul Demeter and my grandfather are involved in this in some crazy way, but I have no idea how or why? I reach a hand behind. "You still here, Aqib?'

Then I hear a door open and a rush of animal energy followed by the sound of claws skittering on plastic, and I know the pit bulls are loose on the ground floor. I keep climbing until there are no more stairs.

Friends

"Aqib, could you stay in here?"

"There are many rooms in which to sleep, Miss."

"I know. Would you stay in here with me tonight?"

Aqib closed the door, looking in her eyes and speaking softly.

"Did you just tell that horrible person I am your *friend*?"

"What? Yeah. Yeah, I guess I did."

Aqib felt the room warm slightly. "The dogs will not come up here. I saw identical bands around their necks. They are probably shock collars limiting them to the space below."

"You sure?"

"Yes. I will go to another room." He shrugged. "You will be fine in here."

"Yeah, I guess. Still, I'd feel better. I am starting to think this might not be a joke. It still has something to do with Paul Demeter, but I can't figure out in what way."

Aqib tried to seem reassuring. He was uncomfortable with Miss' uncertainty. He was used to her being strong and in charge. Taking a pillow off the bed, he placed it on a writing desk in the bedroom. She patted the bed beside her.

"Enough of that. This bed is the size of a small ocean. We could go the entire night and never even touch. And if we did, what the heck? We're friends, right?"

Game Two

Aqib, and our enormous host and I observe the same opening procedure for watching game two. After we file into the home theatre, Aqib and I are swallowed in the same seats, and the big man sits directly behind us.

After that, it actually gets weirder, since a full handful of things are different: our captor shares his popcorn and soda with us; Paul Demeter hits the baseball three times safely in his first three times at bat; I conclude that I am not the focus of an elaborate practical joke; and I realize that dangerous persons do not want Paul Demeter to hit .400.

He hits a homerun in the first inning. He smashes a triple in the fourth inning. During his third at-bat, he singles sharply up the middle of the infield into center field. During the homerun trot, Sumo moans and mutters.

Then, as Paul Demeter chugs around the bases on the triple, Sumo throws the remote against the wall and slaps the popcorn and sodas out of our hands. After the single, he throws a heavy vase that shatters the enormous screen, turning the viewing room into a geyser of glass. He orders us out of our chairs.

Sumo rises before us, absolutely dwarfing us. I imagine steam shooting from his ears. He screams at us in Japanese, and then barks a command. Instantly, the two large men who had taken us from the motel enter the room. They must have been waiting outside the room. Even in the darkened room, they wear sunglasses. Aqib takes my hand.

The courteous treatment is obviously at an end. The men push us roughly out of the room and down the stairs. Aqib stumbles on a step and falls halfway down the flight, and when he scrambles back on his feet, he bleeds from both elbows.

"Hey, take it easy!" I say to the men. "We're moving."

On the ground floor, the men shove us into a room devoid of all furniture but a small plain wooden table and a single chair. Nothing adorns the walls. It has no windows. The rest of the room is bare. The big men leave us.

My eyes scan the room. In addition to the door we have just been thrown through, another door is open to show a half bathroom with a toilet, a sink and a medicine cabinet. A third door must be the access to the room of pit bulls, because we hear and feel the beasts throwing themselves against the door and walls.

Jodie and William

Jodie waited up for him after the game. She fixed her father a sandwich and brought him a cold bottle of beer, while she had tea. They were still up at three a.m. She'd watched game two on TV and couldn't sleep. She wanted to talk.

"You feeling okay?" William asked. "You having a headache?"

"No, I'm fine," she answered, pausing and shaking her head. "No, I am not fine. Going on three days, I haven't seen or heard from my daughter."

"Not at *all*?"

"No. And I am more than a little anxious about it."

William hesitated as he took a sip. He felt uneasy, but he couldn't put a name on it.

"Oh, honey—she's probably fine. Wherever she is, she's going to be okay."

"We had breakfast," Jodie said quietly. "Paul and I."

"Well. Well, how'd that go?"

"Cryptic? As we were leaving, he told me I am a big part of the reason he is hitting so wonderfully. So insane. I don't know what that means."

William rubbed the stubble on his face. "I don't either. So he's saying weird stuff, eh? With all the pressure he's been under, it's a miracle he's not speaking Mandarin."

"Gawd, I know! I can't imagine what it must be like to be inside his head."

"Me either. How did you arrange breakfast?"

She told him.

"Hah." William laughed. "Sounds just like her!"

Jodie laughed too, but the sound was clipped. "That's the last I've seen of her," she said, sipping her tea. "I don't like that she is alone so much of the time. She remains off on her own. She insists in staying in some dive motel. She won't even tell me where it is. She will be as independent as she possibly can, to the end. She is so headstrong… like you."

"Like me?"

"I am worried, William. I can't help it. I got her a new phone. She was supposed to call me after Friday night's game. For all her infernal sassiness, she is as constant as the phases of the moon. She's good to call… well—except when she dropped her phone in Lake Michigan. I was hoping she came to see *you* again. I'm very anxious over this."

"Lake Michigan?" A shadow moved across William's eyes.

"Yes. She dropped her phone in the lake. In Chicago. Why she hadn't called."

William reached for Jodie's hand. "Yeah, that's right. She lost her phone. I forgot." He let the quiet between them lengthen. *Yeah, she lost her phone.* Then, "She is fine, Jodie. I'm sure of it," William said, though he was not sure at all.

"I don't know, William."

"So the kid set you and Bud up?"

Despite herself, Jodie laughed. She nodded. "When he asked me to come to the first game, I thought I might put the whammy on him by going. And he flopped anyway."

"Wasn't no flop. That was baseball," William said. "We won. He helped."

"And tonight the team lost, but he is back to .400..."

"Just!"

"Yes, .4004 to be exact. He went 3 for 4 tonight. Will he play tomorrow?"

William stood close, frowning. "I'll tell you a story. You might find it instructive. Ted Williams' average was .3995, rounded up to .400, going into a meaningless doubleheader end of the '41 season against the Philadelphia Athletics. Neither team was anywhere near the pennant. If he sits Sunday out, finishes .400 for the season, nobody says a thing, right? It's not even an issue."

"Sort of like tomorrow, isn't it?" Jodie said. "Both these teams will go to the playoffs, anyway, no matter who wins tomorrow. So..."

"Exactly."

"So, Paul *could* sit it out."

"Exactly!"

"Let me guess—way back when, on that meaningless day in 1941, Williams *played*?"

"Both games," William said, smiling. "He said if he couldn't bat .400 for the *whole* season, he didn't deserve it. That cat went 6 for 8 in the doubleheader and ended up at .406."

"But Paul doesn't have to play, does he?"

"No."

"Dad?" she asked, looking at him intently. "Are you doing okay?"

William stood in a way that she couldn't see his face. If someone had asked him to express the emotions he felt tonight, watching Bud hit safely and get back over .400, he wasn't sure he could. Still, there was more than a fifty-fifty chance he would fail in the final game tomorrow.

The Astros were going to do something unheard of—they'd announced they were planning on sending Badu Bryant back to the mound, only two days after pitching a complete game. If Bryant only lasted two or three innings, he would likely shut Paul down for at least one at-bat. Possibly two.

William walked to the sink. His back still turned away from his daughter, he groped for the vial in his pocket. He turned it over twice through his fingers. He left his hand on the hard plastic. *The hell with it.* He removed the vial from his pocket. He had trouble opening it. Flicking at the lid with his thumbnail, he didn't feel it budge. He used both hands. The lid came free. Tapping the rim against the sink, he watched the contents run down the drain.

He had a kit locked up in his cubby at the ballpark. It didn't hold much personal stuff because the money took up space. Along with the cash, he had his passport and shaving gear.

Tomorrow, if it all turned wrong, he could ditch his old truck about anywhere. If it turned out he had to go, he thought he would be all right with it. Jodie, the kid and Bud were all he had. No matter what or where, he figured he'd find a way to stay in touch with them… get word to them now and again. Funny thing, though—and it made him chuckle—he knew he would regret not having the chance at the World Series. He'd never been to a real one. *Oh, well.*

He opened a cabinet door and put the folded piece of paper with *Jodie* scribbled on it, up on a shelf by itself where it was sure to be found.

"I'm having something stronger, Jodie. You want a drink?"

"No, thank you."

"It's not my first pennant race, kid," he said. "You needn't worry over me."

"I know you worry like anyone else. I just don't remember actually *seeing* you worry."

"So, maybe you should have looked closer," he said as he closed the cabinet door. "I'll be on the lookout for Sylvia. Last game and all, my guess is she'll make her appearance. We're bound to see her." William sipped at his whiskey and poured the rest of it in the sink. "Any chance you might go to the last game tomorrow? It's in the afternoon."

She walked to him, putting a hand on his shoulder. "Can you help me, Dad?"

"How so, Jodie?"

"Should I go?"

"You know what?" William said, putting his arm around her. "Ordinarily, I'd say make up your own mind, but yeah, you oughta go. Not that you have been the poster child for acting on parental advice, but I think you should go."

"Maybe I will," she said. "I might just do it."

The Final Game

Manager Lavernicus Thibodaux had laid down a hard and fast rule of absolutely no cell phones in the dugout. He loathed social media of all kinds: smart phones, texts, Facebook, Twitter, Instagram—all that junk. If he could have gotten away with it, he would have banned cell phones from the clubhouse, the team bus and even the chartered airplane.

Thus, it was hardly surprising that just as the last notes of *The Star Spangled Banner* faded into the sultry autumn air, every player standing in the Rangers dugout flinched, startled by the text alert on William Kerrigan's iPhone, chirping where it was tucked inside the elastic roll of his pants.

William cursed aloud and then cut his eyes briefly into the players' eyes down the line until he reached Thibodaux's. He only shrugged at his long-time friend, who scowled but said nothing. William unrolled his pants to reach for the phone. He fumbled it, then juggled it and finally secured it. He punched the button, which flashed, "Unlisted ID," before walking to his regular spot in the dugout: far end, second step.

He punched the phone again. It was a message. No—was it a photo? Baseball uniforms have no pockets, so he didn't have his reading glasses on him. He pressed another button and lost the screen. *Damn!* His fingers were too big for this stuff—it's why he didn't text much. He re-tapped the security code. *Okay! There it is.* He didn't lose it. He saw now there were pictures. Three pictures. No message.

He needed more daylight, so he climbed to the top step and leaned, scrolling, losing the screen again.

"Goddammit!" he yelled, groping the phone harder as he re-gained the screen. He could barely make out the images.

His eyes squinted in the sunlight. It was hard to focus, because the quality of the photos was blurred. He finally recognized three head shots—all pictures were of people's heads. No—they were the same person—only the head, a front view of one, and profiles the other two. He staggered, dizzy, and sat. The photos showed the head wrapped in a colorful cloth, like a scarf. Most of the face was covered by the blindfold, including the eyes, but there was no mistaking the hair. His bellow was a long, loud groan, followed by a streak of cursing.

Several Rangers laughed.

"What's up, Fungo?" one said, "Somebody hack your little black book?"

"One of his girlfriends stood him up," another joked.

The phone burned his hands. He didn't dare turn it off, and he didn't roll it back up in his pant leg. Incredibly, Thibodaux let him be.

He studied the phone again. The dark men from the Escalade had Sylvia! *At least we know now why nobody's heard from her. Those people have the kid! Damn!* They didn't trust him, or were hedging their bet, or both? He had never given a thought about anyone else getting in the way. He hadn't seen that from them. Bastard! He'd been selfish, too busy about his own business.

He acted like he was concentrating on the action on the field as he scrolled the photos hard enough to start a blister. He searched the background for clues about where they had her. All he saw was glass. They had taken the photos in the car when they were driving her away.

His skin burned. All of his skin. On the middle of his right forearm, he had a spot the size of a quarter that never healed. An edgy teammate with bad aim had lobbed a Willie Pete grenade too close to a hootch in the ville they were moving through. A VC sniper had popped out of a spider hole and fired a single round that didn't hit anybody, and then just as quickly as he appeared, he di-di mau'd. This wasn't generally considered Indian country, but no hamlet was one hundred percent immune to having the odd, contentious teenager turn Cong on them. William didn't see any use burning an entire, otherwise friendly village just because one Vietnamese kid was sick and tired of large, over-armed strangers tromping over his countryside; so he swatted at the spewing phosphorus canister before it ignited the straw on the roof of this hootch and spread to the whole hamlet. The grenade landed on bare ground and shot burning chemical into the air while Americans and civilians scurried away madly in all directions. Only a speck of the stuff got on William's bare arm, and he brushed it away before it could burn to his bone, but enough of the chemical fire stayed on him to give him the most excruciating pain of his life. His entire body felt this pain now as he stared at the photos on his phone screen.

So… things change. William scanned the faces down the bench, the eager eyes back on the diamond again. The situation was quite different now. The change was drastic. It was no longer only him. It wasn't simply him falling off the face of the earth if Bud managed .400. No more—now they had his granddaughter.

Like a little kid, Jodie had asked him to wave at her during the game. So he stepped clear of the dugout and his eyes found her a dozen rows up, spectacularly turned out in white—white blouse, white capris and a dagger-thin white scarf, slicing a portion of her honey hair, knotted in back. Women didn't wear scarves anymore, it seemed, and it was a pity. She did, and it was perfect. He waved with a big, wide grin displayed on his face, and yet his eyes stopped short of hers.

Her smile was hesitant as he turned his stare toward third base, where Paul fielded a hard grounder and stepped on the base for a force play to retire the Astros' side in the top of the first inning. What would Paul do today? He was just inside .400. If he went hitless, lost .400, everyone would be safe, nobody hurt, no one had to run away.

What was .399, anyway?—it sure ain't chopped liver. Paul would be just about as famous for coming so close.

Yeah—O-for however-many at-bats today—that could happen! Bud's average against Astro's pitching all season was a measly .079, and Houston had his number this year. Badu had handcuffed Paul in the first game, so he was apt to do it again. Paul's success last night against Houston had been an anomaly. His recent history indicated he wasn't going to be hitting the ball today.

Sylvia's voice filled William's head. He shook it violently but could not rid himself of the sound. He hadn't noticed the crowd. It didn't register on him when the other Rangers poked their heads out and over the dugout. Some exited and stood, amazed. A few donned their caps and squinted, as if doing so would give them a clearer picture.

Paul Demeter strode to the plate, fourth up in the inning. Then William noticed.

None of the more than 46,000 fans sat—not a single one that he could see. They rose, all of them—not in a roar like you might expect, but in a hush.

There were no yells, jeers, cheers, boos or catcalls. The silence was so thick and prodigious that it was felt more than heard. William had never experienced anything like it in all his years of big league baseball.

Paul seemed bewildered by it. He rolled his shoulders, trying to shake it off, but he was affected by the throng's reaction. He stepped out, but he did not look around. He kept his head down, swung at air a couple of quick times, stepped back in the box and leveled his gaze at Badu Bryant.

William climbed back to the top step as Paul swung on the very first pitch from the Astros ace and clobbered a liner, headed straight for the left centerfield wall. At the crack of the bat, the hush turned into a buzz that soared to a roar as the ball flew through the sky, headed for a homerun—his 21st, a personal record.

Paul lay down his bat and began his trot. Just as the ball cleared the fence, the Astros fielder, Leo Calderon, leapt and flung his glove into the air so high and hard it almost came off his hand, and he literally hauled the ball back into the playing field. It was a miraculous snag.

The crowd's roar dimmed only slightly as Paul shrugged and jogged back in. Felix Sandoval pounded William's back and screamed something in his ear, but he could not hear a word over the crowd's rumble and the murmur of his grandchild's voice. He swallowed hard.

William's brain and gut had executed identical somersaults by the bottom of the fourth inning. What could he do? His thought process was so intense and singular in purpose that he didn't realize he had sidled down the bench and stood in front of Vern Thibodaux.

"Set your white ass down, Fungo," the skipper snapped. "You're in my way."

William jumped at the sound. Irritably, he scowled. He'd been drowning in thought. As if that was why he had wandered down the dugout, he begged a chaw from his friend.

"Thought you give that shit up," Thibodaux said, handing him the bag.

"I did…" William grumbled, unable to enunciate clearly with a fistful of tobacco in his mouth. "Fifteen years ago."

Yubitsume

Aqib watched the one Miss called Sumo enter the bare room, with another big man following. In one massive hand, Sumo carried a thin, ornately-designed wooden box that he placed on the table. Then he spread a small cloth.

The other man carried a small black leather bag, resembling a medicine kit. This he opened, and from it, he removed a syringe.

Aqib understood what was going on. "I must go to the bathroom," he said, lying. "I must go very badly.

Sumo shrugged his shoulders and grunted, nodding toward the bathroom.

Aqib entered the small room and closed the door. Sitting on the stool, he could easily overhear what they were saying in the other room as if there was not a door between them.

"Miss Kerrigan," Sumo said, "I will ask you now to please sit at the table."

"Why?" Miss said, her voice quivering.

"Please," Sumo repeated.

Aqib heard the movement of chair legs scraping a hard floor.

"Thank you," the deep voice said. "Now please, place your left hand flat on the table surface, palm down. Yes. Just so."

"Okay?" Aqib heard Miss ask, her voice low.

Aqib leaned over, far enough so that his ear was against the door.

"Paul Demeter's batting average is still at .400," Sumo said, "and he only now narrowly missed hitting a homerun today, which is the last game. That is promising for Paul Demeter, but not so for you. William Kerrigan could have prevented what must happen next. He had the means.

Unfortunately, he did not take us as seriously as he might have."

Aqib thought he could feel Miss' fear through the door. Desperately, he summoned his mind to think."

"Fortunately," Sumo continued, "despite Paul Demeter's heroics with the bat, the Rangers lost last night's game, so today's game holds importance to both teams. Paul Demeter will continue to play in this game and risk losing out on his historic achievement. Your grandfather can help us in this matter, but will he? We sent him a photographic message. Regrettably we are forced to send another message to your grandfather. This time, that message will involve some pain."

Aqib listened to Miss' response.

"I know what is in that case you've got there." She was trying to stay brave, so her voice was weak, but unbroken.

"You are an intelligent woman," said Sumo.

"*Girl,"* Miss said, defiantly. "I'm just a stupid little girl who thought she was all grown up. I am not a woman."

"You are frightened."

"Hell yes, I'm frightened!"

Aqib felt his own weakness. He was frantic for Miss, but what could he do?

Sumo spoke in a low voice, just above a whisper. "It will be painful for a short period of time. Aoki will now administer an injection that will help you face the pain."

Aqib acted quickly. He jumped up, flushed the toilet, and flung open the medicine cabinet door. With both hands, he rifled through shelves to find something sharp. Ointments, brushes, tubular items and bottles crashed and clinked into the sink. On his tiptoes, desperately, he felt for the top shelf. At first, nothing. He reached again, banging his hand left and right. Ah! He touched metal hardness.

Yes, this will do!

Fourth Inning

William dared not look at Jodie. Morosely, he watched the fourth Astros pitcher, a left hander, take warm-up tosses in the bottom of the fourth inning, with the score stuck at 1-0, Rangers' favor. This man's arsenal included a nasty slider that broke in on right-handed hitters at the knees, and he had a filthy change-up. Paul had managed one measly hit off him in June: a pop-fly single to right field.

It had taken almost two hours to play three and a half innings—that's what happens when a manager stops a game often to let relief pitchers warm up (the Rangers themselves had used three pitchers). It seemed as if every hitter on each team had decided that his at-bat was the most crucial in determining the day's outcome. Most at-bats saw at least three or four foul balls as batters battled every pitch.

Each pitcher must have felt the same way, since most at-bats ended in outs. The Rangers pitchers gave up only one hit, and the Astros hurlers only two. This game had settled into an un-classic pitchers' duel.

The crowd rose to standing again, the hush firmly in place, when Paul Demeter stepped in for his second at-bat. William stood, squirming as Paul worked the count to 3-2 and then proceeded to foul off five straight pitches. Then the lefty threw him a back breaking change-up that dropped ankle-high just as it reached home plate.

William winced as Paul started his stride to address the pitch but checked his swing at the last instant. Behind the plate, the man in blue thrust his hand toward the first base ump, who hesitated, then threw his arms wide sideways, parallel to the infield dirt in the safe sign.

"Ball four!" the plate umpire screamed.

William swallowed a half cup of tobacco juice. He made it inside the clubhouse door just as the giant wad of tobacco, of its own accord, shot out his mouth like a rocket and splattered the wall. At the sink, he slurped a mouthful of water, rinsed and spit. He stuck his head under the faucet, letting the cold water drown his head and hair.

What are these men capable of? Would they hurt a kid? Would they do worse? Surely not. She is just a child. They might be serious men, representing other serious, powerful men, and a great deal of money, no doubt was at stake, but she was a child, for god's sake. They wouldn't harm her. They were trying to scare him. It was working. He felt sick again and dry-heaved over a toilet.

When he felt a hand on his shoulder, he reached around and eased it off, thinking it was Thibodaux coming to check on him. He turned. It was Eddie, one of the clubhouse guys. "Sorry, Ed. I'm a little antsy."

"Can't blame you, Fungo," Eddie said. "We're all a bit tense. You see that last bit? Dem got himself a break there. That was a complete swing sure as I'm standing right here. If that wasn't a strike, then I am Thomas Stinkin Jefferson. Here. A fella said give this to you."

"Huh?" William asked.

Eddie tried to hand him a sharply-creased small brown paper bag, barely big enough for a kindergartener's lunch.

"What is this?" William asked, frowning, putting his hands behind his back.

"Nothin," Eddie said. "A big fella wanted you to have it. I told him I'd put it in your locker, and he says, 'No—Mr. Kerrigan would want this right away.' I wouldn't have bugged you, Fungo, but he give me this. Sorry."

He held up a one hundred-dollar bill.

"It's fine, Ed."

"But don't worry, Fungo. Like I do ever time anybody wants me to give something to a player, I look in the bag. You wouldn't believe the stuff I find... well, maybe *you'd* believe—girls' panties, hotel keys, death threats, a for real human turd once, a freakin bottle of acid—all kinds of stuff over time. I'm diligent, Fungo. I look after my guys. "

"I don't want it."

"It ain't nothin, Fungo. Just a little box with like a cheap ring in it."

William took the bag. "Eddie?" he asked. "This big man? Was he Asian-looking?"

"Yeah. He was a jap."

William started to give the sack back, but Eddie had already walked off. He could drop it and walk off himself. Instead, he stared at it in his hands several moments. Then he turned the sack over in his hand, and a sandwich size plastic bag fell out. Inside it was the ring box. *What the heck?*

He touched the midnight blue felt box with a finger, opening it, seeing what looked like one of those toy secret-code plastic rings you could get as a kid back in the day with three box tops from cereal boxes. He shrugged and started to close the box when he noticed on the fake velvet material a single reddish brown stain.

What the hell?

He turned the box over. With his nail, he flicked the bottom out of the box. He felt something light inside. At first, nothing plopped out. He shook it. Then a piece of cloth, like a portion of a scarf, poked out. When he pulled on it, it came away. Carefully, he unfolded the cloth. Nothing at first.

He gave it a shake, and the tip of a small, bloody human finger landed on his pristine white, home team baseball pants.

Honorable Friend

I don't remember lying down, but when I arouse, I lie on a cot in the room. The room is windowless, so I have no sensation of time. Somehow, I feel Aqib's nearness, but he is not touching me. I can't see or hear him, but I am aware of his presence. I am positive I dreamed, so that means I slept. Two hours, one hour, not even that? I don't remember the details of dream. I am dazed, but I am not sleepy anymore. I concentrate. Then I remember.

I was at a table on a hard chair. I saw the ornamental case. I saw the long, thin, very sharp knife in the hands of Sumo. I remember the syringe. *Maybe all that is my nightmare.* I lift both hands in front of my face, wiggling my fingers, counting them.

I think I hear a groan, and then the door opens. Sumo's voice fills the small room.

"You have honorable friend, Miss Kerrigan."

Huh? I think. What does that mean? I look for Aqib. Where is he? Had they done something to him? There!—he is not far from me, lying on another cot. Asleep? He is partially covered in a blanket, as I am, but his blanket had slipped to his belt. His right hand clutches the wooden base of the cot as if, even in deep sleep, he is fearful of falling. His left hand lies across his chest, swathed in a blood-soaked bandage.

When I was eight, I was on the playground with Cameron Purcell, a boy in my grade, and we were seeing who could swing the highest. I flew so high that I went exactly perpendicular and stalled out. Gravity took over, and I fell to the hard-packed playground surface, knocking the wind from my lungs. Nothing has ever shocked me or hurt so badly since.

When I see Aqib's bloody hand, I feel like I am in that schoolyard accident again. I have no oxygen. Tears fill my eyes and over flow. When finally I can speak, I whisper. "Aqib, what have you done?"

"He cannot hear you," Sumo says.

"He's only asleep? Right?"

"He is out."

"What did you do to him?"

"Miss Kerrigan. We did nothing. What happened was of his own volition."

"Oh, no. Will he be all right? Please?"

"He will recover," Sumo nods. "Though sadly for your friend, we were not able to alleviate his pain immediately, as we had prepared the one dose and already administered it to you prior to *yubitsume.* While my associate sought a second dose, the women, out of respect, turned the house upside down and eventually located sleeping pills in one of the bathrooms. They forced several down him. He will not be with you for many hours."

I cannot speak. I try, but only a cough emerges. A pathetic burp is all I manage. Sumo walks to the door. He turns. "We leave now. We have to be certain places at the ball game's end, depending on its ending. You will be alone in the house with your sleepy friend..." he says, pausing, "and the dogs."

Fungo and Bud

William fretted the ring box back and forth in his hands while his mind raced. No matter where he looked on the field or in the stands, all he could see in his mind was the tiny piece of finger. He hoped she wasn't suffering.

That poor kid! She was tough and smart, but she was no match for these people. He should have known they would be thorough, and they would permit fortune no opening.

This would undo Jodie. She had been through so much tough stuff, but this might be the game-changer. He cursed himself. This situation was all on him, and it could get worse. He had thought only of himself.

He left the dugout, ostensibly to stretch his legs, and he stole a peek at the box seats. He knew Jodie agreed to attend the game in large part because she hoped she would see Sylvia. Sitting forward in her seat, no part of her touching the back, her face was intent and wide eyed, which was not all that incredible even for a non-baseball person like her, given the circumstances.

A Major League division was to be won and lost; and history possibly made. He stared at the faces around Jodie. He saw anxious, wary eyes—as if everyone was thrilled, but nobody was actually having fun.

In the seventh inning, the score still remained 1-0—Rangers. After the fourth inning walk, Bud remained at .400, rounded up. He was due to bat next. William idled outside the dugout as Paul walked out, swinging his bat and a leaded warm-up bat. For the first time today, boos cascaded and echoed from the seats when people spot him. They didn't want to see him. Fans pushed their hands against the air, as if this pantomime could shove him back in the dugout. Some screamed, pleading with him not to go to the plate.

Paul waved and smiled. "What's up, Fungo? You look like somebody ran over your dog."

"What the hell is there to be happy about?" William scowled. "Bud?"

"This is fun."

"It is?"

"I've never won the division before."

"Are you kiddin me? *That* makes you happy? Listen to the people. They want you out of the game. They'd rather you hit .400 than win. It has come full circle, Bud."

Paul dropped the weighted bat and smiled. "Yeah, I guess it has. Still, I want to win this thing."

William reached a hand toward him. He took him by the arm, looking him in the face. He leaned close to his ear, and said something to him. He had to repeat himself for all the tumult raining down from the stands. Again Paul raised his hand to his ear. William spoke a third time.

To fans watching the two men in the circle, it may have seemed a sentimental, even poignant scene: mentor and student sharing a moment, a father and son moment, even — the two unconcerned by the controlled mayhem in the air; the older man delivering a last word of advice or encouragement.

Fungo mouthed one last word.

Bud nodded. Said nothing.

When Paul Demeter left the on-deck circle with a grim look on his face, the boos had grown loud enough to drown out the public address announcement of his name. Fans begged him to sit out the rest of the game.

A Run For It

When Aqib groans, I jump to his side, stumbling over a pillow that had fallen to the floor. I pick it up and raise Aqib's head, slipping the pillow beneath it. Softly, I touch his forehead, brushing with my fingers lightly, from his brow to his hairline, stroking his sweltering skin. I place my face next to his and listen to his breathing.

What did you do for me, you amazing kid?

I take his wounded hand and place it on my chest. Lightly, I rub the skin not covered by the bandage. I lift his hand to my face, crying. "It's my fault. It is so-ooh me. I got you into this mess!"

I cover him to his shoulders with the blanket and rest his left hand on his chest. I look down at him. But for the wispy mustache, he looks like a child. How could I have possibly thought him a terrorist?

The door is not locked, and I crack it open the width of my face. Sweeping the expansive first floor and foyer with my eyes, I find the staircase. If the pit bulls wear shock collars like Aqib surmised, I will be clear of them if I can get to the stairs.

I had seen no phones anywhere in the place, but there might be one in the many rooms upstairs. There might even be a way out of one of the windows up there. If there is a window I can open, I can tie sheets together for a rappelling rope.

Yeah, and what then? Even if by crazy luck I can get past the dogs one time and make it upstairs, there will be no way I can make it back to the bare room to somehow bring Aqib back up there with me. I will have to do it myself. I will have to make a run for it. But to where?

First things first.

Three monsters are chained near the front door with what looks like about a ten-foot lead. I see no other animals, but I know they lurk. I look again at the staircase and measure the distance with my eyes. The beasts at the door won't have enough chain to get to me, but I'll have to sprint—no matter where the other dogs might be.

As I gather myself for action, I try to dismiss the visual image of what the pit bulls will do to me if they catch me. I try to shoo from my brain torn body parts scattered on the floor and entrails – my entrails - hanging from beastly muzzles. *Quit it!*

My mind turns instead to what Aqib has done for me. I have to try something.

My one almost crowning sports achievement was in first grade when I was picked to represent Woodrow Wilson Elementary in the Mascot Race, which kicked off the annual citywide Little Olympics. I got off to a great start and led all the way in the fifty-meter dash, but slowed down on purpose near the finish to let the others catch up before we broke the string in a bunch.

I estimate the stairs to be about fifteen yards away. I figure I am good to sprint that. I gulp air and take off, with one last look over my shoulder. In that very instant, a gray, mottled dog, with a head like a shot put and the eyes of a serpent, turns a corner and spies me. He gives chase with extreme prejudice. *Too late to turn back now!*

The ferocious chained dogs see me and charge until they run out of chain, causing them to be jerked themselves backward and airborne like throw toys.

Just as I touch the first step, needles stab my ankle and foot. It feels like I have stepped in a live campfire. The big-headed monster has my ankle in his mouth. *I am dead.* At the same time I hear the rush of other paws skittering on the plastic-covered floor, telling me more pit bulls are closing in for the kill.

The dog shakes his head, and my foot with it, as and I brace for the agony. I wonder if he hasn't already ripped my foot from my leg.

Pulling on a bannister, I try to yank my leg from the beast. The dog's own force pushes me up two more steps. *Got to get higher!* I groan and cry with terror as I pull at the bannister. In my horror, I discover a region of power I have never before experienced, and when I give a mighty yank, I fly two steps higher to about a third of the way up the staircase. The big dog comes with me, of course. I pant, needing rest. The great heave saps me.

So as I lie here to die, with the dog pinning me down while his buddies dine on me, I realize this is a sorry end. The other two loose dogs must have a different activation to their collars, for they fret and gnash and nip at each other in frenzied frustration at the bottom of the staircase without trying the steps. No matter, boys; bighead will probably haul me back down to you so you can dig in.

I look down my leg. The dog still has my ankle between his awful jaws. Blood coats his fangs—my blood. I am dizzy and nauseous. If I am lucky, I will pass out and never know about the evil they are doing to my body. I look again in the beast's eyes and see something wrong with them. They don't look so venomous somehow. They don't look natural, animal or otherwise. They look far less menacing even with my foot in his mouth. Then he opens his horrible mouth wider, and I stiffen for the puncture to come. I brace, but nothing happens. The big-headed pit bull does not sink his fangs in me again. I peek. I can't believe my eyes. He is licking me! *What the hell?*

The monster laps at my foot and ankle with his wide floppy tongue, like he is trying to lick the blood away. I try moving my foot. It comes away! He doesn't grab it again, but he does follow and lick it some more. When I ease another step higher, he comes with me, moaning and looking in my eyes.

Straight on now he has a roundish, pie-looking face. He continues licking my ankle. With the blood cleared away, I see the wounds. I expect to see a mass of torn flesh, what used to be my ankle. No. Instead of deep gashes and shredded skin, I see that the pit bull's fangs have barely broken the skin. The gnawing produced a little pain and lots of blood, but it had not really injured me at all. Unbelievable! The beast had been *playing* with me. Then when he thought he hurt me, he tried to make it better.

The monster is a big softy. This is crazy! So crazy I think he just smiled at me. Don't be stupid. Dogs don't smile.

He wants to be my friend, so I laugh out loud. His ears lay back against his head, and his tongue lies sideways out his huge mouth when it isn't licking me. He moans, and then he purrs like a giant cat. This can't be real. What are the chances that, of all the vicious killer dogs, I would luck onto a huge baby?

When I reach down to pat his enormous head, he smiles at me again with his bakery face. *Pie Face.*

"Good dog. Good boy. Okay I'm going higher to get away from your buddies. You stay here. You'll get shocked. Stay, Boy."

The monster moans again and licks my ankle and foot clean of blood.

I move one step higher, and when I settle, the dog steps up, too, and then unleashes a pitiful howl and leaps backward off the staircase in one gigantic movement, like he has been shocked, which of course, he has. He howls with pain, and then he whimpers like a child. I feel awful when he looks up at me like he wants me to help him as he has helped me. He moans once more and tentatively climbs the stairs again, but he stops one step below me.

"I am so sorry, Buddy."

I reach down and let him sniff the back of my hand. I scoot back down the one step and pat his head. "Easy, Pie

Face. I'm going to unbuckle this collar. Hold still. Stay, Buddie. There! Now you are free. Go on now."

I pat his head again and run the rest of the way up the stairs, with him following me. I run down the hallway to every room. Several are as bare as the horrible room Aqib lies in this very moment. None have telephones. I try the windows. All are locked shut and barred with iron. This is hopeless. I am helpless. *We* are helpless. Our future seems certain to depend on the whim of Sumo, or whoever he represents.

The last room I look in is the bedroom where Aqib and I had slept in what now seems like years before. It doesn't have a phone, but it has a TV. Sumo had mentioned Paul Demeter almost had a hit in today's game, and he is still batting .400. Is the game still on? If so, what inning? Is he still over .400? The big pit bull follows me into the room. I need to watch.

Baseball? Is my future hanging on the outcome of a game? That's some badass irony, isn't it?

A more succinct, uneasy realization had begun settling over me as our situation grew more desperate over the days of capture. I shrugged it off at first as craziness, but the more I thought about it and factored in how crazy it was to be abducted and held in this evil way, the less insane it became. Our future hung, not on a game or the caprice of a single person, but on whether or not Paul Demeter hit .400. *Huh?*

Actually, the game is in the top of the seventh, two outs, score 1-0, Rangers, with the Astros at bat. As the camera sweeps the stadium, I see that practically nobody is sitting, even though no runners are on base, and Houston's nine-hole batter is at the plate.

Panorama back to the Globe Life Park crowd—a shot from dead centerfield. Again, practically every fan stands—then to a close-up of the pitcher in his motion. The Astros hitter swings on a change-up and yanks the ball down third base line, headed for a sure double, but Paul Demeter leaps and makes a spectacular backhand catch to end the inning.

He rolls over twice, lands on his knees and holds the ball up in his glove. When he smiles, I see his familiar facial twitch. If he is bothered by the insane pressure hanging in the air around him, you sure can't see it on his face.

The sensational play gives the folksy color guy in the booth an opportunity to bring viewers up-to-date on Demeter's day and an opportunity to add his own opinion on the current situation, just before the screen fades to commercial:

"A remarkable catch by Paul Demeter, fans. A fact lost on most folks, because of his incredible hitting this season, is that Demeter is sure to win his sixth Gold Glove. The man could always play his position. He's still over .400—right this minute—by the skin of his teeth, though he was flat out robbed of a homerun his first time up.

In the fourth inning, he wrangled a base on balls, which we all know doesn't count against him, so he's still at point- three-nine-nine-five presently, which, even without my abacus, I can round up to .400. He is due up at the bottom of this frame, and if I was manager of this ball club, he would not step out of the dugout.

Just sayin. You want to win; that's why you play the game, but .400, people! .400! Just heck is all I can say! .400! I say Paul Demeter needs to stay in the dugout and not go to the plate, but that's me!"

Seventh Inning Stretch

Paul had a couple extra minutes to think before he stepped to the plate, though he wished he had longer. But the crowd had already bellowed *Take Me Out To the Ball Game* and fresh chalk cleanly framed the batter's box. The umpire had swept home plate and pointed his thumb at the Astros pitcher.

Paul took his stance and swung at air a couple of times. Then his eyes took him to the mound, where he watched the short, left-handed Astros pitcher he had never faced before. He watched the hurler toe the rubber and begin his slow, languid delivery. Paul lifted his arms. The bat felt as nothing in his gloved hands. He saw the ball between the pitcher's fingers and noticed its blur as it took flight. He felt his left leg begin its familiar stride.

He would have liked more time to soak up the "boos" from the throng who want him to sit back down so he would hit .400. More time to think about Jodie, who Fungo had just now told him in the on-deck circle was in the stands for her first baseball game since Chicago, so long ago. More than anything, though, he needed time to digest what Fungo had confided in him about Sylvia.

He was so deep in thought his focus abandoned him, and he was unable to move himself as he has been forced to do so many times this season—out of the way of the pitch, a tailing fastball, which plunked him squarely on the butt.

Hitting .400

Paul Demeter is hit by a pitch. The fans go crazy.

He hasn't left the batter's box. He turns and says something to the home plate umpire, who yells at him. The two of them argue. The umpire jabs his finger at first base. Paul Demeter shakes his head. He drops his bat and jogs to first.

I feel sick. The air-conditioned room now feels like a walk-in meat locker. Pie Face growls, but I shush him with a pat to his head.

The Rangers throw a fit, and a couple of players even come out of the dugout, acting all-bad, like they are going to do something, but it quiets down soon. Everybody knows the pitch was not intentional. In a one-run game, when every single pitch has a purpose and can't possibly be wasted, a pitcher is going to throw at a batter? C'mon. The pitch had been a little inside, sure, but it looked like Paul Demeter could have gotten out of the way.

He had looked dazed, like he wasn't paying attention when the pitch came in. Anyway, that was how it looked to me. I also see that his tic is gone as the camera follows him up the base path. I lean in, concentrating. He doesn't look the same. It is a good thing the inside pitch wasn't head-high, or he might have been knocked unconscious, as muddled as he looks. Something seems odd with him. Something is different.

Same as with the base on balls his second time up, a hit-by-pitch doesn't count as an at-bat. I know the math. He is still at .400. Luck favors him today.

Luck. Would that go in my story? *My Story*? What story? I had actually gone a couple of days without the story consuming nearly every thought and action. Now, will I even get to write a story? Where does the story stack up now, anyway? Where does it rank? I am a captive on a bed in a palatial prison, with a large killer dog in my lap, with my future and possibly my life up in the air, and I'm watching a baseball game. How does the story even fit in anymore with this absurd situation?

Paul Demeter is left stranded, and the score remains 1-0, Rangers. Both sides fill the bases the next two innings, but neither scores. In the ninth inning, every fan stands, and the noise in the stadium nears sonic-boom level.

I reach past Pie Face's head, which rests on my thigh, and I grab the remote. I punch mute. I don't need to hear what I can see plainly for myself. Also, I can't stand the sound of the relentless screaming. *Where do they get the energy?*

In the top of the inning, the Rangers get two quick outs, only one out to go, but then a pinch hitter slaps a line drive down the right field line. The ball skips into the corner, ricochets off the bleacher wall and the outfield fence, and the Ranger fielder has trouble picking it up. The Astros hitter is fleet of foot, so what should have been a routine double turns into a stand-up triple. The game-tying run is now only ninety feet from home plate.

On the muted screen, I see fans jumping up and down, dancing, holding hands, waving hands, covering faces with hands, and hugging each other.

Lavernicus Thibodaux calls time out, and, if anything, the crowd goes wilder. People go to their knees in prayer, mothers cover the children's ears, a reverse wave begins with each standing section taking turns sitting down in unison. Instead of Thibodaux, William Kerrigan emerges from the dugout and stomps to the mound. As he crosses the base path, he motions the infielders to join him around the Ranger pitcher.

I lean in. William looks calm and positive in the close up as he talks to his men, speaking to one man after another, jabbing the first and second basemen in the chest with his thumb, and patting the pitcher on the fanny. The only man on the mound he doesn't address is Paul Demeter. He doesn't say anything to him; he doesn't even look at him. The whole confab takes maybe two minutes, tops.

Paul Demeter is due to bat at the bottom of this inning, but the Rangers are winning, so if they get this third out, they won't have to bat. Game over. If that runner on third does not score, there will be no bottom of the ninth … home team doesn't have to bat.

One more out, Rangers win the pennant.

One more Astros out, Paul Demeter will not have to bat again. Ever.

A strike out, Paul Demeter is the last man to hit .400.

One more Astros out, what of Aqib and me?

I can't stand the tension. I hop off the bed to stand in front of the TV. Pie Face whines and stands with me.

My mind sees Jodie. She is at the game. I feel her. She probably thinks she will see me after the game. If I don't see her again, will she think I went away angry with her. I can't stand that.

I think of Aqib so alone down in that awful room. Poor Aqib.

Poor me! I am afraid. What are these spooky men, our captors, capable of?

I feel some peace in knowing my grandfather will stick by Jodie. He will stick. He had better. I know that he has a hand in all this mess. Somehow.

Paul Demeter will hit .400. Something bad will probably happen to Aqib and me.

I don't want to watch, but I cannot pull my eyes from the screen. I turn the sound back on.

The Astros send up a last-ditch pinch hitter. He takes forever to step into the batter's box. He uses the rag to wipe down his bat. He unsnaps and snaps both batting gloves. Once in the box, he digs a small ditch in the right-hand side with his spikes.

Finally he is ready. He fouls off the first pitch. The Ranger pitcher quick-pitches him on the second. He's caught off guard and barely gets a piece of the ball. Foul. Two strikes!

The camera pans the crowd, which is in a state of utter pandemonium. The screams have been replaced by one long stream of noise. Some faces are tear-streaked, some wear the thousand-yard stare I'd seen in pictures I wasn't supposed to look at in William's scrapbook.

The Rangers reliever throws three consecutive pitches that just miss the outside corner.

3-2, full count!

The hitter fouls off two more pitches, the second of which is a screamer that skips off the dirt toward Paul Demeter, who fields it slickly just as the third base ump hollers, "Foul ball!"

One long groan from the Texas multitude.

The Ranger hurler calls for a new baseball and steps off the rubber as he roughs it up. He looks in, gets his sign, winds, and throws. The batter strides and swings. He hits the ball. It is a fair ball!

Piece of cake!

It is an easy three-bouncer hit directly at Paul Demeter, who moves toward the grounder with his usual grace, fields the ball with his bare hand *and there's the smile.* He hops once, as he always does on a simple peg, and makes the throw.

The ball cuts a slightly arced path across the diamond as it sails over the Rangers first baseman's out-stretched glove and into the box seats, three rows up!

The Wait

A Rangers employee in a coat and tie appeared at Jodie's box seat and told her he would escort her to the area where the wives and girlfriends waited. William mentioned that area was probably the best place to meet after the game.

"I'll wait here," she told the representative, "but thank you anyway."

The stands remained deafeningly loud for almost thirty minutes after the game, so waiting where she was, where there would be no awkward questions, would be better.

Then a thought came to her. "Wait. You said 'wives?' So children will be there, too—players 'children?"

Yes, of course."

It would be like Sylvia to find that waiting area. After games in Chicago, Sylvia had begged to visit the area to greet Paul Demeter after games, but Jodie always answered,

"No. We needn't go to that place. We can meet him properly when he comes home." Now it would be just like Sylvia to assert her rightful place and turn up there. It would be the cap to her story.

"So. I believe I *will* go with you," Jodie told the man.

He led her down a corridor, far below the noise of the crowd, to a large room, filled primarily with women and young children. Her gaze was drawn first to the children. Most were no older than seven or eight. Their dads are young men, after all. The kids frolicked, laughing and jumping, bumping into one another, tagging—oblivious, or impervious, to the fact their fathers were world-famous entertainers and had only minutes ago participated in an important competition. Was this the feeling of entitlement Jodie had not wanted Sylvia to acquire?

The wives were dressed as one would expect of spouses of millionaires: stylishly and confident, but relatively conservative. They talked together, slightly louder than needed, and sipped from flutes of champagne because their husbands were winners. The girlfriends were beautiful, as would be expected of the companions of rich professional athletes. They were also stylish, but the pants were tighter, the skirts shorter. They mostly stood alone, drinking from sweaty bottles of beer, wrapped with napkins. It occurred to Jodie that one of these pretty girlfriends was probably waiting on Paul Demeter.

Sylvia was not in the room. Jodie couldn't help herself. Before she knew what was happening, she began to weep, softly. *Damn!* She hadn't realized how much she had counted on Sylvia showing up at the game. She yanked a hankie to put a stop to her tears, or at least hide them, but not before one of the lone girls moved over to her.

"I know," the beautiful girl said, tearing up herself. "The way it ended, right? So awful! If you'd have told me Paul Demeter would make an error that let in the tying run, and then he would strike out on three straight pitches in the ninth, and we would still win, I would've said you were crazy! Paul hasn't done either of those two things in so long I can't remember when it was. What a way to miss out on hitting .400."

"Yes. A shame!"

Jodie's tears hadn't stopped. She dabbed her face and eyes with the hanky, embarrassed. She didn't want to be rude, but she desperately wanted to leave the room. "Excuse me. I don't belong."

"It is a tragedy," the girl said before Jodie could move away.

"I'm sorry?"

"It's not a damn shame; it's a fucking tragedy," the beautiful girl said.

This statement stopped Jodie. "Oh. So, I'm sorry, but I don't know if I would say it is a 'tragedy.' A tragedy would be losing a child, or if a tornado..."

"I don't care," the girl interrupted. "Tragedy is the word. I mean I'm glad we won, sure, but Paul—or anybody—hitting .400 all year and then losing it like he did on the last day? The last inning! Makes me want to scratch my own eyes out!"

"Oh, don't do that," Jodie said, finally dry-eyed.

"Jodie?" William spoke in a whisper from close by.

"Ah, Dad," said Jodie, partially relieved.

She tried to smile. She couldn't. She took her father's arm.

"Let's get you home, kid," William said.

Jodie was afraid of the look on his face. "Yes," she said. "After…"

"After what?"

"After we go to the nearest police station to file a missing person report."

He stopped. He frowned. "We don't have to, Jodie." His words were barely audible.

"Yes, we do. My child has been gone three days. Something is wrong—very wrong. She needs me. A mother knows."

"Let's go home, Sweetheart."

Jodie yanked her arm away. "No way! I mean it, William. If you won't take me, I'll go on my own—even if I have to walk. Something is wrong. You know it, too. Your face is grim. Tell me, because you know, Dad. Is she all right?"

"We will see her soon. I am sure of it."

"I did not ask you that, Dad. Is she all right?"

"She will be," William said.

End of Story

I smile at the first person who passes me on the corner. The woman does not smile back, but she stops. I point my finger.

"What is that place?"

"F'real?" the woman says, a huge frown on her face. "You don't know?"

"I've seen it somewhere before."

"Bet you have. That the movie theater where the po-lice picked up that boy shot JFK. Right in there. Boy watchin *War is Hell.*"

"Oh."

"That dog bite?"

"No, ma'am. Not him."

"That what they all say. Then he bite your ass. Pit bulls is nasty."

"Not this guy. He's a sweetie."

"Umm-hmm. Say—what you doin here?"

"Where's here?"

"This Dallas."

"Thank you."

"Umm-hmm. Nice talkin to you. I got to be going."

"Right. Thank you. Bye."

"Bye now."

After the woman walks away, I stare after her for some reason. About half a block later, the woman stops, turns around and walks part of the way back to me. "How come you don't know where you are at?" she yells, still approaching. "Somebody just drop you off on this corner or something?"

"Yes, ma'am—something just like that."

I give her my widest smile, but she reacts by shaking her head in disgust.

"Why you gotta smile? Ain't nothing funny right here. You fillin all right? You best call on your telephone so somebody come get you."

"I don't have a phone."

"Erbody got a phone."

"I don't. I'm fine."

"Umm, maybe you ain't fine. You wanna use ma phone? Here."

"Thank you very much."

"You're welcome. Hurry up."

After thinking a minute and punching in the number, I hear the voicemail and leave a message. I thank the lady again and cross the busy street. On the other side, I look around, trying to get my bearings. My dog and I walk four blocks… just because we can. I secure Pie Face in a shady place and go in a diner, which is crowded. I take an open stool at the counter.

The Escalade had made one stop previous to the one that dropped off me and the dog.

"What are they doing with Aqib?" I said from the back seat, a scarf covering my eyes.

"You need not worry, Miss Kerrigan," Sumo answered. "My associates have taken him inside a safe-house, where he will get medical attention. He will be taken care of very well for as long as it takes. Then someone will take him wherever he wishes to go."

"Wherever?"

"Wherever."

"I help you?" says the waitress, with a pad and pencil. She doesn't look or sound helpful.

"Yes."

"What, then?"

"All right if I use some of these napkins?"

"You ordering something?"

I turn my pockets inside out and look at what I have.

"Coffee, it looks like."

"Help yourself," the girl says, turning to leave.

"Can I borrow one of your pens?"

The girl sighs and places a pencil in my palm.

"I'd prefer a pen." My eyes say, *please*... "if you have one."

"Sure you don't want me to write the damn thing down for you too, while I'm at it?" the girl says. She reaches in a big pocket on her apron, takes out a sweet Precise V5, rolling ball, extra fine marker and hands it to me.

"Thanks so much."

I stir sugar and fake cream in the large mug of coffee the girl brings me. I sip and feel the liquid burn my throat. The man on the stool beside me finishes his meal, totals up the tip, pays, and leaves.

A half slice of Texas toast remains on his otherwise empty plate. It is untouched, but for a speck of chicken-fry gravy. I realize I am hungry. Sumo offered Aqib and me something to eat before letting us go, but Aqib was sick, and I was so anxious to get moving. We both declined the offer.

I grab the slice and dunk it in the coffee. It is delicious. Time to go to work.

Chewing slowly on the soggy goodness, I select a neat wad of flinty brown napkins, folded and tucked to stand edgewise, next to the shakers of salt and pepper, and bottles of mustard, ketchup and Tabasco.

I test the pen, scratching three fine-line x's on the inside of my thumb. I lick my finger and wipe my thumb clean on my jeans. I unfold one napkin, press it flat on the counter and begin writing. When I fill the napkin with sentences, I unfold another, and then another. I fill that wad of napkins with sentences, and the girl brings me another wad without being asked. I fill that stack with sentences. Then I rest.

I finish drinking my coffee and ask the girl for a glass of water. I pour the water in the empty cup and take it outside the diner for Pie Face. When I return to the stool, a fresh stack of napkins lies on the counter… beside a new cup of hot coffee.

"I love dogs," the girl says.

I have all my Paul Demeter story now, and it is nothing like the one I set out to write. Isn't that the way it is with writers, though? You think you know where you are going, true as scripture, but then events change, people change, you change? The story is all in my head now—the hell with notes and further contemplation! I've just got to get it all down on those stacks of little brown napkins. Who needs a laptop?

On that lazy afternoon in the busy diner somewhere in Dallas, the story flows like water in a Cherokee County stream—furiously over the rocky places, yet smoothly, steadily in the depths. I tell the rest of it straight through, looking up only to accept refills of coffee from the girl, to take the bones she gave to me to my dog, and to think how lucky I am to be a writing person.

PART IV

Sarah

William hadn't gone looking for her… not consciously anyway. He went to the library, looking for help with a simple task. She worked the checkout desk that day. He had noticed her on a couple of occasions before as she shelved books, and he had tried unsuccessfully to come up with an excuse to talk to her.

"Sir, how may I help you?" she asked, smiling. Her name tag said, *Sarah*.

He handed his paperback to her and told her it was one of his favorites, but it was out-of-print and threatening to fall apart. He asked if there was a way to waterproof it and otherwise preserve it, and then he asked if she would like to have a coffee with him when the library closed.

"I'm not a librarian, only a volunteer, but I think there is an answer for your book," she replied. "See that desk in the middle? You can go there, and someone will answer your question."

"Okay, thanks. What about the other thing?"

"I'm afraid not." She laughed.

She squinted at him, pointing to her bare ring finger.

"Yeah," said William, squirming as he stood.

He looked at his hand. "Sure. That..."

"Yes, that?"

"That's not real. I mean the ring is real, but I'm not married."

"Uh huh?"

"Anymore."

"Yet you wear a wedding band."

"Yes. Look, I don't know why I have it on. I really haven't given it much thought. I guess I haven't bothered to take it off."

"I guess you haven't."

"But I can. I will."

"I don't think so."

"Okay. I am sorry I bothered you. No. I take that back. I'm not sorry."

"Okay. Fine. Anyway, no thank you for the coffee."

He walked out, feeling like a fool.

He let a full two weeks go by before he dared return to the library. Sarah was on a stepladder in the biography section at the end of the first floor. He looked at her. She turned and saw him. She climbed down and began walking toward him. *Too late.* He didn't know what to think. He didn't know what to say. He turned to walk out.

"I hoped you would drop back in soon," she said to his back in a library voice.

He stopped.

"You did?"

"I must apologize to you."

"I don't know why you would do that? Was me that made the fool."

"Marjorie, our assistant chief librarian—she's my friend."

"Yeah, I know Marjorie. She's a big Rangers fan. I bring her stuff sometimes."

"Yes, she told me. But I would hardly call it *stuff.* You bring wonderful jerseys and bats and balls the players have signed, and she auctions them off to buy audio visual equipment for the children's department. That is so good of you."

"Ahh, it's easy asking guys for their autographs. I like Marjorie."

"She likes you, too. She thinks you are a good guy. She also told me about your wife. I am very sorry."

"Thank you."

"You took off your ring."

Fungo looked down at his hand. The sun had not yet completely tanned over the skin, so long hidden from light. "Yeah, I guess I did," he said, "I don't know why it took me so long. I just kinda left it on, y'know?"

"Yes, I think I do," Sarah said. "Would you consider it fresh if I come right out and asked you to ask me for coffee again?"

"Exceedingly fresh," Fungo grinned. "Sarah, would you like to go have some coffee with me?"

"If you would make it a glass of Merlot instead, I would love to."

On their first real date, they went to see Stephen Stills at the racetrack. She apologized about the venue. "It is a bit of a stretch, imagining an icon of Woodstock with NASCAR. I know."

"Aw, I don't know," William said. "I guess if Bob Dylan can play the Choctaw Casino, up on Lake Texoma, anybody can be anywhere."

Thursdays and Saturdays

Paul Demeter arrives at Jodie's house off Riverside at precisely 7:15. He sits at the bar with his coffee, sesame seed bagel and Sudoku while Jodie wolfs down her onion bagel and finishes dressing Willie.

Then Paul takes Willie to pre-K—not in a Thunder Chicken, but in a Honda Accord. At noon, Paul returns for him and takes him across the Arkansas to the West Side, where they hang out the rest of the day.

Paul is lay coach for the Sand Springs Sandites High School baseball team. For away games, like today, pick-up duty falls to me. I often swing by my office at *Llanos* afterwards, with Willie and Pie Face in tow.

Sometimes, like today, I can't take my joyful, vigilant eyes off Willie, the little imp. He amazes me. When he smiles, I laugh out loud—every time! I can't help myself. His young, miraculous life is one of exquisite overindulgence.

Usually, he gets whatever he wants, and right now, what he wants is to stand on the copy machine, having reached that elevation by crawling up on Pie Face's back, then hoisting himself the rest of the way with his strong little arms. From there, he easily reaches the framed award on the wall and knocks it, crashing down to the floor.

"Young man, please get down from there," I say in a carefully-measured voice to my little brother.

Someone has to be the grown up, since neither Jodie, Paul Demeter nor William can be bothered to do anything but spoil the child.

"What a mess! No, don't touch it; there's broken glass. No, Pie! Stay!"

The American League Most Valuable Player award went to the man who hit .399 for that magical season, four years ago. Paul Demeter, William, and the Rangers made it to the

World Series, but they didn't win it. As promised, Paul retired from baseball after Game Seven in St. Louis. He said he was thinking about moving to Oklahoma, and Jodie said she thought that was a good idea.

Jodie refuses to accept any of the $2.4 million Paul Demeter calculates as her part accrued in their life together and apart, but she *does* accept him in her home for supper two nights a week. Occasionally she will come to his Berryhill apartment for a meal he has grilled.

Jodie does all right without Paul Demeter's money. She remains the reading specialist at her school, and her long dormant writing career recently received a pleasant, much needed wake-up call, after she delivered a collection of related short stories to her agent.

The agent told Jodie the stories are the best she has ever written and that, re-arranged as chapter sequences, and with minor editing, she believed she could represent the book as a remarkable and very marketable first novel.

Aqib calls me every week, or I call him, and we visit each other whenever work takes me close to Chicago, where he and his partner live. He is co-founder and president of a company that arranges LGBT student tours abroad.

He sends money regularly to his family back in Peshawar, but he has not yet convinced them to rejoin him in America. His mother has forgiven him, and she writes that his father has as well, but that he is still angry with him.

"His anger has not prevented him from spending your money, though," his mother writes, "and telling every person who will stand still long enough how successful his son is in USA. Your little brothers miss you terribly," she adds. "Perhaps when they are older, they will be with you in America?"

My grandfather is still in baseball.

"William will die in the dugout," Jodie says.

He is manager of the Springfield Cardinals of Double A. He likes the job, but he hates staying in *Missour-ah,* as he calls the state. Sarah visits him often, which takes some of the sting off the place, and in the off-season, he stays with her in her rambling home in Arlington.

Of course, I have a standing invitation to the twice-weekly dinners at my mom's, and I enjoy attending when I am not out of town on assignment for the magazine. We three adults jabber back and forth with each other, usually pleasantly, but sometimes we are snippy if one of us has had a trying day—sort of like a family—while we combine to arrange the meal: my dad, always with the silverware and napkins, me, pouring the wine and warming the bread, while Jodie does the entrée.

Funny, though—once at table, none of the adults seems to have much to say. Each of us is comfortable with the general quiet and subtleties of our own thoughts and the precious sounds of a child's prattle.

The End

ABOUT THE AUTHOR

Beesley is the author of *Vietnam: The Heartland Remembers* (University of Oklahoma Press and Berkley) an Outstanding Non-Fiction Book, *Dallas Morning News,* and a *Junior Scholastic Magazine* bookclub selection.

"This is a hard, strong book."–*New York City Tribune*

"Highly recommended."–*Publishers Weekly*

"This is a dark walk down Memory Lane. Take the walk."–*Topeka Capital*

Beesley also wrote *Sweetwater, Oklahoma,* which won OU's College of Liberal Studies Outstanding Master's Thesis Award.

"Beesley is a strong, talented, witty writer whose work is likely to show up in anthologies and in future textbooks"–*Sunday Oklahoman*

Beesley served with the U.S. Army's 75th Rangers in Vietnam and Cambodia. Today he teaches school and lives with his wife in the Southern Plains.

ACKNOWLEDGEMENTS

The author expresses his gratitude for
the faith of his wife, Denise; for the editorial assistance
of Brandey Alexander and Jim Dempsey,
and for friend, Frank McCall, whose literary eye
never strayed, early or late.

He thanks Bradley Beesley, Christopher Moebs,
Michael Ray Little, and Tracey Zeeck
for their artistic contributions; and
Heath Payne for his expertise on the art of pitching

The author gives special thanks to his big brother, John,
who at age thirteen, took the clipboard
from their mother and father
in the Yale, Oklahoma maternity ward,
and named him for Stan Musial and Warren Spahn.

CPSIA information can be obtained
at www.ICGtesting.com
Printed in the USA
FSOW01n0943060218
44238FS